Nantucket

NANTUCKET

The Life of an Island

By EDWIN P. HOYT

The Stephen Greene Press

BRATTLEBORO, VERMONT

Nantucket

First published in 1978 by
The Stephen Greene Press, Inc.
Published simultaneously in Canada by Penguin Books Canada Limited
Reprinted 1980, 1981, 1987
Distributed by Viking Penguin Inc.,
40 West 23rd Street, New York, NY 10010.

(CIP data available)

Printed in the United States of America by
Halliday Lithograph Corporation, West Hanover, Massachusetts

Contents

Illustrations

Following page 118

Nantucket

I

The Early Ones

E V E R Y O N E discovers Nantucket in his own way. The island's original European discoverers were probably Viking sailors, who—though no one can be certain of it—may have visited the island over a thousand years ago. The Vikings' accounts of voyages west from their outposts in Iceland and Greenland include descriptions of an island where they landed. That island sounds very like Nantucket.

In the ages before these first European visits, and for several hundred years after them, the island belonged to the Indians, whose name for it—*Nantucket*—meant "the faraway island." Indian legend tells that the island was once the home of a great man-eating bird who swooped onto the Massachusetts mainland for his prey. One day the bird plummeted down on Cape Cod and seized the two children of a giant named Maushope. The great wings beat, and the bird flew up and away to the southeast to its lair on the hidden island.

Maushope was furious. He seized a club and waded out through the sea to Nantucket, where he began to search in the forest for his children. He found their bones beneath a huge oak tree. There he waited in vain for his enemy, the great bird, to reappear, and as he waited he brought out his pipe to smoke and compose himself in his sorrow. He searched the island for tobacco but found none. He did find several stalks of poke, which the Indians smoked when there was nothing else, and he sat down, struck flint and lit up. Up from the pipe came a huge cloud of smoke that quite obscured the island. Although Maushope soon enough went back to the mainland to pick up the threads of his life, the smoke remained. And from that time on, whenever the fog drifted in over Nantucket island, the Indians who settled there would look out to sea and then up into the heavens.

1

"There comes old Maushope's smoke," they said.

And in the twentieth century Maushope's smoke was still coming, winter, spring, fall and summer, on days when the weather man had assured all the world that the islands would be clear and sunny. What did mere humans know of such things? How could they tell when the Spirit of Maushope might look down on the cradle island of Nantucket and blow his smoke to remind men of the tragedy of so long ago?

When the Indians' legendary giants were gone from Massachusetts, the Algonquin people settled comfortably in their tracks, and they, too, discovered Nantucket in their own way, coming by canoe from Cape Cod and Martha's Vineyard. They lived in the forests and glades, around the fresh water ponds. Legend says Nantucket was forested then; early history speaks of Tuckernuck Island as being almost totally covered with woods, and of Nantucket itself as heavily wooded with oak. The Indians were hunters and fishermen. They found plenty of fish and shellfish in the waters, and game in the woods and fields (although island author Nathaniel Benchley has heard there were no deer on Nantucket until about 1920). If they planted, they did so little of it that the practice never caught the attention of early writers. The Indians were primitive people, living simply. There were about 1,500 of them according to the best counts on an island of 30,000 acres, about 14 miles long and about 3.5 miles wide on the average.

The Indians lived on the higher ground all over the island, under a number of sachems, chiefs who controlled various parts of the land. One sachem, for example, controlled the land from Tom Nevers Head to Siasconset and Sankaty for nearly a mile inland. Another had the land abutting, from Sankaty Head to Squam to Coatue Point. And the rest of the island was thus divided into a number of "Sachemates," with the chiefs together choosing a chief sachem who was the final arbiter of Nantucket affairs in Indian days.

Those days began to draw to a close in 1602, when Captain Bartholomew Gosnold set out from England in a small ship with a crew of thirty-two on a voyage of exploration to Virginia. Navigation being what it often was in those days, Captain Gosnold fetched up off a cape one stormy day, saw his ship surrounded by codfish, and called the place Cape Cod.

As the wind lashed the sails, and the sun began to fall in the afternoon, Captain Gosnold prudently retired out to sea for the night. Soon he saw before him the white cliffs of a promontory. He was gazing upon Sankaty Head. The captain avoided the shoal water, skirted the island carefully until he found the safety of the depths, and there waited out the night. When the voyage was finished, Gosnold's discoveries went into the hands of the geographers and cartographers of England, who were drawing rudimentary maps of the new world.

The Indians of Nantucket remained unmolested, however, for another forty years. As England's kings divided up the American discoveries among their subjects, the island was deeded as a part of New York. In 1635 it came into the hands of the Earl of Sterling, who had not the slightest interest in visiting Nantucket, then or ever. In 1641 his agent sold the island to Thomas Mayhew and his son, Thomas Mayhew, Jr., English colonists then living in Watertown, in the Bay Colony. The island was a mere nothing to the Earl, hardly worth bothering about: he owned all the lands from Cape Cod to the Hudson River, and this little speck of sand and shrubbery did not interest him.

The Mayhews were merchants and missionaries. They really cared little for Nantucket, though they were interested in the souls of the Indians. The Mayhews were not against turning a profit on their island property, however, and so were receptive to offers from would-be buyers. Before they could sell, though, they had to make some arrangements with the island's Indians, and this they did in the summer of 1659. The leading sachems of the day were Wanackmamack and Nickanoose. These chiefs sold the Mayhews the rights to much of Nantucket's land, maintaining camps and hunting privileges. To cement the deal, the Mayhews paid twelve pounds on the spot, and promised that they would return the next summer to pay another fourteen pounds. (Thirty years earlier another Indian island, Manhattan, had been sold off for less than half the price the Mayhews paid for Nantucket; but, then, Manhattan was only a *little* island. . . .)

Having confirmed their title to Nantucket from the Indians, the Mayhews sold to other colonists all the rights to the island that the Indians did not claim. The names of some of those who bought Nantucket land from the Mayhews would forever go down in island history, and be repeated in succeeding generations time and again. The principal buyers, or First. Purchasers, were nine: Tristram Coffin, Thomas Macy, Christopher Hussey, Richard Swain, Thomas Barnard, Peter Coffin, Stephen Greenleaf, John Swain and William Pile. Coffin,

Macy, Hussey, Swain—those are the names that would be repeated, and for very good reason, because it was the First Purchasers, with the partners they took in, who settled on Nantucket and began to beget.

The Mayhews decided to keep a foothold on the island for themselves. They sold most of the island for thirty pounds and new beaver hats for Thomas Mayhew, Sr., and his wife. But they kept one-tenth of the land, and reserved Quaise for themselves.

By the fall of 1659, when all the land dealing had been completed, Nantucket was ready for the white men. The First Purchasers took in ten partners, in many cases relatives or friends who wanted relief from repression on the mainland.

Thomas Macy was the first man ready to leave the Massachusetts mainland and move to the island. He had the definite feeling that Massachusetts was becoming overpopulated with the wrong kind of people. It was not that Thomas Macy was a bigot or a racist. As events were to prove, he got on very well with Indians. Nor was he a religious bigot. He had already proved that; in fact, that was his whole trouble. Thomas Macy was a kind-hearted man who did not like being stepped upon by authority. And that is why his eye fell on Nantucket as a refuge; the land came up for sale just at the time that he was having a problem with the politicians in Boston, who also happened to be the religious leaders.

Macy's worries stemmed from the fact that he was a Baptist living in a community dominated by Puritans, who were evincing in the New World no more tolerance than the English church authorities who had caused them to leave the Old World in the first place.

Macy was an Englishman born and bred. He came from Wiltshire in 1640, hoping to make a new life in the New World. He seemed to do fairly well. One report said he acquired a thousand acres, a house, and all that went with such holdings. But in 1657 the Massachusetts authorities passed a law making it a criminal offense for anyone to "entertain" Quakers. The vigorous advocates of the Society of Friends had come to the New World, too, seeking freedom and prosperity, and their appearance in Massachusetts put the fear of God into the shirtfronts of Puritan authority.

Macy was suspect anyhow, with his "anabaptist" belief, so he was ripe for trouble in 1659. One rainy day that summer, four men came up to the Macy house seeking shelter from the storm. Macy looked at them. From their dress and speech, he knew well they were Quakers. He should, by law, throw them off the property. But Macy also looked at the sky, which appeared ready to burst, the gray clouds lowering and scudding in the rising wind. It was already raining hard. Macy had come in from the fields, soaked to the skin. He told the four men they could stay. They remained in the front room, while Macy went into the bedroom to change his clothes and see if his sick wife needed any attention. She never even saw the strangers; by the time Macy came out, the rain had stopped and they left the house.

But someone saw them, and soon enough the authorities came to investigate. Macy was called to Boston to account.

He delayed for a time. He pleaded that he was "destitute" and could not afford to buy a horse to take him to the seat of authority. But eventually he had to appear, and he did. The magistrate reminded Thomas Macy of the law: the punishment for entertaining Quakers came to five pounds for every hour they were under one's roof. After hearing Macy's story, authority pondered, and fined him thirty shillings for his momentary lapse of kindness to those four Friends.

Macy went home, chagrined. He was a lucky man to get off so lightly—the proof came a few weeks later when two of those Quakers he had harbored in the rainstorm were hanged in Boston for professing their religion. Mainland Massachusetts was not a very pleasant place to live, Thomas Macy decided. And like many another since, he decided to get away from it all, by moving to Nantucket. He bought into the island with Tristram Coffin and the others, and prepared to remove.

Macy's first voyage to the island, in the fall of 1659, was slightly different from those of the present day. No ferry from Woods Hole or Hyannis for him; he bundled his wife and five children into a boat. They were joined by his friend Edward Starbuck, one of the ten new partners and a Baptist from New Hampshire. Starbuck was also in trouble. He had been taken to court a few years earlier charged with "the profession of anabaptism," so he found mainland New England no more hospitable than did the Macys. Isaac Coleman and James Coffin, who could speak the Natick language, were also aboard on Macy's first crossing to Nantucket.

They sailed down around Boston Bay, and then out and around the tip of Cape Cod. Thomas Macy never looked back. He was giving up

his house, his land, his personal property and his neighbors, for whatever they meant to him. He was heading into desolate Indian country
where he knew not another white man lived.

They encountered the bad weather for which the Atlantic around
Cape Cod and the islands is notorious. The wind howled and the
rain came down, and they were soaked in the little boat. Macy's wife,
Sarah, became frightened and appealed to her husband to do something to save them before they were swamped and drowned.

"Woman, go below and seek thy God," said her husband—indicating
that Baptists talked just like Puritans in the fury of the storm. "I fear
not the witches on earth or the devils in hell."

And Thomas Macy sailed on.

Starbuck and the Macys headed for Madaket harbor on the outer
island, that "heap of glacial drift" where the Macys would put down
their roots.

The manner in which Macy and the others spent that first winter of
1659 is not well known. They may have dug a hole in the ground and
built a roof over it, or they may have built a rude house of native
timber. They arrived in the autumn, the loveliest time of year on the
island, when the breezes were warm and the yield of nature bountiful
in the Indian summer. They made friends of the Indians, and had no
trouble at all.

When spring came and the ground dried, Macy and his male
companions set out from the shelter near the Madaket shore where
they had spent the cold winter, each man bent on finding himself a
more comfortable spot. Thomas Macy located his second house at
Watercomet, near Reed Pond. Edward Starbuck found a place near
the head of Hummock Pond that appealed to him. So they began to
settle in more permanently.

That year Edward Starbuck went back to mainland Massachusetts,
and then to Dover, New Hampshire, where he had been an elder in
his church. His purposes were several: to bring his family back to
Nantucket, because he had decided to make his life on the island;
and to proselytize for other settlers to come and join them, to make
their lot a little easier in numbers.

The Starbucks then returned to Nantucket—kit and caboodle, except
for two Starbuck daughters, who had married mainlanders and would
stay on. Their proselytizing soon brought others who were in trouble

with authority, or were somehow dissatisfied with life on the mainland. Richard Swayne, for example, had been fined even more heavily than Thomas Macy for entertaining Quakers. When Starbuck returned to Nantucket he brought ten more families.

Houses were built. How they were built is a question that has never been answered. Some historians say that by the time the white men came, Nantucket and Tuckernuck were virtually denuded of timber. It may be true; the Indians could well have cut down most of the trees for fuel in those damp, cold Nantucket winters. Perhaps some of the lumber came from Peter Coffin's sawmill at Exeter, New Hampshire. It has also been said that one of Tristram Coffin's points of interest in the island was that a settlement there would supply a good market for son Peter's business.

Certainly if there was timber on the island for the original houses, soon enough it was used up, and supplies began coming from the mainland, to Madaket, then the center of the white population. Soon John Bishop, a carpenter from the mainland, was persuaded to come to the island, in return for a half-share allotment of land. Peter Folger of Martha's Vineyard came over for another half-share, to be miller, weaver, and interpreter. He was also a joiner, and his son Eleazer was the island's shoemaker. First Purchaser Tristram Coffin came over, and was appointed the first magistrate of the island, while Thomas Macy became town clerk.

There was very little interference from the outside in these early years. In law, Nantucket island belonged to New York Colony, but it was nearly a decade after settlement before New York Governor Francis Lovelace paid any attention to the island or its people. Even then the attention was not much: Nantucketers paid a tax of four barrels of fish to the colonial government.

The islanders built their houses, traded with the Indians, planted their Indian corn, and fished and hunted for their food. Since there were so few of them they intermarried frequently. Coffins married Starbucks and Macys married Husseys until the whole island population seemed to be closely interrelated. Years later, after the decline of Nantucket had dropped the population from a high of 10,000 to half the number, Maria Mitchell, the island's famous astronomer who taught at Vassar College, was accosted by another scientist at a meeting.

"I met your cousin," said Maria's friend.

"Which one?"

"Your cousin from Nantucket."

"I've five thousand cousins on Nantucket," said Professor Mitchell.

These Mitchells and Macys and Starbucks and Coffins worked together well, for the most part. Their system of land ownership almost made it imperative that they be close and co-operative. For from the beginning, Nantucket's land was divided into two kinds. First was the house-lot land, suitable for building on. This was sold and parceled out to the settlers. But the rest of the land held by the whites on the island was owned and used in common.

From the early days when land ownership was vested in twenty-seven proprietors, allotments were distributed according to Nantucket's own system. Each original proprietor—the First Purchasers and their partners—held 720 acres of the commons for sheep. Given twenty-seven proprietors, this made 19,440 acres of common land. In the future, any land sales had to take the early system of land division into account. In later years ownership would be figured in such complicated fractions as 45/19,440 of the common land, or "45/720 of a share in Squam." Together the original owners were known as the Proprietors of the Common and Undivided Lands of Nantucket, and the system of land-holding they inaugurated continued without much change for 150 years until one of the richest men of the island got greedy and land hungry, and went to court with the mainland people to break the system.

Mary Coffin was the first white child to be born on Nantucket, in 1663. She grew up and married Nathaniel Starbuck, and they built one of the finest houses on the island; Parliament House, it was called, because it had the biggest room available for public meetings.

As the new settlers begat, so they farmed, and Peter Folger ground their grain, in the water mill at Lily Pond. The dam burst one year, and put that mill out of business, but another was soon built, and Peter Folger ran that one, too.

The first islanders got along famously with the Indians. The Mayhews, as missionaries, had done a lot for the Nantucket Indians before the place was ever settled by whites. The settlers came to be friends, and kept it that way. King Philip, of the Indians on the mainland, came over to Nantucket in 1665 seeking assistance of the island's tribesmen in a war with the English in Massachusetts. The Nantucket Indians gave him short shrift. Philip was also seeking the scalp of an Indian enemy named Assassamoogh, whom the whites protected. Assassamoogh had committed an unspeakable crime against an Indian taboo. He had once spoken aloud the name of Massassoit, Philip's father. For that the penalty was death. The whites did not accept the Indian verdict. In fact, Thomas Mayhew sent Assassamoogh to Harvard College, and he changed his name to John Gibbs. Assass-amoogh–Gibbs then became a preacher who served Nantucket and Martha's Vineyard missions for twenty-five years.

The Indians seemed happy enough with the whites, in the begin-ning. Sachem Wanackmamack was regarded by everyone as a fine figure of a chief, and Wauwinet, another of the sachems, was also held in high esteem. Nickanoose, the son of Wauwinet, was a scan-dalous fellow, however, who deserted his wife and children and went to live with another woman. Perhaps he was under the pernicious influence of firewater: even in the happy community of Nantucket, there were some who made or imported *spiritus frumenti* and sold it to the Indians.

Conditions among the drinking Indians sometimes went from bad to worse in the early years of white settlement. The Indian Quence divorced his wife in the white man's court—to which the Indians had equal access by law. Another Indian, Machoogen, turned out to be a burglar. Debdekcoat was "a fraudulent creditor." The most famous of the early Indian characters on the island was Korduda, or Kadooda, called James Shouel by the whites. After the sachems lost control to white law, Korduda became the instrument of that law on the island, and he was appointed magistrate of Indian affairs under the town government. He investigated burglaries and thefts. He checked into stories about Indians hyped up on firewater. Indeed, on Nantucket, he was the power among the Indians.

As time went on the Indians began making one complaint after another as the whites encroached on their territory and their old rights. The Indians soon learned that the courts might help them where argument would not. But Korduda then stepped in. If an Indian complained against another Indian, Korduda's decision was usually that they both be given a whipping. It was remarkable how the level of complaint was reduced by Korduda's management of affairs.

Korduda was called upon one day to adjudge a particularly trouble-some matter involving an Indian who claimed he had been wronged and wanted to go straight to see Squire Bunker, the magistrate for the whites.

"*Chaquor keador y taddator witche conichau mussay chaquor?*" asked the interpreter, turning to Korduda: "*What do you think about all this?*"

"*Martase couetchawidde neconne sussaurupte nehotie moche* Squire Bunker," advised Korduda: "*Maybe you'd better whip him first, and then let him go to see Squire Bunker.*"

By the time the interpreter turned around, the offended Indian was long gone.

Life was indeed quite manageable on Nantucket.

II

Saints and Sinners

WHEN THOMAS MACY and his family came to
settle on Nantucket, one reason the Indians were so friendly was that
they were used to white men already. The Mayhews had worked
among them for five years as missionaries, and converted several
hundred Indians to Christianity. In a few years the Indians had a
church of their own and a number of "praying men" besides the
Harvard-educated John Gibbs. Indians, in fact, seemed to be the best
educated people on the island. Joel, the son of Sachem Hiacoomes,
was sent to Harvard to join the class of 1665, along with Caleb
Cheeshahteaumuck. But the coming of the white men had already
begun the disruption of Indian society. Nantucket's two tribes had
lived at peace for years, ever since a line was drawn along the middle
of the island, north and south, delineating their territories. Five years
after the white man's coming, firewater and other foreign pressures
of an acquisitive society were making themselves felt among Nantucket's Indians. Joel came home for summer vacation in 1664, and
was murdered by a gang of robbers. Caleb was victim of another
gift of the white men: he died of tuberculosis shortly after graduation
from Harvard.

There were already great sinners as well as holy men on the island.
An exaggerated example of all the evils that had come and would
come to the Indians was a preacher named Hoight, who was genial
and friendly, but who succumbed to the evils of the flesh. He became
addicted to rum, and he chased squaws. "Do as I say," he counseled
his flock, "not as I do."

Still, there was no greater sinner on Nantucket against the purity of
the Christian ethic than Tristram Coffin, the leader of the proprietors,

who had acquired the island property in the first place. Tris Coffin suffered from the sin of pride, and before he was finished pride would lead him down a thorny path.

Love of power and possessions, that was the problem. The Nantucket settlers were anything but rich men. When Nathaniel Wier died in the spring of 1680, he was about as well fixed as the average islander. He left ten acres of land, his house and outbuildings, two steers, one cow, and six heifers, plus his personal and household effects. After the long winter, the family's provisions were down to seventeen cheeses, "20 weight of bacon," and a dozen bushels of grain.

Tristram Coffin was better off than that, by far, because he was a "proprietor," while Wier was a "half-share man," one who had been given a half-sized land allotment as an inducement to settle on Nantucket. Coffin lived at Capaum in a house he named Northam. He had extensive interests and connections on the mainland, including the lumber that must be brought from New Hampshire and Maine to build the houses. He controlled three of the twenty-seven proprietors' shares on the island.

Coffin and his wife, Dionis, were parents of nine children, and three-quarters of a century after they came to the island, their descendants numbered 1,582. By the middle of the twentieth century Nantucket Coffins had spread all over the world: the name Tristram Coffin was not at all uncommon throughout New England, and many other areas of the United States. But on Nantucket, in his lifetime, there was but one Tristram Coffin. He was the island patriarch.

As magistrate, Tristram Coffin was a hardworking, god-fearing taskmaster. Urged by Thomas Macy, he managed, a few years after the white settlement had begun, to secure passage of the first Blue Laws in America—prohibition of liquor, but only for the Indians. Coffin had a dream, too, of a class society in which he and his family would be the leaders. That dream accounted for the odd manner in which Nantucket's lands were held. The proprietors of the island were supposed to hold the common lands in perpetuity, and thus to assure the control of affairs by the landed gentry.

Tristram Coffin and Thomas Mayhew had influence with Governor Lovelace, who was a dandy of the court of Charles II in London. In 1671 Coffin went to a meeting with Mayhew's son and the governor. Coffin represented "the house of Coffin" as Mayhew represented the

Mayhews. Thomas Macy came along as well, representing "the people" of Nantucket.

In these early years, Coffin and his family were a little bit apart from the lesser men of the island. Yet Tris Coffin's dream was thwarted by the press of external affairs over which he had no control. His power was first challenged in 1672, when England and Holland went to war, and the Dutch regained temporary control of New York. When the English returned, Sir Edmund Andros became the new governor.

Such change was precisely what some of the people of Nantucket had been awaiting. After fifteen years, all was not harmony in Thomas Macy's paradise; and the difficulty was again sinfulness. The sin in this case was pride run up against the covetousness of the people who had been brought in by the original proprietors because of their special skills. These artisans, like Nathaniel Wier, had been granted half-shares, but they had no part in the common lands, and therefore no equality with the proprietors.

The leader of the half-share men insurgents was John Gardner, who had come to Nantucket in 1672 from Salem on the mainland as a professional fisherman. Gardner was an able man; soon he was chosen a selectman, along with Edward Starbuck, John Swain, Tristram Coffin and William Worth. Starbuck, Swain, and Coffin were proprietors, Gardner was not. Worth was Thomas Macy's son-in-law. The arguments began, for the ambitious half-share holder wanted full equality, and Worth was somewhere in between.

Maneuvering and scheming followed. Tristram Coffin lost his influence when Governor Andros came to power, for the new governor knew nothing of the history of the island. John Gardner managed to secure the new commission as captain of militia and his brother, Richard Gardner, became chief magistrate. The "new boys" thus held both political power and the muscle to enforce it.

In the spring of 1673 the Gardners traveled to Fort James on the New York mainland to receive their commissions. While in New York, they asked for permission to buy some of the Nantucket land still held by the Indians to enlarge their fishing business. So innocent a request, it might seem, so simple and straightforward. The governor granted them the favor without a qualm.

When the news hit Nantucket, it roused a storm that put the fierce nor'easters to shame. For it had been the intent of the proprietors

that no individual should ever be allowed to buy land from the
Indians. The Indian land was to be acquired in "the common interest,"
which meant the interests of the proprietors. If the half-share men
were to be allowed to acquire land for themselves, there was no telling
who would get control of Nantucket.

The island split into two camps. Tris Coffin and his fellow proprietors began bombarding New York with letters. The Gardners and their
friends wrote their own letters, charging that the original purchasers
were guilty of fraud. It was a power struggle, pure and simple. Coffin
had always claimed the right to vote the shares of his two sons, who
were proprietors, although they did not live on the island. The
Gardners insisted on the principle of "one man, one vote."

For two years they struggled. The Gardners controlled the courts
as well as the police system, so the Coffin faction's appeals were all
to higher authority.

In November 1674, Tristram Coffin took his case personally to the
governor, accompanied by Matthew Mayhew of Martha's Vineyard,
who had a similar problem. John Gardner and Peter Folger went to
New York, too, to represent the interests of the half-share men. Apparently Coffin won the case, for the governor reaffirmed the legality
of the land sales and the system of shares. Actually, however, the
balance of power had shifted to the half-share men. Perhaps they
could not get the property, but they outnumbered the proprietors,
and could exert political control. The situation deteriorated, as far as
old Tris Coffin was concerned, because Thomas Macy "turned traitor"
to his class, and joined the Gardner faction. In 1675 Macy was made
chief magistrate. Later on he and Worth quarreled with the Gardners,
and went back over to the proprietors' side. Peter Coffin then showed
up on the island, having been driven off the mainland by Indian wars,
and Tristram Coffin secured his son's appointment as assistant magistrate, even though Peter was a newcomer. Property had its privileges,
said the proprietors.

That appointment infuriated the Gardner men, among whom was
Peter Folger, the clerk of the court. He refused to carry out his duties
or to give up the court records, and so was ordered to prison.

Nantucket's prison in 1677 was also the community pigsty, and
when Magistrate Macy ordered Folger to jail, the hog in residence
had to be evicted. Although Peter Folger was a half-share man, he

had lived on the island for fifteen years. He was sixty years old, a respected artisan, citizen and local statesman, as well as an author, poet, interpreter, schoolmaster, preacher and father (he would be the grandfather of Benjamin Franklin). Altogether, Folger was a considerable man on the island, and the non-proprietors were furious to see the old fellow in the pigsty. Tris Coffin and Thomas Macy made it even worse, by losing not a moment in appointing their crony, William Worth, as the new clerk of the court.

Peter Folger remained in his pigsty for a year and a half awaiting trial, a martyr to the cause of freedom. Meanwhile the proprietors rode roughshod over their enemies. Gardners and their allies were convicted of the heinous crime of speaking evil of authority. Indians came up before Peter Coffin, who did not know them or their ways, and they did not like his judgments. In the opinion of the Gardner faction, life on Nantucket was becoming startlingly similar to the life on the Massachusetts mainland that most had opted to give up.

In 1677, it seemed that old Tris Coffin's victory was complete. He was made magistrate again, and the power was securely in the hands of the proprietors. Or so it seemed. The Gardners had been writing to New York during all these troubles. There was difficulty of communication because of the war on the mainland between King Philip's Indian followers and the colonists. Governor Andros was really too busy to pay much attention to Nantucket until the war ended. So old Tris Coffin and his friends rode high, but they went too far. They hailed John Gardner into court, and he refused to appear, so Tris Coffin fined him eight cows and sheep, and the authorities took away his civil rights.

That word got to New York just about the time that King Philip's War was coming to an end. Andros dismissed the court actions against Peter Folger and John Gardner, and Gardner's civil rights were soon restored.

Not long afterwards, Gardner was able to buy the land he wanted from the Indians, and in 1680 he became chief magistrate of Nantucket. He had conquered his old-time enemy, Tris Coffin, completely.

Around the same time, pride and greed led Tris Coffin into sin just at the moment he was at the height of his power. In September 1678, a French merchant ship was wrecked on the east end of the island. Two days later Coffin's son James and John Coleman asked the magis-

trate if they could salvage the cargo. The crew had failed, and
declared it too dangerous to attempt, they said. Magistrate Coffin
gave them permission, and the pair unloaded two thousand hides,
worth about four shillings apiece. They also took off sails and hawsers
and an anchor. In all, the salvagers made off with more than £400
worth of goods. When one considers that two years later Nathaniel
Wier's total worldly possessions were valued at £35, it is not hard to
see that Coffin and Coleman salvaged themselves a small fortune.

The matter was not treated lightly by Tristram Coffin's enemies,
and soon charges were made to the governor that the magistrate was
cheating higher authority in behalf of his family. The governor called
on Coffin to account. Coffin stalled for a while pleading "windye &
could raw weather," his own weakness of old age (he was seventy-
three) and confusion. He finally sent off three salvaged guns, and
pleaded that there was nothing else of much value: a few pieces of
small hawser that were hardly worth saving, a handful of shrouds,
most of them cut up, and forty hides, so rotten that they were worthless.

Events overtook Tristram Coffin. The governor summoned a Board
of Admiralty. The order came through in the summer of 1680, when
Coffin's bitter enemy John Gardner was chief magistrate, and Gardner
was appointed to the board! So were a pair of sea captains. And when
the truth came out, the court ordered Tristram Coffin to pay back
more than £300 for the hides taken unlawfully from the wreck.

Tristram Coffin again pleaded innocence, old age, and poverty. His
son James, who had done the salvage job, paid off seventy-five pounds,
and the governor reduced the fine so that it would be cleared by
another seventy-five. Apparently the governor was persuaded to this
course by John Gardner. The taste of victory was sweet, but the taste
of charity sweeter. And so, after all those years, the lion lay down
with the tiger, and a certain unity was restored to Nantucket island.

III

They Lived and They Died

IN 1729 A NANTUCKET man named Ebenezer Barnard tilled five acres of sandy pasture between Long Pond and the west end of Nantucket town. The land had always been regarded as indifferent in quality, and so it proved in the autumn when the corn was ripe. Barnard reaped a crop of 250 bushels, and was not overly pleased. But what was one to expect from farming on an island that was little more than a sandspit? Fifty years later the people of the island had so overworked the land that a Madaket planter felt pleased enough to get twenty bushels to the acre. And from there it was all downhill. By the 1970's Nantucket farmland was reduced to a few gardens, a few livestock farms, and the big truck gardens of Bartlett Farms. There was just about enough gardening potential to help out with the summer pressures on the grocery supermarkets.

Small wonder then, that as early as 1690, when some Nantucketers were standing atop Folly House Hill, looking out to sea, they observed with grave interest the spouting and play of a school of whales just offshore.

"There," said one graybeard to another, "is a green pasture where our children's grandchildren will go for bread."

They were not to wait nearly so long. Whaling would become Nantucket's major industry in the lifetime of their own children.

Although it was hardly an industry among them, whaling had been part of the way of life of the Indians before the white man came to the island's shores. The Indians went out in their canoes—many, many canoes—and struck at the whales with bone harpoons fastened to ropes of bark. When the whale tired the hunters shot him with arrow after arrow until he was dead, and then dragged him ashore to cut up the blubber and the meat and divide it among the families. Indian whaling was incidental; the Indians never went offshore after whales specifically. If the whales came to them, they would hunt them, but otherwise they were out in their boats fishing for cod and bluefish, scup, haddock, striped bass, herring, and many other varieties, some of which have thinned out and disappeared over the centuries. The Indians were not very efficient fishermen; they used lines of twisted grass and big bone hooks that would attract a school of frenzied blues, perhaps, but must have been eyed askance by many another fish. In fact, say the historians, the Nantucket Indians were incompetent fishermen before the white men came to teach them their methods.

The whites taught the Indians to fish efficiently, and the Indians taught the whites how to whale. It was a few years after the original settlement before the first whaling adventure happened. It was really an accident all around. A whale strayed into Nantucket harbor and remained there for three days. The villagers got the blacksmith to make a harpoon of steel with a wooden shaft, and they went out in boats and harpooned the beast. They managed to kill the whale, dragged him back to shore, and cut him up. The success whetted their appetites, and so in 1672 the settlers of Nantucket began looking around for a professional whaler, whom they proposed to attract to the island by the offer of a half-share of land, as they had attracted others with useful skills. Long Island had a tradition of whaling from the shore, so the Nantucket men turned there, and made a contract with a whaler named James Loper to come to the island. The contract was the usual agreement of its day: ten acres of land and the right (for a fee) to pasture in the common land, if Loper would come for at least two years. Loper never came, but later John Savage did, and he became Nantucket's first whaler. Still later, the islanders turned to Cape Cod, where the settlers had gained more proficiency in whaling, and about 1690 they brought over Ichabod Paddock.

Nantucket's Indians became whaling specialists, and soon many of the boats were manned entirely by Indians. They were also good fishermen, once they had the white man's equipment, for whaling and fishing fit well into their old way of life, as few things about the new community did.

Before fishing and whaling took hold, the settlers had mostly built their houses away from the sea, seeking whatever shelter the forests and hills would give them against the cold winter winds. But with the advent of whaling and fishing, they built shacks near the shore, and put up a tall spar fitted with cleats so a lookout might climb to the top of it. The lookout station was manned by whalemen during the season. When whales were sighted, the boat stations were roused, and the chase was on. In the autumn, and even the calm days of winter, the shore whalers sometimes went so far out to sea that they were out of sight of the island. They were successful year after year, for Nantucket was in the feeding grounds of the right whale, a species that frequented the coasts and so was fairly easy to hunt. The Nantucket men took fifty or sixty whales a year with this simple system.

Having sighted a whale, chased, harpooned and killed it, the whalers "saved" it, bringing the beast in as close to the shore of the island as possible, and then attaching it to a "crab," which was a capstan placed on the shore. Once beached, the animal was cut up with flensing knives, and the crab was attached to the strips of blubber, which were then cut and torn from the carcass, and hauled up on the beach to be loaded into carts and carried to the try-houses where fires were lit and the blubber was boiled down for its oil.

Huts, and later houses, were built near the shore. Two villages sprang up from the whaling and fishing, and one of them, Siasconset —called " 'Sconset"—survived long after shore whaling ended, eventually to become the summer colony it is today.

The settlement continued, and headed steadily toward the area of the island that would become Nantucket town. In the beginning it was known as Wesko, for a certain white rock that lay at the foot of what is now Straight Wharf. The watermen in particular favored Wesko—this is where John and Richard Gardner built their houses, and where they tried to acquire land from the Indians, thus creating all the fuss with patriarch Coffin.

Very early the settlers began laying out roads and streets. Richard Swain and Thomas Coleman were the surveyors in 1664. The next year grand plans were afoot—to dig a trench and drain the Long

Pond, for the dual purpose of accommodating a fish weir and creating more meadow land for feed. The Indians were to take charge of the fish traps, if they would do half the work, and for their trouble they were to have half the fish. It was always hard to keep the Indians working, and they were beaten often for failing to take care of their corn. The poor Indians did not prosper at all among the white men. They were not equipped to compete in a vigorous Anglo–Saxon society. Little by little they sold off their lands to the whites. Little by little they sickened and died with fevers and malaises of various kinds, most of the sickness very improperly understood.

Life had been simple before the whites came. The Indians fished and hunted and grew enough corn for their needs. But the whites had so much greater needs, and the Indians were whirled into a society that demanded more houses, more roads, more services.

The common land of Nantucket was used to support the livestock of the settlement. The proprietors had certain rights for pasturing and tillage, but for fees the artisans and others who came could use the common lands. It was a full-time job keeping track of animals and pastures, what they ate and what they were supposed to eat. Four geese equalled a sheep, and it went up from there in terms of what a man could run on the land. They raised geese and chickens, cattle and sheep, hogs and horses.

Twenty years after the arrival of Thomas Macy and his family, that old devil Incest was beginning to show his face on the island. In *Nantucket Odyssey,* Emil F. Guba waded gingerly into these deep waters. If Maria Mitchell at the end of the nineteenth century indicated that she was related to nearly everyone on Nantucket, the truth was not too far away. In the nineteenth century one minister, pondering the future of so ingrown a community, said that Nantucket was nearly a third Folger, with large doses of Coffin, Gardner, Ewer, Starbuck, and Cartwright. Ewer and Cartwright were new names, they were latecomers to the field, but the others will be familiar enough. One reason that Tris Coffin and John Gardner made up their differences must have been the intermarriage of their families. Nantucket was so ingrown by 1693 that Matthew Mayhew wrote about the situation to the governor of Massachusetts (the island had become part of Massachusetts by an act of 1691). The cause of justice was hardly served on Nantucket these days, Mayhew wrote. Intermarriage was so general on the island that it was difficult to get a jury that was not related to a principal in any case. Later Coffins and Folgers and Husseys were not all so very smart, either. The governor listened, and decreed that thereafter all capital cases would be tried by a special court, and all appeals were taken to Boston.

The same situation held on Martha's Vineyard, where Alexander Graham Bell later discovered that intermarriage had resulted in the creation of a huge deaf-mute population (4 percent of the island). Nobody ever had the courage to survey Nantucket, and the idiots, imbeciles, and feeble-minded of the families were kept sequestered. Nantucket always tried to take care of its own.

But there was the other side of the inbreeding issue—the transmission to the lucky ones of the strong traits, as with the Coffin–Gardner combination, which, if it produced sparks, would also produce high spirits and plenty of determination.

Thus was created the Nantucketer: a fiercely independent soul. How else? For consider the difficulties under which people of Nantucket lived. The sea around them was barrier as well as provider. They had come because of the barrier, the first of them, escaping the strictures and unpleasantnesses of life in a strictly Puritan community. On Nantucket sometimes they forgot that fact in their attitude toward their fellow men. The people who came after the proprietors had a different motivation from theirs. For the most part they were attracted by economic opportunity, and tolerance was not even a part of what they sought on the island. John Gardner, when he was in power in Nantucket, opposed and discouraged the spread of the Quaker belief. In land dealings, some of the white settlers took unfair advantage of the Indians, obtaining much for little, and perhaps that little paid in rum.

By the third generation, around the turn of the eighteenth century, the people of Nantucket had begun to acquire characteristics that set them apart from others. Speech was one. About two centuries later E. K. Godfrey noted the difference in the Nantucket speech sounds. "Bar" became *bah,* "yonder" became *yondah,* "here" became *heah,* and "wharf" became *whaahf.* This was in distinct contrast to the speech of Martha's Vineyard, only thirty miles away and Cape Cod, where "bar" was *baer,* "wharf" was *whaerf,* and "yonder" was *yondehr.*

There were other characteristics. Nantucket people were more

friendly than Cape people; as a visitor left he was always asked to
come again. That is logical enough, of course: by 1700 Nantucket still
numbered only around 700 white settlers, and new faces offered one
of the few diversions on the island.

In the culinary department, said Mr. Godfrey, old Nantucket had
several idiosyncrasies. By New England standards, the Nantucketers
never learned how to make clam chowder.

Oh, they could cook clams, all right, *but they left out the potatoes!*

Either Mr. Godfrey was misinformed, or in the years since his time
the Nantucketers have mended their erring ways, for the cookbook
put out by the Nantucket Old People's Home Association, the cookbook issued by First Congregational Church, and Mary Allen Havemeyer's Nantucket cookbook of 1976 all use potatoes in their chowder
recipes.

As the years went by, Nantucket cooks developed so many special-
ties that whole cookbooks could be devoted to them, and were. The
real Nantucket items, of course, stem from the food resources of the
island: fish, shellfish, corn, beach plums, cranberries, rose hips. In
the hard times of the beginning years very little was wasted, and thus
developed the Nantucket specialty of "chitlin's and britches." They
have nothing to do with Maryland or Virginia chitlin's—this dish comes
straight from the codfish: the britches are the roe.

Nantucketers also ate wonders—doughnuts without a hole, and
various kinds of corn meal pudding, ranging from Whigpot, a break-
fast dish of cooked corn meal, molasses and milk, to Mendon Bannock,
which is a mixture of corn meal, eggs, sugar, salt and milk, cooked
on a griddle.

The recipes of the modern Nantucket cookbooks have been changed
to fit modern cookery, but the surnames of the donors tell the story
of their heritage. Eliza Hussey Gardner contributed a recipe for
scalloped clams, which probably came down from the days of her
forbear, John Gardner. It consists of clams and crumbs and butter.
And there was Lizzie Folger's Meat Loaf Surprise, Louise Hussey's
Kale soup, and that catchall group of Old Nantucket Recipes, for
jellies of rose hips and beach plums, and blueberries and cranberries.

As the island entered the eighteenth century, Nantucket town had
not yet become the islanders' metropolis. Capaum was their harbor,
until a storm closed it up and they moved to the present Nantucket

harbor. Their craft were so small at first that they needed very little harbor, and, of course, there were so few of them.

So few, indeed, were the settlers in the beginning that the first dead were buried on their own lands. In 1662 Richard Swain's wife, Jane Bunker, died, and was buried near her house. The next year, young Jethro Starbuck was crushed to death by a cart, and he was buried on the family grounds. These were tragedies, people dying before their time, as was the terrible shipwreck of a young party in the spring of 1669. John Barnard and his young wife Bethiah Folger Barnard wanted to go to the more populous island of Martha's Vineyard to buy some household goods that were not available on Nantucket. They were joined by Bethiah's brother Eleazar and Isaac Coleman, all of them young people in their twenties. They set out one fine June day in a cruising canoe owned by one of the Indians, who had agreed to take them over and bring them back in the next day or two, depending on the weather. They made the journey safely, and bought what they wanted, then headed home. But on the homeward journey, the wind struck up, as it can so quickly in Nantucket's waters. Soon the sun was hidden behind glowering gray clouds, and the waves were slopping over the canoe's sides. The storm worsened even as they headed for safety. The canoe finally capsized on Tuckernuck shoals, and all were thrown into the water. Eleazar Folger clung to the canoe, and was washed up half dead on an island just off Cape Cod many hours later. All the rest were drowned. The little community mourned its dead, but of course the young people had simply faced the dangers of the life they lived. That life would go on.

In the last years of the seventeenth century, the original settlers began to pass along. Tristram Coffin died in 1681, Thomas Macy in 1682, and Peter Folger and Edward Starbuck in 1690.

When death began to come naturally, and the population increased, the settlers of Nantucket set aside a burying ground on the hilltop overlooking Maxcey's Pond and the moors outside the village that was developing there, called Sherburne after 1673. To the north of their first burying ground now stands the Wannacomet water tower. The graves were marked, but over the years the inscriptions weathered, and by 1875 the only one still legible was that of John Gardner, who died in 1706. The graves of Tristram Coffin, Thomas Macy and Peter Folger might as well have been unmarked altogether.

Sic transit gloria mundi.

IV

The Quakers

THE ORIGINAL SETTLERS of Nantucket were god-fearing men for the most part, but their religious beliefs were so divergent that for half a century there was no church nor any minister as such on the island. Some islanders were Baptist. Some were Presbyterian. Some professed the faith of the Puritan fathers.

Usually Nantucket people did not quarrel over religious matters but left each other alone in this regard. Their arguments were over more worldly matters; for example, when the settlers met to discuss the invitation to Peter Folger to come and live with them, John Bishop, the carpenter, offered the only objection. Folger was being brought in to run the mill, and Bishop had plans of his own along the same lines. Again, the long quarrel between the Gardner faction and the Coffin faction had nothing to do with religion. Moral issues, yes. The reason Thomas Macy changed sides in that fight, starting with Gardner and ending with Coffin, was his disgust when he discovered that the Gardners gave rum to the Indians. That was moral, but not religious.

The settlers were, in a sense, drawn together even in their times of quarrel by the Indian wars on the mainland, and the tightening in the 1670's of the Massachusetts colony's religious restrictions. The wars brought relatives and friends to the island seeking shelter, and their common problem gave them a new tolerance. Even when he was in deep trouble with the Coffin authorities in 1676 Peter Folger stood for such tolerance. On April 23 of that year, Folger wrote a long epic poem which he called *A Looking Glass of the Times*, and which Benjamin Franklin, his grandson, later called "homespun versifying." The poem was occasioned by King Philip's depredations among the folk of the mainland, the burning of settlements, the murder of white settlers, their wives and children, and the general air of anger and despair that filled the northern colonies in these desperate days.

> *Let all that read these Verses know*
> *that I intend to something show,*
> *About our War, how it hath been,*
> *and also what is the chief sin*
> *That God doth with us contend. . . .*

Like most of those old settlers, Peter Folger was much concerned with his immortal soul and those of his relations. Next year, lying in his pigsty prison, feeling his sixty years, Folger wrote his son-in-law, Joseph Pratt, a long letter devoted entirely to matters of the soul. "I am now past the 60th year of my age and know not the day of my death, but this I know, that whenever it be it will be a joyful time to me. . . ."

Three years later, Peter Folger embraced Quakerism.

He was not the first Quaker on the island. John Swain was a Quaker, and so was Stephen Hussey, his brother-in-law. But when the proselytizing brethren of the Society of Friends visited the island they were deeply distrustful of this pair. For one thing, Swain and Hussey seemed unable to agree between themselves on matters of religion. Hussey was considered to be rich and overly concerned with wealth. Somehow the visitors had the idea that neither man was held in especially high regard by his fellow Nantucketers.

The settlers of the island had long known a good deal about Quakerism. The Macys certainly would never forget the embarrassment of trial and fine by the authorities for doing the Christian duty of sheltering Quakers from a storm. John Gardner wanted very little to do with the Quakers, and he tried when he was in authority to discourage them from coming to Nantucket. Quakers came to visit early. Historian Douglas Lithgow says a Quaker named Jane Stokes came in 1664, which was just as the settlement was really getting started. But it was thirty-five years more before Quakerism began to have much impact on Nantucket.

The surge of the religion of the Friends began with a Quaker named Thomas Chalkley, who came from England in June of 1698. Chalkley was an educated and intelligent man, and a very persuasive one. His coming was an event of importance, for seldom did such distinguished visitors arrive on island from across the sea. A public meeting was called, and Chalkley found the people of Nantucket "tender-hearted" and prepared to acknowledge his religious truths. Another meeting was held, and a full two hundred people turned out to hear Chalkley talk. It went very well.

"Oh, how was my soul concerned for that people," said Chalkley. He preached with fervor and effect.

Despite his coolness toward Quakerism John Gardner asked Chalkley to hold a meeting at his house, and Chalkley did. Afterwards, Gardner got into a religious argument with the Quaker. He had argued religion with Quakers before. The important result of Chalkley's visit, however, was the later conversion of Nathaniel Starbuck, one of the most highly respected citizens of Nantucket. Many others were at least half-convinced, and so when Chalkley and his party left, a large crowd saw them down to their boat, and called to them to come back and visit again. That was the Nantucket way, of course, but Chalkley took it seriously, and reported that there was fertile ground for the Society of Friends on Nantucket island. The stream of Quakers continued.

Two years after Chalkley's visit to the island, Starbuck and his wife Mary were both converted to the belief of the Friends, and they began to spread the doctrine. Mary was impressive: she was a very strong character, mother of ten children and manager of a household. The Starbuck house with its big room suitable for meetings became the center of Quaker activity on the island. Mary Starbuck was a celebrated preacher, and she converted many of her fellows to the new faith.

Chalkley came back to Nantucket for a visit in 1704, and found a growing quarrel between the island's Quakers and the Presbyterians, who spoke up loudly against the Friends. Starbuck took him to the house, and they held several meetings there. They went out to visit John Swain and found him with a crowd of Indians in the middle of a house raising. They held a meeting that evening, and were pleased with the results. Young Nathaniel Starbuck, son of Mary and her husband, put them up at his own house, since there was no inn or any public accommodation on the island. But for meetings in town, they almost always went back to the elder Starbuck's Parliament House.

Seeing how matters were on the island, Chalkley persuaded Mary Starbuck to take the responsibility for preaching and proselytizing, and thus was established the first Quaker Meeting on Nantucket. Mary Starbuck was fifty-nine years old at the time, but she did not spare herself. Four years later the Quakers were fully established as Nantucket's leading sect, and were in touch with other meetings at Sandwich on Cape Cod and in Rhode Island. In 1711 there were so many Quakers on the island that they secured a lot from the authorities for a meeting house and a burying ground, and constructed both, just southeast of the ancient burying ground where John Gardner lay. By the time Mary Starbuck died in 1719 the community of Quakers had become the moving force on Nan'ucket. By the end of the eighteenth century half the people of Nantucket belonged· to the Society of Friends.

As the Quakers gained influence, Nantucket changed, in habit and in speech. The Friends did not use the names of the days of the weeks as others, thus a Quaker would read to his children of Robinson Crusoe and his good man Sixth Day. One wag suggested that the Quakers would "Bowdlerize" even simple, homely poesy:

> *Third Month winds and Fourth Month showers*
> *Soon make way for Fifth Month flowers.*

And there was the true tale of the Quaker schoolmaster on Nantucket who set up the copy for his class in Spencerian handwriting as "Beauty fadeth soon, like a rose in Sixth Month."

It was a good thing the Quakers were not afflicted with a sense of humor—and they were not: humor generally was regarded as much too worldly for Nantucket Quakers.

Being islanders, the Nantucket Quakers picked up some odd notions of their own. Quakers in England and on the American mainland knew that the nominative, or subject form of address was Thou. "Thou knowest the First Day," one Quaker might say to another. But not a Nantucket Quaker. "Thee knowest," said the Nantucketer, and he made an absolute botch of thou-ing and thee-ing, almost always using the objective, Thee, for all purposes. It became endemic with Nantucket Quakers.

It was odd how Mary Starbuck brought the religion of the Friends to Nantucket, for there was nothing in her family background to suggest any such proclivity. She was the seventh child of old Tristram Coffin, and most all the Coffins were irreligious. There is a bit of doggerel from a Nantucket man who married a later Coffin that tells something about the families:

The Rays and Russells coopers are;
The knowing Folgers lazy;
A learned Coleman very rare,
And scarce an honest Hussey.

The Coffins noisy, fractious, loud,
The silent Gardners plodding,
The Mitchells good, the Barkers proud,
The Macys eat the pudding.

The Swains are swinish, clownish called;
The Barnards very civil;
The Starbucks they are loud to bawl;
The Pinkhams beat the devil.

Or, as the old Nantucketer told a young man who asked for his daughter's hand in marriage:

"My daughter, sir, has in her veins some of the blood of all of the original settlers of Nantucket, and a queerer lot God never made!"

No one ever claimed that the Quakers were not as queer as anyone else. But at least they were serious about it, and as time went on the deadly seriousness of the Society became apparent. The men who chose to fight in the American Revolution were almost uniformly disowned by the Quaker Meeting for their actions. Reuben Barnard was disowned for becoming a privateer. He was captured by the British and put aboard a prison ship; that made no difference to the Meeting. David Coffin, Jr., was disowned. He drowned at sea, and it was just as well: his family, Coffins or not, could never have gotten him into the Quaker burying ground. Elihu Coffin was disowned, and so was Job Coffin, and Obadiah, and Tobert, and Valentine. So it went, on down the line to Asa Folger and Benjamin Folger and John and Obadiah Folger and Obed and Reuben and Robert and Simeon. Even Paul Hussey was disowned, although his great crime was that he went on an armed ship to negotiate the exchange of prisoners with the British at New York in 1778.

Sometimes people wonder why Nantucket was generally neutral in the war of the Revolution, which she was. Well, since more than half the 5,600 people on the island were Quakers, and the Brethren had that nasty habit of throwing offenders out of the faith, and anyone who bore arms, for whatever cause, was an offender—there wasn't much wonder about it, after all.

There just wasn't any compromise. A Quaker could marry only another Quaker, unless he or she wished to be disowned. "On Nantucket," said one reporter, "this fostered blood marriages and violations of God's natural law." It certainly did. Other Quakers elsewhere were not nearly so stiff, but that was not Nantucket's way. Of the forty-seven Quakers who fought in the war, forty-seven were disowned, including one who served under John Paul Jones on the *Bonhomme Richard*. The Quakers of Nantucket just didn't give a damn!

V

The Indians' Revenge

OLD TRISTRAM COFFIN had always held that strong drink would be the undoing of Nantucket, but the Coffins were notoriously loquacious and so very few people paid much attention.

When the Quakers began to assume moral ascendance on the island, they kept public morals fairly well under control. Unlike many towns, and even villages, on the mainland, Nantucket did not sprout rum shops or suffer from public drunkenness. Nevertheless, drink did have its evil effects, and the Indians of the island were the first to suffer. By the beginning of the eighteenth century the Indians were on the decline, led by the Demon Rum, and sometimes by the infamous Preacher Hoight.

Drunken Indians soon became sick Indians, prey to smallpox and diphtheria and tuberculosis. The lesser spirits among them discovered that they could attach themselves to the whites and get by with very little work. Many were reduced to outright beggary. The Gardners and other fishermen hired the Indians, and took care of their families. Although Nantucket's Quakers soon declared themselves firmly opposed to slavery, the condition of the Indians on the island was not far from it.

Among the Indians there were some god-fearing Christians, touched by the Mayhews and their spiritual descendants. At one time the Christian Indians had four meeting places on Nantucket, one near Gibbs swamp at the east end of the island, one at Miacomet, one near Polpis, and one near Plainfield, inshore from Siasconset. The Mayhews had arranged for distribution of Bibles written in the Natick language, and those Indian Harvard graduates, at least, could read them. The religious Indians took up white ways; they built houses of wood with brick chimneys, just like the whites. They bought cows and horses and sheep, they kept fowl, and they lived like the whites. It did not save them. The Indian population kept going down, down, down, until by the middle of the eighteenth century there were fewer than 500 Indians on Nantucket. Then in 1763 they were stricken by disaster. In August of that year either plague or yellow fever came to the island. The whites seemed to have immunity, but not the Red Men. The Indian population was already reduced to 358, and in a matter of weeks the little community was practically destroyed. All told, 222 Indians died, which left only 136. Accident, the rigors of the sea, sickness and drink soon enough did for the rest of them, and in 1822 the last full-blooded Nantucket Indian died.

The white population grew as the Indians declined. In 1719 there were 721 whites on Nantucket, but just before the outbreak of the Revolution someone counted 4,545.

Nantucket, then as now, was ever changing. Around 1720 the town moved from the Wannacomet area to the present site, centered around the old Wesko. Windblown sand had closed the harbor at the original settlement, and the need for decent port facilities had arisen once more. The Wesko site provided a fine harbor for small craft. The fact that there was a bar two miles off the beach did not make any difference to the boats and small ships Nantucket men were using in the eighteenth century.

When the townsmen moved to Wesko, they moved their houses with them. There were already some houses in the area. The Gardners had settled here, and so had some other newcomers. The house known today as the island's oldest was located here, although by the time the mass migration to Wesko occurred, it was being used as a storehouse for hay and grain. It was built by John Gardner and Peter Coffin for Mary Gardner and her husband, Jethro Coffin. Captain Gardner contributed the land, and Peter Coffin brought lumber from his New Hampshire mill in his own ship. Jethro Coffin did much of the building himself of the two-story house. When finished, it was regarded as one of the finest places on Nantucket.

The Quakers moved with the others, and built a new meeting house. They were among the first Abolitionists in America, their public condemnation of slavery having begun in 1716. That year the Nantucket Meeting went on record as holding it was "not agreeable to truth for

Friends to purchase slaves and keep them for a term of life." Quaker
Elihu Coleman was a leader in this movement, and in 1729 he read a
treatise before the meeting—"A Testimony Against That Anti–Christian
Practice of Making Slaves of Men." Of course not all Nantucketers,
by far, agreed with that philosophy. The Swains, for example, were
slaveowners. So were many other Nantucket men who professed either
Presbyterianism, the Baptist faith, or more likely, nothing at all.
"Nothingarians" they were called, and the Coffins led the list.

The Congregationalists had a foothold on the island. So did the
Methodists toward the end of the eighteenth century. As time went
on there were Arminians, Episcopalians, Roman Catholics, and later
Africans and Universalists. As the Nantucket society grew, it became
well churched.

The hard and regular life seemed to lengthen the lives of the white
settlers, and many of them lived into their eighties and nineties, in
spite of the diseases that visited the island. Worst of these were
pneumonia and tuberculosis. Smallpox ravaged the island several
times, but the moment it began the islanders were ruthless in seques-
tering the victims. They built a hospital on Gravelly Island, and they
practiced inoculation. They feared smallpox perhaps more than any
other ailment, for these hard old New Englanders knew that if the
word got out that smallpox had hit the island, the price of off-island
goods would jump. So the poor sick ones were sent away and prayed
over, and kept out of sight.

There was not much crime on old Nantucket, at least among the
whites. There were disputes, and court cases, but the worst crimes
were committed by the Indians. In the first century of settlement,
ten people were hanged for murder—all ten of them Indians. The first
such incident was the murder of the young Indian Joel, the Harvard
student, and the last was a multiple murder, crime and punishment
indicating how far along the path of society Nantucket had come by
the autumn of 1767.

By that time the Indians were in a sorry plight, and they recognized
it. In the 1750's, the Indians were restless and threatening. The whites
learned of an Indian conspiracy to rise up and assassinate the whole
settlement of Nantucket, and the sheriff took fifty men out to the
Indian settlements to make a show of force and quiet them down. The
show worked well enough, but the Indians then complained to Boston

authorities that they had been cheated of their lands. Of course this was true, but the Nantucket Indians had been cheated no more than any others: the pretense of purchase and sale had always been carried out, even though the value of what the Indians received was transitory, while the land remained. By mid-century, when the poor savages realized that all their lands were gone, it was too late. The deals had been sanctified by time, and the petition to Boston was answered with a long speech by an English judge who came to the Nantucket Meetinghouse to hear the case. Everything the whites had done was legal, according to the King's laws. Indeed, the learned judge said, Nantucket land records were the best he had ever seen—the land deals were legally even more correct than most of those on the mainland.

The unhappy Indians had no recourse left except to get what they could how they could, and so burglary, robbery, and murder appealed to more of them as the rum flowed.

Nantucket's economy grew handily in the eighteenth century, and the reason was those fields of blue surrounding the little island, which that one forefather on his hilltop had so wisely observed would be the plowing field of the Nantucket men of the future. The onshore whaling gave way to offshore whaling in the first quarter of the century. More people came to the island. Boats were built, and then ships, and soon so many were the latter that there were not enough young men and Indians to man them, and off-islanders were hired as seamen and whalers, men from Cape Cod, and men from Long Island.

The whale was a valuable creature. His fat made oil for lamps and for street lights in cities and towns. His bones made stays for ladies' corsets. His meat could be fed to Indians and animals. (There are not any notable recipes for whale meat among the Nantucket cookery books.)

At first, during the onshore whaling days, Nantucket shipped its surplus oil to Boston. The Boston merchants then shipped to England and made large profits. Nantucket men were just as good Yankees as Boston men, though, and some of them had capital; they decided to build their own ships and send the oil to England themselves, and let the devil take Boston town.

The islanders had learned a good deal about whaling before the middle of the century. The chief object of their hunting continued to be the right whale, however, until the day a sperm whale washed ashore on the island. When the islanders cut it up, they discovered in the head the "case," which contained many barrels of the finest, lightest oil they had ever seen. This was a beast worth chasing!

In 1712 Christopher Hussey was out whaling one day in an open boat, when he ran across a school of sperm whales, and killed one. What excitement that brought! The men of capital fitted out vessels of thirty tons and more, and began sending them out to deep water to search for sperm whales. It was a cautious business. The little ships went out for not more than a month and a half, and if they got a single whale, they cut up the blubber, and then brought it back to the try-pots on shore. Half a dozen of these ships were working in 1715 off Nantucket. A few years later Straight Wharf was built, and in 1730 Nantucket boasted some twenty-five whaling vessels fit for deep water.

It was 1745 before the Nantucket merchants were willing to chance a trading voyage of their own. That year they sent a load of whale oil directly from the island to London, and the ship returned with a cargo of hardware and manufactured goods without the extra expense of the middlemen in Boston. The merchants looked at the profits, and that settled it. From now on, Nantucket would seek to become *the* whaling port of North America, and the Nantucket men would handle their own business without "help" from the Boston merchant bankers.

The business had its ups and downs. In 1755 three whaling sloops were lost around the Grand Bank off Newfoundland. In 1766 another three vessels were lost, and six others were captured by the French during one of the periods of war between England and France, the crews and ships being taken off to France. The answer must be bigger and better vessels, to stay offshore and out of trouble, and soon Nantucket was manning square rigged ships and barques of a hundred tons. They moved from Davis Strait, in the waters southwest of Greenland, and from the Gulf of St. Lawrence, to the coast of Guinea and the mid-Atlantic. Every year there were more whales, more oil, more profits for Nantucket.

Indian sailors manned many of these vessels, and with or without firewater, the Indians nursed their grudges as they saw the whites in possession of their tribal lands. One whaling man, Benjamin Russell, sailed with several Indians in his crew, and did not seem to have any particular trouble with them until the fall of 1767. On the night of October 4, Russell moored his schooner, *Sally,* in the harbor at Nantucket, and went ashore. He spent the night with his family. The mates, Robert Ellis and Bryan Gall, remained aboard the ship in the cabin, while the Indians and the other members of the crew stayed in the forecastle. The mates went to their bunks that night and slept.

At 1:30 in the morning Ellis was awakened by dreadful sounds coming from the forecastle. Robin Narro, one of the Indian crewmen, was at the gangway, yelling his head off. The others were murdering each other up forward, he said. Ellis roused Gall, and the pair rushed forward and found Peleg Titus dying from a knife wound in the back, while the Indian sailors Nathan Quibbett and John Charles stood watching, both armed with knives. When Ellis demanded an explanation, Quibbett said he had stabbed Titus in self defense.

Self defense! Just then Isaac Jeffrey, another Indian, stuck his head up, and Quibbett saw him. He rushed down into the forecastle, crying that he would kill Jeffrey, too. He went below with his knife and proceeded to do just that, while the white men stood on the deck and listened to the woeful cries of the man being murdered below.

Quibbett reappeared, all gory and panting, and admitted that he had killed Jeffrey. The way he held his knife indicated to the others that Quibbett might not yet be through with his murdering. Mate Ellis grabbed him, and tried to get the knife, but in the struggle the weapon went overboard. Finally, three of them managed to overpower Quibbett and lock him in one of the ship's compartments for the night.

Next morning Coroner Timothy Folger held an inquest, and Quibbett and Charles were put in jail to await trial. The governor in Boston was informed.

In jail, Quibbett ran amok and killed John Charles. So Timothy Folger held another inquest.

Quibbett stayed in jail then, a ward of Sheriff Benjamin Tupper, until Chief Justice Thomas Hutchinson and Justices Peter Oliver and Edmund Trowbridge came from the mainland for the trial, on May 4, 1768. The town meeting chose a jury panel of forty-four men. This time they did not have their old trouble in finding an impartial jury, because Quibbett was an Indian, and not related to anybody except other Indians.

The grand jury indicted Quibbett, and the petit jury found him guilty. A Gardner was foreman of the grand jury, and a Hussey was foreman of the petit jury. Any Indian knew what to expect from that crowd; Quibbett offered no defense. Thomas Hutchinson was a hanging judge, and so on Thursday, May 26, 1768, a party of Coffins and Gardners and Folgers and Husseys and the rest gathered at the gibbet near the first milestone from Nantucket town on the Siasconset road. There Sheriff Tupper presided as they hanged Nathan Quibbett.

   Any Indian could have told you that was what was going to happen.

VI

Progress

NOT EVERYBODY who came to Nantucket was happy. In the middle of the eighteenth century, some Nantucketers moved away. A whole wave of them went to Nova Scotia after the French Acadians were expelled by the British, beginning in 1755. Another group moved to North Carolina. Some tried the Hudson River Valley. Some of them lasted there, some did not. But at least they were away from island life, which did not agree with everyone, by far.

Those who stayed on Nantucket and profited were not necessarily the scions of the old island families. In mid-century, for example, the biggest figure in the whaling business was William Rotch, who had several ships sailed by Coffins and Gardners, Folgers and others of the old crowd. Tris Coffin's dream of a landed aristocracy had not even survived a generation.

William Rotch was a Christian man, and a fellow of many parts. He did not write tracts about slavery, like Elihu Coleman and others who liked to preach. He did something about such matters.

Rotch owned the whaler *Friendship,* and in the crew was a black man named Prince Boston, a slave who belonged to William Swain, one of the Nantucket slave holders. When Swain died, Prince Boston became the property of the Swain heirs, even though he was at sea at the moment aboard the *Friendship.* She sailed out in 1769 on a whaling voyage that lasted less than a year, for the ships were still not venturing far away; there were whales aplenty off the Azores and in nearby waters in those halcyon days.

In 1770, when *Friendship* put in, all greasy, to Nantucket harbor on the return, Rotch from his countinghouse gave the men their "lays" or

shares of the earnings of the voyage, whaling always being a co-operative venture in which every man divided the luck according to his
station on the ship. The Swains objected mightily. Prince Boston, they
said, belonged to them, and so anything he had earned on the voyage
also belonged to them.

William Rotch did not believe in slavery. He took the case to the
court of common pleas, and he acted as lawyer for Prince Boston in
the suit. He won it. So thus a Quaker Nantucket whaleman struck the
very first blow for emancipation of the blacks ever managed in the
Commonwealth of Massachusetts, and shortly thereafter the blacks
of Nantucket became free men. If they went out a-whaling, they had
their lays just the same as an Indian or any white sailor.

The truth was that on Nantucket people were probably more nearly
equal than on the mainland. The Quakers kept reminding one another
and everyone else that every day brought a man that much closer to
the grave than he had been before, and even old Tristram Coffin had
never figured out a way to take it with him when they laid him in that
long-lost grave. Literally thousands of Quakers were buried in their
burying grounds in unmarked graves—that was how much regard they
had for mammon.

Quakers did have a fine regard for education, and under their
influence Nantucket provided better education for all than almost
any other place in the commonwealth. With occasional exceptions the
schools were run privately. The boys went to boys' schools and the
girls went to girls' schools; the boys were taught by men and the girls
by women. The Quakers had their own schools, following a tradition
that has come down in America to the present time. The blacks were
educated and so were the Indians, as long as they lasted. Orphaned
and poor children were educated by public charitable subscription.

Those Nantucketers took their obligations seriously. They had a
real community. At first there were not even very many lawsuits, because the people all knew that suing was an expensive luxury. They
adopted a system that we would call conciliation and arbitration.
When two men disagreed, they called in their neighbors and declared
a sort of holiday while they settled their differences amicably. That
done, it was back to work again, always remembering that man only
labored toward the grave.

In 1716 the Nantucket town meeting voted to hire Eleazer Folger as schoolmaster for one year, at a pay of three pounds. But for the next century the educational process was handled privately. The Reverend Timothy White, the first congregational clergyman to come to Nantucket, ran a school for fifteen years, beginning in 1732. He married a Gardner, the daughter of John Gardner III, but Gardners were not all rich. Timothy White had a hard time scratching a living on the island with his minister's pay, and that is why he turned to school teaching.

Teaching was a special province of the preachers, in whatever denomination. The Rev. Bezaleel Shaw kept a school, and so did the Reverend James Gurney. The Friends had their school in the old abandoned meeting house, and later in the house of the preacher Benjamin Coffin on Pleasant Street. As the island's population grew, so did the school pressures, until in 1800, when the island housed some 5,600 souls, Nantucket Academy was built up on the top of Academy Hill.

In the years before the Revolutionary War, the land of Nantucket was managed almost entirely by the original proprietors and their heirs, through their corporation. The artisans and others who had come later simply had to conform to the way of the men who owned the undivided lands and held them in common. Theoretically then, Tristram Coffin's plan was sound. Actually, the management became more complicated every year, and particularly every generation, as the number of inheritors grew and the available lands remained the same.

Nantucket was, after 1695, a Massachusetts county, a governmental entity in itself. Early in the next century Tuckernuck, Muskeget, and the Gravelly Islands became a part of Nantucket County. But that was the total extent of land acquisition that could be accomplished; there was not any more. Indeed, the erosion of the island's shoreline through the years indicated that there would be rather less land than more.

Before each spring, the proprietors met and established the tillage lots for the year. These were kept separate from the sheep's commons, which were used for pasture. The system was never a very good one, ecologically speaking, because no one had any real, continuing responsibility for the land: the man who planted corn on a plot in 1700 did not have to worry about that piece of ground in 1701, because it would be given to someone else for another purpose. Thus everything was taken from the soil, and nothing given back, and eventually the land began to show it. Before the end of the century the land was in poor condition.

The sheep pastured in common on one part of the forage land, and the cows and horses pastured elsewhere. Each year in June the sheep were flocked and brought to two shearing places, one at Washing Pond (which would later become the Nantucket town water reservoir) and the other at Gibbs Pond. They were sorted out by their owners, according to earmarks. The new lambs were marked and the old ewes and bucks were shorn.

Sheep, horses, cattle, hogs were all allowed to run at large, and the owners paid virtually no attention to them all the year around. The death rates were high, the steers became wild, the horses wilder, and hundreds of sheep died from lack of attention. The haphazard breeding policies developed a species of mutton that any self-respecting farmer on the mainland would have been ashamed to own; the sheep were small and yielded little wool. Nantucketers were poor farmers; by mid-century they were averaging about twelve bushels of corn to the acre, while good farmers on the mainland were getting eighty to a hundred bushels an acre. Just before the Revolution, Nantucketers complained that although there were more than 5,000 people on the island, "its produce was scarce sufficient for the maintenance of twenty families."

It was just lucky for the people of Nantucket that they had the sea to plow.

In the middle of the eighteenth century, whaling began to come into its own. That first venture to London in 1745 had proved so successful that the vast majority of the people of the island turned to the whaling trade and its supply and end product industries. Young men learned to make sails, to make barrels, to make lances and knives, to build ships, and to make rope, to make candles. Soon the wharves and the dock area of the island were sprouting sail lofts and cooperages, and smithy shops and warehouses.

The whaling industry took a while to develop, but the sperm whale was the key to success. The English wanted sperm oil for their city street lamps, and they would pay as much as eighteen pounds per ton.

That sum would keep three schoolteachers for a year. The lesser oil from the right whales went to Boston or to the West Indies.

At first the Nantucket whalers did not separate the fine oil of the sperm whale's head-case from the oil that was extracted from the whale's blubber. But they were taught by candle manufacturers on the mainland, and by mid-century they had learned. The case oil brought the highest price of all. Of course once the Nantucketers had learned this much, they set out to steal the formula for spermaceti candles, the closely guarded secret of Obadiah Brown of Providence. In time they learned, and set up extremely profitable candle works on the island, which continued as long as whaling prospered on Nantucket.

Just before the Revolution, when Mother England was trying to keep her colonies in line by frequent use of the rod, Nantucket had grown very prosperous from exploiting the sea. The London price of whale oil was up to £40 per ton for sperm oil, and £50 for head-case matter. The whaling captains went out in their boats, and brought home 26,000 tons of oil. The owners settled up on the basis of £35 for sperm and £44 for head matter. Then they shipped to London.

A whale might produce 120 barrels of oil, and 2,000 pounds of whale bone, which sold to England at around fifty cents a pound. So there was plenty of money to be made for those so fortunate as to be able to find the capital to invest. Whaling was always dangerous, but Nantucket men would gladly face the danger for the profits involved.

One July day in 1761 Captain Peter Folger was out a-whaling in his vessel, when one of his men committed a "foopaw" that was worthy of a "coof," the Nantucket word for off-islander. The worst "foopaw" a whaler could commit was to do something to miss the whale, and harpooner John Meyrick did just that. They were hunting whale, and for a time all they could see was a pair of ships off to the eastward. But then someone spotted a school of sperm whales, and the Folger crew was off in the boats after them. Folger's boat came up on a whale, the harpoon went home, and the beast spouted blood. "She went down and there came a snarl in the tow line and catched John Meyrick and over-set the boat, and we never saw him again afterwards.

"We saved the whale."

Captain Peter Folger knew what was important, all right.

Before the Revolution, the number of Nantucket vessels at sea rose to 140. Eight ships brought provisions to the island and took off what little besides whale products was produced. The rest were engaged in whaling, and they ranged from the iceberg seas of the north down to the Falkland Islands in the remotest South Atlantic.

In many a way, whaling changed the island. In Nantucket village, for example, the hill that slopes down from Main Street to Washington Street was relatively smooth in contour. But in the 1730's, when the harbor was being improved to handle the surge of whaling vessels, the land was dug away from Quanaty Hill to create the bank that falls down from the eastern side of Orange Street to Union Street.

The fishermen of Siasconset were still at work, providing cod and haddock and other fish for the islanders. The island's four big windmills ground the grain that was grown and brought in on their Mill Hills southwest of town. In 1745, the men of the sea gave serious thought to improvements, and Brant Point light was put up.

All Nantucket was prospering because of the new whale industry. There was trouble with the French in the 1750's and 1760's, but the end of the Seven Years War finished that, and the years just before the Revolution were the best of all. The islanders wanted peace, continuation of their business, and as little to do with government as possible. The Quakers among them objected to paying taxes even more than most businessmen did; once they had refused to pay the commonwealth's tax agent, and he had gone among the islanders collecting silver spoons and other valuables, until he had what he thought was right. The Quakers disliked the whole idea of a general government. A Hussey was sent to Boston to the General Court, and the elders decided it was unseemly for a Friend to sit there. When he continued, they disowned him.

Nantucket was highly regarded in London in these years, and Parliament, which had imposed restrictions on other Massachusetts fishermen, exempted Nantucket from the same restraints. But Nantucket could not escape the pressures of the times, no matter how much Nantucketers kept to their own ways and their own business. In 1773 three ships sailed from Nantucket to London loaded with whale oil; in England they were loaded with tea for Boston port. Two of the ships, *Dartmouth* and *Beaver*, were owned by Nantucketers: in fact the principal owners were the Rotches, the kindly entrepreneurs who had brought about the freedom of Prince Boston, the Swain slave. A Rotch was captain of *Dartmouth,* and *Beaver* was commanded by Hezekiah Coffin, another Nantucketer.

When *Dartmouth* arrived in Boston harbor at the end of November, the people of the town were up in arms about England's newly proclaimed Tea Tax, and after a meeting they began agitating for the tea to be sent back to England. They would not pay the duty Parliament demanded. For two weeks the argument continued, Bostonians on one side, and Governor Hutchinson and the authority of the King on the other. Captain Rotch was right in the middle, meeting with Governor Hutchinson, and also with Samuel Adams, the principal agitator of the revolutionaries. Under the law, a vessel could sit in harbor twenty days with its cargo unclaimed and intact. But at the end of the twenty days, if the tax on the vessel's cargo were not paid, the cargo could be seized for nonpayment of customs duties. December 17 was the twentieth day that *Dartmouth* and *Beaver* lay in the Port of Boston. On December 16, Captain Rotch had one last conversation with Governor Hutchinson, who declared that the law was the law and it would stand: the tea tax must be paid. Rotch so informed Sam Adams. That night a band of revolutionaries disguised as Mohawk Indians boarded *Dartmouth,* and dumped Captain Rotch's tea into Boston harbor.

Nobody could ever say Nantucket wasn't in the "thick of things."

VII

That Miserable Revolution!

THE BOSTON TEA PARTY was troublesome enough to Nantucket ship owners. There was precious little profit in picking up a cargo in London and having a bunch of wild men throw it into the harbor, insurance or no insurance. So when the Shots Heard 'Round the World were fired at Concord and Lexington less than two years later, there were very few rejoicers on Nantucket isle.

The Quakers were a majority on the island, and they absolutely forbade their members to take up arms and do violence to anyone. There were no Nantucket Minutemen. There was, however, one legitimate Nantucket hero in the Revolution: Reuben Chase, who served as a midshipman on John Paul Jones' *Bonhomme Richard*. He was made prize officer of the British brig *Mayflower,* and sailed it into the French port of Lorient on the Bay of Biscay before the fireworks with the *Serapis,* which Jones captured and took into port in Holland.

There were other brave men who went to sea, too, although most of the real Nantucketers preferred to serve on privateers and get a share of the loot. John Barnard was a cabin boy on the brigantine *Massachusetts.* Tristram Barnard bought the brig *Hannah* in London and manned her with American prisoners whose freedom he purchased. He brought a cargo of supplies to Boston. Peter Boston, a black man, was a seaman in Massachusetts colony's navy, and served for a time under Captain David Porter. Jonathan Briggs served in the army.

And there were others, including some fifty members of the Society

44

of Friends, who were disowned by the Meeting for their adherence to the American cause.

Benjamin Bunker, one who chose to fight for the Americans, created quite a stir on Nantucket when he flatly opposed the neutral policy of the Quakers. At one point, Bunker outraged the gentle Friends by capturing a British privateer off Great Point. He took his prisoners to the mainland, because to bring them to Nantucket would have been downright foolish.

To the Quakers and the other businessmen, the war was a real tragedy. For years until the 1770's Nantucket shipping had staggered under the blows of Spanish and French privateers. All that had ended, and the seventies brought a prosperity that gladdened the hearts of the householders of the town. The last thing they wanted was for this prosperity to be blighted by war with their chief trading partner, England. Still, Nantucket had its own revolutionary Committee of Correspondence, consisting of a Coffin, a Gardner, a Hussey and a Folger, plus Josiah Barker, one of the newcomers to the island.

When the hostilities began, the woe in Nantucket was great. Nantucket learned almost immediately of the events at Lexington, for a young man named Fred Crow brought the news from the mainland on April 21, 1775.

"All business was immediately at a stand," wrote Obed Macy. The people gathered in little knots and bemoaned their fate. They worried about the men at sea, those hundreds off a-whaling, who were husbands, brothers, sons and lovers. They worried about the ships and about trade.

"A common distress pervaded all hearts, which was in no way relieved by anticipations of the future."

No one had any idea how they were going to carry on business. That was the worst of it. Some hoped that even though there had been bloodshed, soon it would be business as usual. Others knew better. It would be a "long and terrible" contest, they said.

As the whalers came home, the ships were unloaded and then moved into the inner anchorage to be laid up. No one knew what to do. They could not go out whaling again in the face of privateers of both sides. In they came: Abner Briggs from Guinea with 100 barrels, and then Robert Hussey and Stephen Gardner; Nathan Coffin came in with 270 barrels.

One of the Swains left the island for the mainland. Several ships came from Boston and other ports, bringing people who believed there would be more safety among the Quakers of Nantucket than in America. It was confusion, and more confusion. Nantucket simply did not know what to do. In Philadelphia the Continental Congress knew. Nantucket was a damned nest of Tories, said Congress, and Massachusetts acted. On May 23 a ship entered Nantucket harbor carrying a hundred soldiers. They landed at the wharf and marched into town, shouting and muttering about the "Tories." They came to seize a supply of flour they suspected the Nantucketers were saving for the British. They stayed a few days and tried to recruit, without noticeable success. They seized the flour and other provisions, and went off with fifty of the island's whaleboats. Behind them, islander Kezia Coffin Fanning wrote in her diary:

"God save the King!"

In the summer of 1775 Massachusetts called all towns to send representatives to a general meeting at Watertown. But the town fathers of Nantucket were afraid that to do so would be to court attack from the British. The islanders had already had a taste of war—from their own American side—and they continued to show a distinctly cool side to the revolutionary mainland. Down in Philadelphia they began to like the Nantucketers less and less, and anyone from the island was presumed to be a Tory unless he could prove otherwise.

Nantucket began to suffer. In August 1775 Massachusetts interdicted future whaling voyages from the island. A handful of Husseys, Mitchells and Coffins protested, and tried to get special whaling permits. Some of them did. But soon enough Nantucket was in trouble again, because sharpers on the island were using the food permits to buy supplies which they then sold to the British. Governor Trumbull of Connecticut was furious, and demanded an explanation.

There was an explanation, although not one that would satisfy Governor Trumbull. Those Tories on Nantucket were trading with the enemy! A British man-of-war anchored off the Nantucket bar that fall. She ran out of supplies, and Nantucketers brought her bread.

Dr. Samuel Gelston was the go-between. He was caught by the Americans, and taken off-island to Plymouth jail. He escaped. He was recaptured at Newport and taken back to be held for trial. Gelston was charged with trading with the enemy and threatening to spread smallpox! He denied everything and asked to go home to his wife and eight children on Nantucket. He promised to reform. The mainland authorities let him go.

Nantucket men tried every slippery trick they could to keep on trading with the enemy. They sent ships to Trinidad and Tobago and to Grenada for supplies. Congress was angrier than ever, and outlawed any trading with the West Indies without special government permission. The independent Nantucketers went anyhow, braving the threat that their ships would be seized by the Colonial authorities. A Captain Fanning brought a load of supplies to Nantucket safely, and the rumor soon spread throughout Connecticut and Long Island that the supplies had been sent to the British in Boston. Kezia Coffin Fanning, a tireless diarist, said it was absolutely untrue. She was probably right—she seemed to know all the gossip of the island, and her heart was with the British, so there was no need for her to lie. But the point was that Nantucket's reputation was so bad in revolutionary America that the Continentals would believe any story of Nantucket treason.

At the end of 1775 Nantucket was in a serious plight. The success of the whaling trade in the past ten years had caused nearly every family on the island to base its personal economy on some aspect of whaling. Suddenly, whaling was impossible; if the Continentals did not cause problems, the British would. This was Nantucket's difficulty throughout. More than any other place in the colonies, Nantucket was dependent on British good will. She had herself made it so with the whaling trade, lured by those bright prices offered in London. The disregard the Nantucketers had shown for agricultural pursuit now settled down to haunt them. Nantucket began to suffer in the war.

Massachusetts asked Nantucket to contribute to the general good by using the islanders' gold and silver to buy Continental Currency, so the state and Congress might finance the war. Stephen Hussey, the agent of the state government, had to report back that no one on the island was willing to give up gold or silver for Continentals. Shrewd Nantucketers! They knew in 1775 that Continental dollars "weren't worth a Continental"; but the refusal did not endear the island to the Colonials.

During 1775, of course, it was still acceptable to hope for a reunion with the Mother Country, although reconciliation was looked on askance by the hotheads who wanted outright separation. In January 1776, the blow came: Massachusetts issued its own declaration of independence from Great Britain, and Nantucket shuddered as it read the fateful words, "God save the People," which appeared at the end of the proclamation, where always before the words had been "God save the King."

The worst fears of Nantucketers were realized almost immediately. The island could not produce enough food to feed itself, and several vessels were sent to the Kennebec River to secure supplies, as had been done for years. Back came the word from America: the supply vessels had been seized.

A few brave souls had gone, and would go, a-whaling. David Rand sailed for Iceland on a whaling voyage, but news was received that he had been captured by the English and sent to Halifax. A few more went out, but it became apparent the war was real and not a flare-up; the ships stopped sailing.

Nantucketers were considered to be of one particular value to the American effort; their relations with England made them useful as go-betweens. Early in the war Captain Seth Jenkins was entrusted with letters by some English friends of America to the Congress. For the moment there was a certain value in keeping such lines of communication open. The plight of Nantucket was very clearly shown in Jenkins' voyage. Seth Jenkins, George Folger, Alexander Coffin, and one of the Gardners were all caught short by the opening of hostilities. They had all sailed, that spring or summer of 1775, from Nantucket to London carrying cargoes of whale oil, in the pious hope that by the time they arrived all would be settled satisfactorily.

But by the time the Nantucket captains reached London, affairs had so deteriorated that they were in danger of losing their vessels, and perhaps even of being imprisoned. The captains sold their ships as well as their cargoes, and tried to find passage back to Nantucket on some vessel. They soon learned that no vessels were clearing for Nantucket, or any other part of America, except the instruments of war.

Of course, all these Nantucket captains were British subjects, and quite legally they could buy a ship and set out on a trading voyage. They did so. Through the influence of friends in high places they managed to buy a brig. They named her *Sherburne,* and loaded her with a cargo they said was destined for those parts of the new world that were not in rebellion. Most important, they managed to have their ship registered in London, which would save them from seizure by British customs, or by the blockading British fleet once they got into the Atlantic.

The American agents still in London gave the Nantucket captains a number of important letters to John Hancock, John Adams, Benjamin Franklin, and others. They sailed on May 23, 1776. After they were safely through customs, they took on a Major Morris, an English officer who had sold his commission and was going to America to fight on the side of the revolutionaries. They then headed across the Atlantic and sold their cargo in the West Indies, turning disaster into profit as a good Nantucket captain should do. They loaded with rum, sugar, and molasses and in mid-July sailed again. Their manifest indicated they were going to Halifax; in fact they were heading for home.

On July 20 the brig was stopped by a ship that ran up the Union Jack. She was the *Congress,* said her master Captain Cragie, and she was part of Lord Dunmore's blockading fleet. As *Congress's* boat came to board, the frantic captains tore up the bill of sale of their ship, and several other papers that would incriminate them as Americans and revolutionaries.

On coming aboard, however, Cragie announced that his flying the Union Jack had been a ruse: he was a revolutionary privateer out of Philadelphia.

The Nantucket captains did not believe Cragie. They did not know what to believe, and so they stayed with the story they had told originally, and their ship was taken as an English prize. Ten days later *Congress* came up on a French merchantman carrying a cargo of gunpowder for the Americans. Captain Cragie let the Frenchman go. The Nantucket captains were now convinced that the raider was an American, not a captain of Lord Dunmore's trying to trap them, and they identified themselves to Cragie.

Cragie was a privateer, and he had captured a valuable vessel and a valuable cargo. It meant a fortune to him. He scoffed at Jenkins and the other Nantucketers. They offered to bring out the letters to Hancock and the others, if he would let them go on the French ship

to Philadelphia. Captain Cragie refused; he was damned if he was
going to lose a prize just because these Nantucket men claimed to be
Americans. Their vessel was a British bottom, was it not? Their cargo
was contraband bound for Halifax, was it not? Cragie ordered all the
captains aboard the privateer. He had them and their belongings
searched, and he seized all the gold and silver they had amassed in
the sale of their whale oil, and their cargo in the West Indies. He sent
the brig into Egg Harbor, on the New Jersey coast, to be sold as a
prize.

The captains went aboard the *Congress*. They managed to conceal
the identity of Major Morris, thus saving his life, perhaps. But they
were on the privateer, outward bound, as prisoners. It did no good for
Jenkins and Coffin to complain that their letters to Congress were
vital, and that they also carried verbal messages that were so delicate
they could not be entrusted to writing. Off went the privateer, with
its unwilling passengers, in search of more booty.

Captain Cragie was an industrious and lucky privateer. Being short
of water, he headed into the port of Abico in the Bahamas, and there
encountered a whole fleet of merchantmen, which he seized. He sent
one ship to America with a cargo of salt. He stripped what he wanted
from several other ships, to refit his own and add to the booty. Luckily
for Jenkins and the other captains, there was a Nantucket ship among
the little fleet, and Cragie put his passengers aboard her and sent
them off home. They arrived on September 5. Captains Folger and
Jenkins and Major Morris headed immediately for Philadelphia to
deliver their messages, while Alexander Coffin petitioned the various
authorities to return their brig, their cargo, and above all, their money.

They never got a dime.

Nantucket fretted. Stephen Hussey, a revolutionary patriot, undertook
to enlist men for the revolutionary service, and secured some non-
Quakers. Some of the young Quakers went to Dartmouth, Nova Scotia,
early in 1777, hoping to get a whaling ship out of that port, but they
had no luck. Nantucket's source of livelihood was most effectively cut
off.

The war made itself known in many ways. Some of the whalers were
turned into fishing vessels. Some of the whaling families turned back
to the farm for the first time in decades. Some families moved to New

York, and others to North Carolina. By 1777 the pinch was on. If the fishermen were successful, they needed salt to preserve their product, and there was no salt. A few hopeful souls established a salt works at Brant Point, but it produced precious little salt from the sea. There was not enough sun to evaporate sufficient quantities of seawater. Another group put up a salt works at Polpis, and made plenty of salt, until they discovered it was costing more to make it than they could get for it.

By absolute necessity, then, Nantucketers became smugglers, braving the privateers and warships of both sides. The money so easily earned in whaling in years past was ventured now in desperate ways. Combines outfitted trading vessels, and crews sailed for the Indies, to buy salt, sugar, molasses and farm tools, which last had previously been so little used on the island that they were in short supply. Salt sold for four dollars a bushel, where it had been about fifty cents before the war. Molasses was a dollar a gallon; it had sold at about sixty cents.

As the war progressed the tales of sorrow began to filter back to Nantucket. In 1777 a number of Nantucket men were released from English prisons and prison ships and sent home. Charles Nuenkins, who had sailed out in 1776 for Philadelphia for a load of flour to make Nantucket's bread, was captured, imprisoned at New York, and finally came home the next year. But Barnabas Coffin, who had been with him, got smallpox on the prison ship, and died. Barzilla Swain sailed bravely for the West Indies for supplies, and the next anyone heard of him he was dead in Boston, "a physical wreck" after months of imprisonment in the cold and dank jail at Halifax. Just after Christmas that year came the unhappy news that Barnabas Gardner and Abel Gardner had died aboard the stinking prison ship *Jersey* in New York harbor.

Most of Nantucket's seamen went back to the sea out of sheer necessity. They were smugglers, preyed upon by both sides, risking the dreadful British prison ships, and the seizure of their vessels and cargo by the Americans. Some got through, but as the war continued, attrition cut the Nantucket fleet week after week. The British occupied New York and Rhode Island, and that increased the danger. The British added to their blockading fleet, and that increased the danger again. Nantucketers began sailing small open sloops, which could run fast and low in the darkness, and they took the salt and rum and sugar that these sloops and brigs brought from the Indies at such danger, and traded them on the Connecticut shore for what Nantucket must have. Corn went from sixty cents a bushel to three dollars; flour jumped to thirty dollars a barrel. Soon the savings of Nantucketers were exhausted, and by 1778 real hardship had set in.

How would they heat their houses in the cold winter? That was a real problem. In the past firewood had been brought from the forests of Maine and New Hampshire, for the island had not for many years depended on local timber. But no captain was going to run all the risks of a sea at war for so unprofitable a cargo as mere cordwood. Nantucketers began cutting down the island's scanty scrub oaks and the soft pines, which had been imported from Scotland. Some burned brush. They burned juniper and cedar. Some burned peat. Many nearly froze as the biting winds of winter whistled through their uninsulated shingle houses. By the end of the Revolutionary War, the island was fairly well stripped of usable timber.

Always the war was with them. In the winter of 1777 a ship struck on Great Round shoal, and when the boats came in, it turned out to be an English vessel, taken as a prize by an American privateer and manned by a mixed crew, some privateers, some Englishmen. The wife of the English captain was aboard; the ladies of Nantucket took care of her and entertained her.

Benjamin Tupper was an outspoken Nantucketer who had no use at all for the Revolution. He spoke his mind freely in the early days. He continued to do so after the Declaration of Independence. He was arrested in the summer of 1777 and imprisoned in the jail at Barnstable on Cape Cod, for trading with the enemy. Friends secured his release, but only after he had put up a bond of £600, promising to refrain from helping the British in the future.

In 1778 Nantucket was badly split between Quakers, who were determined to remain neutral, and patriots, who wanted Nantucket to join the rebelling Colonies. The Americans on the mainland were most distrustful of Nantucket, and the British were, as well. Islanders trembled in the fall of that year, when they heard of the English plundering of Martha's Vineyard in September. (They carried away 10,000 sheep and 300 cattle, burned the salt works and six ships, and took 23 whaleboats.) Nantucket was next on the schedule, but the wind changed, and remained foul just long enough for Sir Charles Grey to become discouraged and head back for New York. It was Nantucket's closest call to disaster thus far.

In 1779 the raids came. Seven vessels appeared off Nantucket harbor one April day. Two of them came into port, and made fast at the wharf. They were manned by Loyalists, some of them Nantucket men, who had been empowered by Lord Howe, the British commander in chief in the colonies, to visit Nantucket and destroy the property of rebels, although they were not to disturb those who professed loyalty to the King.

In the next few days many old scores were settled. George Leonard, a Tory, was in charge of the Loyalists, and he led the plundering. William Rotch, who was cordially detested by the "patriots" because he was one of the most powerful advocates of neutrality, was still plundered by the Tories. Those summer soldiers marched about the island, threatening men and women and even children with musket and bayonet, until the people were furious. Deborah Chase went out to the spring for some water one night, although her father warned her a sentry stood near by and she might get a bayonet in her belly. Sure enough, a Tory sentry tried to stop her, whereupon Deborah smashed him in the face with her bucket, knocked him down, and left him bleeding on the ground while she filled her pails and then went home.

After several days of this harassment, William Rotch got word to George Leonard that unless the Tories left the island, there was going to be real bloodshed. Leonard cursed, but the seven ships left Nantucket. Not long afterward, news came to Nantucket that the Tories were going to return, encouraged by General Richard Prescott, a vile-tempered officer who hated rebels with all his soul, and had no compunctions about any punishment that could be given them. In 1775 Prescott had captured Ethan Allen, who was trying to foment a rebellion of Canadians in Quebec, and had very nearly hanged Allen. In the spring of 1779 Prescott was in New York.

The people of Nantucket sent William Rotch, Samuel Starbuck, and Dr. Tupper to New York, on the premise that it was best to send Friends to treat with the British. Prescott would have nothing to do with them, until Dr. Tupper stood up to Captain Dawson, the naval commander, a much more amenable and civilized man. Finally they

were able to persuade Prescott to call off the Tories. They did so well,
in fact, that Commodore Sir George Collier issued an order forbidding
any British vessel from raiding Nantucket!

The islanders' path between the British and the Colonials was
narrow and tortuous. Hardly had this threat been overcome, than the
Colonial General Horatio Gates received information that Nantucketers were planning to sign a separate peace with England. The
Massachusetts legislature demanded an explanation from the town
forthwith. This time Nantucket sent Stephen Hussey, who was known
for his pro-American views, and he managed to quiet down the rebels,
at least to the point that they refrained from sending an occupation
force to the island.

Yet Nantucket's troubles with the organized Tories were not over.
In August 1779 Leonard and his men were back again on the island.
This time they were accompanied by several English privateers,
which stood in and out of the harbor, capturing such small vessels as
they could. They took Captain Stephen Gardner's brig, bound for the
West Indies. They took Abishai Swain's sloop, bound for the Kennebec
to get a load of wood. Two of the vessels stayed in Nantucket, waiting
for prey.

One day in the middle of September an American privateer headed
in toward the harbor; suddenly the ship veered away and anchored.
Inside, the Tories were furious. They took a cannon up on the Cliffs
and fired several shots at the ship, but did not hit it. Next day Leonard
insisted that the Nantucketers had signaled the American vessel.
Several Nantucketers known not to be enemies to the British were
called on to negotiate with Leonard on the issue, and did so.

Then came a counter-complaint, from Thomas Jenkins, who had lost
most of his fortune and belongings to Leonard and the other Tories
on their first visit. He had moved to Lynn on the mainland, and there
he made a formal complaint to the Revolutionary authorities about
William Rotch, Samuel Starbuck, Dr. Tupper, Timothy Folger, and
Kezia Coffin Fanning. Trading with the enemy was the charge again.
It was certainly true that Jenkins had suffered. He had lost 260 barrels
of sperm whale oil, 1,800 pounds of whale bone, 2,300 pounds of iron,
1,200 pounds of coffee, and 20,000 pounds of tobacco—a goodly fortune. But so had others lost, and it came out in the proceedings that

Nantucket was suffering hard. Of the seven hundred families on the island, two-thirds were completely out of firewood. They were short of flour and meal, and they continued short, because the other colonies placed embargoes on food products. In the south, the harvest was good in 1779 and Virginia and Maryland and the other states had surpluses. But the embargo persisted, and Nantucket went hungry.

The matter dragged on for months, and was thoroughly aired before Jenkins withdrew the complaint. The only positive result of the furor was that at least some of the officials of Massachusetts began to understand the pressures under which Nantucket was living.

Nantucket continued to be harried. No sooner had Tory Leonard disappeared, than Major Joseph Dimmick and his Continental raiders would show up, to do the same to the suspected Tories on the island that the Tories had just finished doing to the suspected Yankees. In May 1779 Dimmick's men made a raid and took furniture and whatever else they could find. Had it not been so serious, the coming and going of the two sides might have been funny.

By winter, that year, nothing was funny. The food supplies on the island were so low that many families suffered from hunger. Wood was virtually unobtainable off-island, and men scoured the moors and the meager forests for what might burn. To make matters worse, the winter of 1779–80 came early, and was very cold. The harbor froze over in December, and people could walk on it to Quaise. All the ponds froze and so did the brooks. Snow covered the bogs, and ice made peat-digging impossible. Men, women, and children searched the island, and traveled to Coskata over the ice for juniper and scrub oak.

Smuggling was all that saved the island. The rich were able to bring in much from the bumper harvests on the mainland. The poor went hungry and depended on the charity of their neighbors, and many of these poor were women and children whose men were in the Colonial forces or on English prison ships.

By the spring of 1780 Nantucket was desperate. Timothy Folger went to New York, represented Nantucketers as innocent victims of the war, and asked for help. Nantucket wanted to send twenty fishing boats out to sea, and four whalers, and ten vessels to bring firewood and food to the island. This proposal was not received well in Philadelphia, and soon Nantucket was appealing again to the revolution-

aries for help and safe-conduct. They did not mention that the British
had given them permissions, and when at last they went to sea they hid
their British papers if stopped by American ships. Then, the next year,
they had to plead again with the British for fishing permits, but they
got them, twenty-four in all. The Americans, of course, called this trading with the enemy.

In 1781 Leonard and Dimmick were back again, conducting their
raids on the people of the island. In July, they came at the same time.
Leonard and his Tories arrived early in the month, and on July 9
Major Dimmick came after them. They staged a skirmish. One man
was killed and two were wounded, but the Tories got away, only to
come back in force in September for plunder. Dimmick was there, and
he drove them off.

It was the same in 1782: raids and smuggling, ships sent to sea to
be lost to privateers or naval forces. Nobody loved Nantucket. In
March, William Rotch and a dozen others headed for the Quaker's
quarterly meeting at Sandwich on the mainland. Their ship was captured by a British privateer with a small boat in tow. The British
ordered Rotch and his companions into the smaller boat, but Rotch
refused to give up his property. The captain of the privateer shouted
down to the prize master.

"Why don't they go?"

"They will not go," was the answer.

The captain then sent a man with a cutlass to drive them into the
little boat.

Rotch and Samuel Starbuck stood their ground.

"Be gone into the boat or I will cut your heads off," said the Britisher
with the cutlass.

"I am not afraid of thy cutting my head off," retorted William Rotch.
"We are prisoners. Treat us as such, and not talk of cutting our heads
off."

And soon enough, along came an American privateer and took the
British privateer, and the Nantucketers. Rotch got his vessel back
from the Americans by paying salvage.

That is how it was for Nantucketers. They paid and paid.

The year 1782 brought the first break for Nantucket in the misery of
the war. The people of the town that year managed to secure permits

from both the British and the Americans to go whaling once more. It was a grand moral victory, only slightly tarnished by the fact that the war came to an end at about that time.

At last Nantucket could begin to repair its fortunes.

VIII

The Apostasy
of William Rotch

WHEN THE WAR was over, the people of Nantucket picked up the pieces of their lives. The whaling fleet was virtually destroyed. In 1775 the island had boasted a fleet of 150 ships. During the war years fifteen ships were lost at sea and 134 were captured by the British or the Americans and thus lost to their owners.

The island's crop land was over-planted and worn out. The sheep population was reduced from 12,000 to 3,000. Privation, captivity, and death had reduced the population of the island to about 4,200, and there were 200 widows and 340 orphans.

But Nantucket was ready for peace, ready to get back into the whale oil business in a big way. William Rotch's *Bedford*, a whaling ship, had gone out to work during the last year of the war, secure with its permits from the Crown. She returned at the moment of peace, and was immediately dispatched to London, arriving on February 3, 1783, under Captain William Mooers.

In London *Bedford* created a sensation! She was the first ship flying the Stars and Stripes ever to enter an English port, and no one from Gravesend to London knew what to do about her. She was reported at the customs house on February 6, but the authorities did not yet let her land. She lay at Horselly Down, just below the Tower, and the curious came to gawk at her, while the Lords in Council decided what to do.

The problem on Nantucket, as everywhere in America, was capital. In earlier times capital had come from England, but no longer. The

English investment in America had ceased with the cannon fire. Those, like William Rotch, who had amassed large fortunes before the war and survived it, were able to go back into whaling. Others were not so fortunate. Nantucket men estimated that the island had lost a million dollars in the war.

For the lucky ones who could take it up again, the whaling seemed to be better than ever. For the six years of the war the whales had been left virtually unmolested, and their numbers had increased. The oil was in short supply, and commanded a ready market and a good price.

Real estate on Nantucket was depressed. A good house on the island before the war would have been worth $2,000. The price dropped to $500. Farm property dropped even lower, as the young men went back to the sea. For an able-bodied hand, opportunity at sea was far greater than on the land. A laborer could earn about 65 cents a day on land. At sea, a successful year's voyage might bring a man $500, or almost twice as much. And he should be able to count on advancement.

Nevertheless post-war whaling was not without its financial risks. In 1786 disaster temporarily struck the industry. The price of whale oil dropped, and many who had risked their slender capital found that a successful voyage did not pay all the expenses of mounting it. It cost £25 per ton of oil brought in to make the voyage, and owners were getting £17 per ton at Nantucket. The market had simply dried up. During the war years, when whale oil for candles was not available, Americans had been forced to use tallow candles, and they had grown used to them. At the end of the war, the United States was no longer tied to Britain, and so American whale oil in London was subject to an import duty of £18 per ton—or as much as the same ton had sold for before the war. The British had their own whaling industry, and the Americans could not compete with them in the protected British market.

Nantucket appealed to the Massachusetts legislature, and secured a subsidy for the whaling trade, £5 per ton for sperm oil and £2 for ordinary whale oil. This subsidy made whaling profitable again, but it also encouraged whalers from Sag Harbor and half a dozen other towns on the mainland to enter the business. The competition cost Nantucket dearly. The young men of Nantucket who had fought and been imprisoned in the war came home to find a shabby, unhappy community, offering little opportunity. The whaling business was what they knew, and the whaling business seemed destined to die. Some went into fishery, but fishery never caught on with Nantucketers.

Soon enough Nantucket whalers had an offer from the English, who wanted to establish their own American whale fisheries now that Nantucket was no longer a part of their empire. The British set up a whaling port at Halifax, and invited the Nantucketers to come and man it, and to live in Nova Scotia. Many did. They moved in across the harbor from the city, and built their houses and wharves, in the district called Dartmouth. The future seemed bright. The drain on Nantucket's manpower was great, but Nantucket did not have much to offer its boys just then.

So there were Bunkers and Gardners and Colemans and Coffins and Husseys and Macys in Halifax.

William Rotch was one of those most hurt by capture and destruction of ships during the Revolution. His losses were about $60,000. With the coming of peace, Rotch had expected to recoup quickly, but the state of the American economy, and the interdiction by tax of the English whale oil market, put a severe crimp in his plans.

First Rotch considered the possibility of removing his whaling operations to Bermuda. He made arrangements with suppliers on the mainland to produce barrel staves, hoops, boat supplies, and all that would be needed to carry on the whaling trade. He made offers to several people on Nantucket to join the operation. The purpose, of course, was, by operating out of English Bermuda, to avoid that £-18-per-ton tax that precluded profitable sales from America to the big English market.

When other Nantucket whaling men heard of the Rotch plan they were annoyed and worried. Already Nantucket had been raided once for the Halifax operation. One islander particularly incensed was Alexander Coffin, who had fared so badly in the voyage of the *Sherburne* at the beginning of the war. He had certainly suffered nearly as much as William Rotch, and yet he was not suggesting that Nantucket be deprived of its preeminence in the whaling trade. He wrote to Samuel Adams in Boston, outlining Rotch's plan, and asking the help of the Massachusetts legislature in forestalling it. The legislature accommodated the objectors: soon a bill was passed outlawing the export to Bermuda of the specific articles that Rotch proposed to import.

Thus frustrated, Rotch sought other avenues to repair his fortunes. In July 1785 he sailed for England to see what encouragement he might get in London. After taking lodgings in Grace Church Street, he went to the western shore seeking a proper whaling port, and settled on Falmouth. Using all the influence at his disposal, Rotch secured an appointment with William Pitt, then Chancellor of the Exchequer. First, as a Quaker, he spoke of the neutrality of Nantucket during the war (which was only partly true) and of Nantucket's loss of two hundred vessels worth £200,000, which was at least some exaggeration. Pitt heard him with friendly interest, particularly when Rotch suggested moving the whole whale fishery to England. But nothing happened. After a four-months' wait with no word on his proposal from the British authorities, Rotch asked that someone be empowered to deal with him, and his request was honored. The Privy Council appointed Lord Hawksbury. They could not have chosen a greater enemy to America.

Hawksbury objected to paying £200 each to bring a hundred Nantucket families to Falmouth. He also objected to bringing in American ships ("our carpenters must be employed"). And after two meetings, William Rotch was so annoyed that he decided to go to France and see what could be arranged there.

Rotch landed at Dunkirk and headed for Paris, where the French ministers of Louis XVI offered the Quakers freedom to practice their religion, and exemption from any military requirements, "as they are a peaceable people and meddle not with the quarrels of princes."

When Lord Hawksbury learned that Rotch had gone to England's prime enemy, he tried to made amends. William Pitt sent word that Rotch could write his own terms for importing Nantucket whaling to England. But it was too late. The die was cast.

Soon some eighty Nantucket captains in eighty ships headed eastward across the Atlantic to make their homes and headquarters in French ports, notably Dunkirk. In the fall of 1786 the settlement began. Rotch sent his son-in-law to France, and remained on Nantucket four more years, winding up his affairs. Then he, too, moved to Dunkirk.

Meanwhile, the British were distressed with the turn of events, England needed whale oil for her street lighting, and she wanted to augment her own whaling fleet. In the spring of 1786, after the fiasco with William Rotch, the British government began to discourage the whalers at Halifax, by ordering the end of immigration there of American whaling men, and outlawing the registry of American ships as British. Some forty Nantucket ships were now operating out of Halifax, and another eight or so out of France. The whole American whaling fleet was down to about eighty ships, while within two more years, backed by the British government, the British fleet numbered more than 300 whalers.

Britain wanted still more. The government in London encouraged the establishment of a whaling port at Milford Haven in Wales. The Halifax whalers were invited to come to Milford Haven, and so in 1792, a number of them did. Samuel Starbuck and Timothy Folger led a fleet of thirteen whale ships across the Atlantic, and soon twenty-five families originally from Nantucket were in Wales.

In France, it was not long before the safety and welfare of the Quaker community at Dunkirk was threatened. The Revolution flooded across France in 1789, and the revolutionaries did not feel bound by the immunity to military service granted by King Louis' ministers in the past. New laws required every man to bear arms in defense of the country, and one reason the Quaker whalers had come to France was just to escape such strictures. William Rotch led a delegation carrying a petition to Paris, and appeared to present it before the Assembly.

Going to the building they were offered cockades for their hats, to show that they belonged—so they would not be molested by the Parisian mob that congregated outside the government buildings. Rotch and his friends refused, on the basis of their religion. The puzzled French let them through anyhow, then became more puzzled when Rotch presented the petition. They wanted to be exempted from bearing arms. They wanted acceptance of their own registers of births, marriages, and deaths, instead of the public records. They wanted exemption from oath-taking.

President Mirabeau of the Assembly registered the puzzlement:

"Since we have procured liberty for you, and for ourselves, why should you refuse to preserve it?"

Rotch and his Quaker friends spent several days in Paris trying to answer that question to the satisfaction of the new France. They felt they had succeeded, at least in part. But events rushed headlong. In 1792 came war with Austria, and riots in Dunkirk. The Quakers shut their doors, and their houses were unmolested, but the families began to worry.

Arrests proliferated throughout France in 1792 as supposed enemies of the Revolution were brought to account. International tension grew. William Rotch saw that war between France and England was not far off. He was in a strange position. Since his refusal to locate in England, he had been persona non grata there. When Rotch's ships were stopped by English captains, they were taken into port as prizes. He would lose the ships *Ann, Canton, Falkland* and *Maria.*

Because of all the trouble the Nantucket men began leaving France. Some went to the new British whaling port of Milford Haven. Some went home to Nantucket. Two days before the French revolutionaries cut off Louis XVI's head, William Rotch sailed for England to try to mend his affairs. Less than a month later came war between England and France, and a siege of Dunkirk by the English that quite put an end to whaling, at least for a time. Nevertheless, in the long run, the Nantucket–Dunkirk whalers persisted and prospered, until the decline of all whaling shortly before America's Civil War. From time to time they continued to draw on Nantucket for new blood. The whaling families kept in touch, and one might say there was a bit of Nantucket embedded far off in French soil.

Soon Rotch's son, Benjamin, and his family left France for England. By this time Rotch had made his peace with the Crown, and some of the ships were transferred to the Milford Haven whalery.

William Rotch headed home in 1794, but was so dissatisfied with what he found in Nantucket that within a year he moved to New Bedford, which was establishing its own whaling fleet. Many of his ships operated out of New Bedford thereafter for the next thirty years. Benjamin Rotch remained in Wales and prospered. He built a big house called Castle Hall, and became an English squire. Sir William Hamilton, who had developed the whole Milford Haven whaling scheme, became his friend, and the Rotches often entertained Hamilton and his wife, Emma—and her lover, Lord Nelson. The Rotches even mingled with royalty.

Alas, the Rotch glory was short-lived. The War of 1812 brought such complications to the family's fortunes that in England Benjamin went into bankruptcy, and lost Castle Hall. The royal welcome was withdrawn, the whaling enterprise failed, and the docks at Milford Haven were closed. The English Rotches were reduced to simple Quaker life again.

Nantucket whalers heaved a sigh of relief. That would teach the worldly and ambitious to play fast and loose with the island's welfare!

IX

The Golden Days

SLOWLY, AFTER 1787, the depression that had overtaken Nantucket began to lift. The opening of whaleries in Canada, England, and France helped extend the market for whale products. The concerns of an expanding world with navigation brought about the establishment of many lighthouses, and whale oil was still the best illuminating product in the market. The popularity of spermaceti candles created a new demand for the finest oil.

Removal of most of Nantucket's leading whaling families to France and England added a new pressure to the island in the 1780's. It was hard to find enough Nantucket men to man the Nantucket ships, so lesser persons were employed. Whaling ships hired men from Martha's Vineyard and the New England mainland ports, and still did not have enough. The Indian population of Nantucket was almost extinct, but Mashpees and other Indians from the area found employment on the ships. Finally, black men found an opportunity in Nantucket whaling, and came to the island to settle down. Some were free men. Some were slaves who escaped their masters in southern states, and often found sympathetic assistance from Nantucket Quaker captains visiting southern ports. They built a cluster of houses on Nantucket. Aptly enough, they built in the southern part of the town. The settlement came to be known as New Guinea, after the slave territory of West Africa.

The nature of whaling changed in the last few years of the eighteenth century, for as the whaling fleets of the world increased, the schools of whales that came close in to North America and Europe were quickly decimated. The whalers began venturing further out to sea, south of the Azores and down the "gullet" of the South Atlantic. The far northern waters produced fewer whales, so the whalers turned to the far southern waters. In 1787 an English whaler rounded Cape Horn and discovered the whaling grounds of the Pacific. Four years later Nantucket sent its first whaling ships into the Pacific, to cruise along the western coast of South America. There were plenty of whales out there; the trouble was that a whaling voyage now extended to two years and more. This meant bigger ships, around 250 tons, bigger crews, around 20 men, and—everyone hoped—bigger returns.

In 1791 Captain Paul Worth set out from Nantucket in the new ship *Beaver* bound for the Pacific. The ship cost $10,200 when she was fitted out for the voyage. She carried seventeen men overall, which meant she mounted three whale boats, each boat carrying four oarsmen and an officer who wielded the harpoon. Two men, usually the cook and a boy or the cooper, remained on board as "ship keepers."

Beaver's cargo consisted of 1,800 barrels of whale oil, most of them knocked down; 40 barrels of salt meat; 3.5 tons of bread; 30 bushels of dried beans and peas; 1,000 pounds of rice; 40 gallons of molasses; and 24 barrels of flour. She was out for seventeen months, and her only supply purchase was 200 pounds of bread. She did only fairly well, bringing 650 barrels of sperm oil, 370 barrels of sperm head-case matter, and 250 barrels of oil from lesser whales. Still, it was a profitable voyage, and the ship paid out on her first trip.

That's where the profit was—in *owning*. The only danger was to a man's pocketbook, and the possibilities of profit were so tremendous that the risk seemed worth it. For compared to the owner's profits, the shares of the brave men who went out for as long as three years were almost insignificant.

Take the whaler *Lion*. The accounting of one of her voyages tells almost the whole profit story:

Lion carried a captain, first mate, second mate, seven Nantucket sailors, a cooper, nine black sailors, and a boy. Each, from captain to boy, had a share in the earnings of the voyage. The captain's share was 1/18 and the boy's, 1/120. In between were all the others. The first mate got 1/27, and the second mate, 1/37. Not far behind were the two boat-steerers, or harpooners, who each got 1/48 of the proceeds. The white seamen got 1/75 and most of the blacks got 1/80, a discrimination that may have been based on ability and experience, but probably was not.

Lion had a good, or "greasy," voyage, and when the ship came home, she was carrying more than 37,000 gallons of sperm whale oil, 16,000 gallons of head-case matter, and 150 gallons of "black oil" from some small creatures.

The captain's share of the voyage came to $2,000. The first mate earned $1,300. The harpooners came back to collect $750 each. The blacks made over $450 and the boy, low man on the roster, earned more than $300, or as much as a grown man could expect to earn as a day laborer in a year.

The captain could buy a house on Orange Street with his share, and get married and leave his wife with enough money to take care of her until he returned from his next voyage. And on the basis of the success of this voyage, he could bargain for a larger share, or "lay," of his next. Soon he might be able to buy into a ship, and eventually, if very lucky, to become a proprietor.

That was where the money was. For on the voyage of the *Lion*, after every man was paid, the proprietors earned a profit of $24,000! That profit would buy, equip, and send to sea another two ships and leave $5,000 over for insurance.

A man like William Rotch, with twenty ships or more, could be a millionaire in a year or two at a time when a million dollars would have bought all Nantucket, with Martha's Vineyard thrown in for good measure.

Beaver sailed in 1791 and *Lion*'s voyage was in 1807. In between, Nantucket whaling had changed considerably. The long, slender whaleboat was developed early, built to speed through the water on the track of a whale. Early, they carried a harpooner and four men at the oars, as did *Beaver*. But by *Lion*'s day, the bigger whaling vessels, moving further afield from Nantucket, had changed their style. The newer ships put three whaleboats in the water instead of two, and they manned them with two officers and four oarsmen. For in pursuit of efficiency, the whaling men learned that it was important to have a skilled hand steering the boat, and another specialist in the bow, throwing the harpoon. Thus harpooners, also called boat-steerers, were the equivalent of ship's officers. On some whalers they managed watches. Always their "lay" was just below that of the mates, and in some cases, an experienced boat-steerer might earn more than a green junior mate.

As the ships grew larger and the voyages longer, the profits rose. Sometimes there were losses, though, as with Captain Jesse Bunker's *Commerce* in the spring of 1806. She was seen near the equator by another vessel, homeward bound with a good full cargo of oil. But she never arrived. That was one of the tricks of fate for which Nantucket men and Nantucket wives had to be prepared. The "widow's walks" atop the houses near the harbor were not merely for ornament, and many an anxious wife got her exercise moving restlessly atop the little platform, looking out to sea.

In the early days, Nantucket built some of its own boats and sloops and even schooners. But as the whaling ships became larger and more difficult to build, the Nantucket proprietors turned to mainland yards for their ships. The cost of bringing all boat-building supplies to Nantucket was one reason. Another was the paucity of shipwrights and such skilled craftsmen. In 1802 Nantucket men built the whaler *Rose,* and over the years they built another four whaling ships. But most of the fifty ships of the fleet in the early part of the nineteenth century were built off-island.

The increasing size and weight of the whaling ships in these years created a new problem, one that would eventually bring about the demise of Nantucket as a port. It was the problem of the bar that extends in front of Nantucket harbor. As the big whalers returned, heavily laden with oil, they found the bar impeded their progress. One solution was to send lighters out beyond the bar, to relieve the ships of enough weight of oil to let them pass over. This was expensive, delaying, and could be dangerous if the weather suddenly changed in the middle of transfer.

In 1803 Nantucketers sent a committee to Washington to ask Congress for help in digging a channel from Brant Point out past the bar. Congress agreed to make a survey of Nantucket harbor with that end in view. The surveyors came. They recommended the construction of piers. One pier should extend from the northwest point of Coatue to the southwest corner of the Black Flats. The other pier would begin about a third of the way from Brant Point to the Cliff, and extend to the northeast corner of Cliff Shoal.

Virtually everyone on the island had an opinion on the subject of the harbor. Some believed in the pier idea. Some believed that digging a channel would suffice. Some wanted to build jetties. No faction would give in, and so the surveyors returned to Washington disgusted enough to give a bad report, and Congress went no further in support of the deepening of Nantucket harbor.

That failing, the major shipping owners soon devised a new plan. Outward bound, Nantucket ships would sail unloaded to Martha's Vineyard, where they would put in at what is now Edgartown. There they would take on provisions, barrels, and some crew members. On return, they would also put in at the Vineyard, and unload enough to lighten ship and allow them to clear the Nantucket bar.

In the first few years of the nineteenth century, Nantucket seemed on the road to a new prosperity. The hope was suddenly dashed once more, and again in a way the Quaker islanders found most disgusting— because of force and violence. On "the twenty-second day of Sixth Month, 1807," the British frigate *Leopard* stopped the American frigate *Chesapeake* just as she was coming out of Hampton Roads, Virginia, not really ready for sea, virtually unarmed. The British arrogantly demanded certain "deserters" who, they claimed, had taken refuge in the American vessel. Captain James Barron refused to give them up, *Leopard* opened fire, and Barron surrendered rather than let the British destroy his unready ship.

The *Chesapeake–Leopard* affair was merely the latest in a long series of incidents between Americans and the British on the high seas. The fact was that the British resented the independence of the colonies that had escaped them, and the Americans resented the British at least as much. It was all of a piece with William Rotch's encounters with the government in London. There was no love lost.

The result was President Thomas Jefferson's Embargo Act, which outlawed all export from the United States, including that of whale oil. Although the embargo did not forbid the actual practice of whaling, it dried up the English oil market, and many an owner laid up his vessels. Nantucket suffered once again.

Yet it was in this period that a Nantucket captain went down in world history for solving one of the most intriguing and romantic mysteries of the sea.

The uncertainties of whaling had driven Captain Mayhew Folger of Nantucket into the sealing trade, for in the nineteenth century there was an American market for sealskin. Gentlemen of the cities, in particular, affected sealskin coats.

Captain Folger set out on a voyage in the spring of 1807, before the *Chesapeake–Leopard* affair, and sailed his ship, *Topaz*, for the Cape Verde Islands, off the Atlantic coast of Africa. Then he turned southwest, until he was off rocky Trindade Island, which juts forth off the Brazilian coast. From there he headed south into unknown waters, searching for islands about which he had heard from other captains, but which did not appear on any charts. These islands were supposed to be literally alive with seals.

Topaz sailed through unknown seas deliberately, by the intention of Captain Folger, to find a rich sealing ground. But the weeks went by, and Captain Folger saw no land at all. In these southern latitudes he encountered storms and snow. *Topaz* was badly battered in one blow, and began to leak, and some of her boats were stove. In the middle of September, Captain Folger rounded Cape Horn and came to Desolation Island's rocky and forbidding shore. There he decided to stop and investigate the sealing possibilities. But another storm came up, and he was afraid the ship would be driven ashore on the rocks, so he headed out to sea, and steered for Tasmania, where, weeks later, he landed at Adventure Bay. There in the shelter of the land, he took on water and firewood, and the crew did what they could to put the ship to rights.

The British on the island were hospitable, and it was the first week of November before Captain Folger sailed again. Then he went sealing, across the Tasman Sea, around Stewart Island south of New Zealand, and to Pitt Island, where he took a few seals. Just before the first of December *Topaz* headed for the Antipodes islands, where the Captain knew there were many seals. Captain Paddock of Nantucket had taken thousands of skins there the year before. But Captain Paddock had apparently gotten all the seals, or had frightened them to a new breeding ground, for when Folger reached the island, not a seal was to be found. The South Pacific was proving no more lucky than the South Atlantic had been.

In January 1808 Captain Folger headed north. He was badly in need of fresh water, and so he steered for an island discovered in 1767 by H.M.S. *Swallow*. It was named for the man who had sighted it: Pitcairn Island. It was uninhabited, but was supposed to have fresh water.

On February 6, 1808, Captain Folger reached the island and lay offshore until the next morning, when he put over two boats to go in and search for water and look for seals. On approaching shore, the men saw smoke. Going closer, they were met by three men in a canoe. They were dressed like the natives of the south seas.

Then came the hail, in British English.

"What ship is that?"

"It is the ship *Topaz*, of the United States of America. I am Mayhew Folger, her master, an American."

"You are an American? You come from America. Where is America? Is it in Ireland?"

Captain Folger continued the interrogation. They were Englishmen, said the "natives," born on that island. How could they be Englishmen, when England did not own the island? Because their father was an Englishman, they said. And who was their father?

"Aleck," said the youths.

"Who is Aleck?"

Soon then, Captain Folger learned he had discovered what had happened to the British warship, H.M.S. *Bounty*. Taken by mutineers in 1789, sailed from Tahiti out into the broad Pacific, the *Bounty* had never been heard from again, although its captain, William Bligh, had led a search party, armed with the vengeance and the power of the King's navy, on a fruitless search of the South Pacific for the mutineers.

Captain Folger went ashore, and on the island he met Alexander Smith, the last of the mutineers. He learned how Fletcher Christian, the *Bounty*'s mate who led the mutiny, had died, and how the male servants the mutineers had taken with them from Tahiti had risen up and murdered all the other whites; how Smith and the women had killed the Tahitian men. He met the islanders, some forty of them, Smiths, and Christians, McKays, Youngs, Williams and Quintlas, children of the mutineers. The names were different, but the closeness of the ties the same: it was almost as if the American captain were home again among the Coffins and Macys and Gardners and Folgers of Nantucket.

X

A Very Successful Bank Robbery

ONE JUNE DAY IN 1795, a fair-sized sloop of the variety that was often moving in and out of Nantucket harbor came to rest at the North Wharf. Three men began working on deck, handling corn and other foodstuffs that came up from the south before the New England harvest began.

No one in Nantucket gave the three much more than a second look. The sloop, *Dolphin*, had been there before, and so had the three who handled her. This was the third voyage this spring. The islanders knew a bargain when they had one in hand, and they did not question too deeply into the origin of these supplies. It was enough for them that the three "coofs" were selling off their cargo at well below the usual delivered cost on Nantucket. If they were fools, so much the better for the island.

The three vegetable purveyors were not as big fools as they seemed to be, however. In fact they were not fools at all, but knaves. The leader was Seth Johnson, a Massachusetts man with several aliases and a long criminal record. He had brought with him John Clark, Jr., the son of an old partner in crime, and Zebulon Wethers, whose current alias was James Weatherly. They sold their corn and other supplies with a will, and grinned when the islanders' eyes popped at the prices. For the trio had something else very much on their minds than feeding Nantucket at a loss.

Nantucket, they hoped, was going to feed them in return, and for a good long time to come.

This Nantucket matter was really young Clark's caper. All spring he had been casing the Nantucket Bank and learning something about the community and its habits. First he had come in March in another sloop with provisions. These were stolen from a vessel in Norwalk, Connecticut, and sold at cheap prices, but for a nice profit to the thieves. The second trip had been with stolen corn and flour from Staten Island. And now on this third trip, Clark knew a good deal about the town and its people. He and the others were ready to act.

For several days they peddled their produce quietly. At night they went ashore to Joel Barnard's tavern, where they quenched their thirst and had a meal.

On Saturday, June 20, the trio announced that they were sold out and would sail back for the mainland on Monday morning with the tide. That day John Clark went to the bank to cash some drafts, and while he was there he managed to get hold of one of the keys to the vault for a moment. He made a pattern, or at least that was his story later. Back on the sloop the three conspirators made duplicate keys from pewter spoons.

Anyhow, that night the three sailors rollicked in the tavern for a time, and reaffirmed their intention of leaving town on Monday. Then they left, apparently to go back aboard their boat and sleep, but really to hasten to the Nantucket Bank, close by the North Wharf, on the south side of Main Street (where Buettner's Dry Goods store is now located).

Their keys opened the front door of the darkened building, and the inner door to the countinghouse. But in approaching the vault, they encountered an unexpected problem: a shiny new padlock for which they had no key. Clark and his accomplices were delayed for two hours while they manufactured a key to fit the padlock. It worked, and they were in the vault shortly after one o'clock in the morning.

The next day being Sunday, the robbers had plenty of time, yet they did not know who might be walking the streets after dawn, and they determined to leave the bank before daylight. That gave them not quite four hours to get their loot.

During the night, then, the shadowy figures slipped from the front door of the bank one by one, each carrying a heavy bag, delivering it to the sloop, and then returning. It was slow going, but as dawn began to break, and they agreed to quit, they had taken nearly $21,000 from the vault. There was more money in the bank, but there was no time if they were to play it safe. The robbers stopped short as the sky turned pink, and made the sloop ready for sea. As the sun began to rise, they were moving out of the harbor, past Brant Point light. Once outside they set their course for New Haven.

At New Haven John Clark took his share of the loot, about $8,000, and concealed it in his own hiding places. The sloop moved to a small island near Greenwich, and more of the loot was buried there. Then *Dolphin* moved down to New York, where she went into a shipyard, and the band separated.

The robbers were lucky, because when the bankers came to work on Monday morning and discovered the theft, they were so upset they kept the loss a secret lest there be a run on the bank. It was, after all, a very new enterprise. The bank had been chartered for less than two months, and Nantucket people were still not certain that a bank was necessary in their town. Certainly one could borrow money from the bank rather than from associates, but the concept of the "check" was so foreign that some Nantucketers refused to accept bank checks as payment.

Although the robbery was discovered on Monday morning, June 22, it was kept as quiet as the officers of the bank could keep it, while they tried to determine on a course of action. When the robbery was revealed, it triggered a bitter intra-island battle, with political and social overtones that stemmed back before the Revolution, as far as the old struggle between the haves and the have-nots of the island.

Nantucket was very much a class society. The fourth and lowest class comprised blacks, Indians, and common laborers, usually from the mainland. The third class was possibly no better off, but they were "islanders," and proud, even arrogant. The second class consisted of ship captains, shopkeepers, and other trades people. The first class was made up of ship owners, merchants, and professional men. The society as a whole was mobile and upward-oriented, but it still had a very real class system.

In addition to having this social structure, Nantucket was divided into Quakers and non-believers; the Quakers tending to belong to the upper classes. And then there were differences of loyalty and political interpretation. During the Revolutionary War, the island had been sharply divided between loyalists and revolutionaries, and these differences tended, after the war, to produce Federalists on the one hand and Democrats on the other, as American politics developed national parties.

Old enmities existed among Nantucket's population because of all these differences, and they were as sharp and honed as only those of a small restricted community can be. For example, Kezia Coffin Fanning, the notorious Tory diarist, was the richest woman on the island during the Revolution. She was an excellent businesswoman: she used her business for political ends, and she used her influence with the British during the war for business ends. At the end of the war, Kezia held first mortgages on much of the valuable property of the island—she had milked the islanders dry with her control of the necessities of life, which could come in only with British assistance. She had a town house on Centre Street, and a country place at Quaise. (Top that for arrogance!)

But when war ended, and the revolutionaries triumphed, Kezia's enemies ganged up on her. She fled to Halifax, but left her affairs in the hands of her son-in-law, Phinehas Fanning. He was instructed to foreclose every mortgage if he did not have payment, and to sue where necessary. The debtors won in the end. When all the mortgages were foreclosed, and the properties sold at auction, the bids were ridiculously low; soon the properties returned to the hands of the old owners. Not realizing much value, Kezia could not pay her own debts. The handsome house on Centre Street was lost and the country place at Quaise went into the hands of others. She was imprisoned in Halifax, and her husband, John Fanning, a well-meaning and kindly man, died of a broken heart on the island.

Old bitterness, like that which surrounded Kezia Coffin Fanning, continued and translated into political struggle between Democrats and Federalists. The Nantucket Bank was organized by an uneasy coalition of both sides. The uneasiness perhaps accounts for the delay in the public announcement of the bank's robbery. It was finally revealed almost a week after the fact, on the Friday following the robbery. That very day three Nantucket men were arrested and charged with the theft. They were Randall Rice, a butcher, and a "coof"; Joseph Nichols, the clerk of the court of common pleas; and Nichols' son, William. They were all good friends, Federalists, and members of the Union Lodge of Masons, which had its own political and social overtones. The three men were put in "jail" in James Barker's store, and guarded by directors of the bank.

On the following Monday, George Folger, Jr., the cashier of the bank, offered a $1,000 reward for the recovery of the money.

Nantucket soon lined up on two sides over the question of the guilt of the accused. The accusers were Quakers and Democrats. The accused were unbelievers and Federalists (and, of course, Rice was worse than that—he was a coof!). Rice was "fingered" by Walter Folger, Sr., one of the richest men on the island, a spermaceti candle manufacturer, and a student of The Science of Physiognomy. He was also a Quaker, a Democrat, and an old enemy of Randall Rice's. Folger had seen Rice early on Monday morning as Folger walked down the street toward the wharf. Rice had seen him coming and had crossed the street to avoid him. Rice looked guilty. As a student of The Science of Physiognomy, should Walter Folger, Sr., not know guilt when he saw it?

Very quickly, Folger also implicated Samuel Barker, Joseph Barker, Jr., and Jethro Hussey. All of them, needless to say, were as much Folger's enemies as Randall Rice, who was arraigned in Massachusetts' Justice's Court on June 27, 1795, and then he went home to bed. He had caught cold in James Barker's drafty store the night he was held there.

Nantucket erupted. Neighbor accused neighbor, and enemy accused enemy. Several Nantucketers pointed fingers at Rice and others. Libbeus Coffin, an illiterate and moronic laborer whose word had never meant anything to anyone, became a folk hero by claiming he saw Randall Rice, Jethro Hussey, and several others go into the bank on the night of The Robbery, and come out with heavy parcels. William Worth, a ne'er-do-well blacksmith (but also the nephew of the president of the bank) said he heard Rice and the others plan the whole robbery one night just after the annual sheep-shearing holiday. Rachel Gardner testified that she heard Randall Rice talking about dropping his handkerchief in the bank. These and many other would-be witnesses turned up, all of them suddenly recalling suspicious activities by the accused.

The island smoked with the fires of character assassination all summer. Officials came and searched the property of several men under suspicion, but they found nothing. Randall Rice sued Walter Folger for libel. Then, in September, the real action began.

The Massachusetts State's Attorney sent an assistant, James Prescott, to hold a court of inquiry on Nantucket. The court opened on September 18, 1795. The accused were only Rice, Jethro Hussey, his son, Josiah, and Samuel Barker. The flock of eager witnesses was called. Some denied their previous stories; some stuck with them. After four days of conflicting testimony, Prescott ordered all but Josiah Hussey held for trial. Jethro Hussey and Barker posted bond and were released. The Nicholses had been freed earlier. Randall Rice was not so fortunate. With his accusation his creditors had begun to close in on him, and he could not raise bond. He went to jail.

But the Rice faction was not entirely undone. William Worth, Libbeus Coffin, and Rachel Gardner were all indicted for perjury in their testimony against Rice and the others.

That really set the town's juices in motion.

Meanwhile, outside Nantucket, the identities of the real criminals were pretty well known. Johnson and Weatherly showed up in Philadelphia with large amounts of gold and spent like sailors. The news of the Nantucket robbery had spread like prairie fire across the new states, and the two were arrested. But since no one on Nantucket seemed interested in the real crime, they were freed for lack of evidence.

The political struggle on Nantucket continued. And political it was. The accusers were led by the rich Quakers, Democrats politically, who had lost their political power in the state and on the island with the triumph of Federalism in the region at the time. The defendants had the power. Peleg Coffin, Jr., the leader of the pro–Rice group, was the most prominent Federalist politician on the island, and a United States congressman at the time of the robbery. Emil Guba, the expert student of the Nantucket Bank Robbery and its overtones, says that if Coffin had been on the island at the time of the robbery he would have been accused himself.

The case dragged on. In the spring of 1796, John Clark, Jr., one of the real robbers, was brought to Nantucket by an interested citizen named Joseph Chase, who did not believe in Rice's guilt. Clark told the true story of the robbery. But Nantucket was not interested in mere facts. The fight had gone too far for that. The Clark confession was never even used as evidence. Phinehas Fanning, one of Rice's lawyers, was jailed for debt—at the instigation of their faction's enemies. He spent two weeks in the lockup with Clark and Weatherly, who had also been brought over to answer Nantucket charges. They told all. But very strangely, the prisoners escaped from the jail one night and disappeared.

A year had now passed since the robbery. The struggle was just as spirited as ever, the enemies going at each other's throats. Hussey, Rice, and Barker were ordered before a Boston grand jury. So were the perjured witnesses against them. In September the grand jury laughed the case out of court. But that did not end the struggle. Everybody, it seemed, was bent on suing everybody else. The accused, having been let off by the grand jury, thought it was their turn now. Jethro Hussey sued Libbeus Coffin. Randall Rice sued Rachel Gardner. Walter Folger's property was attached. Albert Gardner sued Uriah Swain for slander because Swain had said in Nantucket's town square that Gardner was connected with the robbery. Rachel Gardner, Mary Barnard, and Elizabeth Barnes all told various people that the defendants were still guilty. The defendants retorted that they were notorious women—they all had bastard children.

Everyone on Nantucket, it seemed, was itching to do everyone else in. Rice sued just about everybody, including schoolmaster Edward Burke for nonpayment of his butcher's bill.

The bank directors were very unhappy with this turn of events. They wanted to "get" Rice and the members of the other party, so they started all over again. They tried to bribe Rice's lawyer, Fanning.

Rice lost his slander suit against Folger, and that destroyed the poor butcher. Soon he was deep in debt. Sam Barker ran into Libbeus Coffin in front of the courtroom in Nantucket, and Barker knocked Coffin down. Next day Rice saw Isaac Coffin in the square, and smashed him in the nose. Everybody, it seems, was watching, for in a minute or two some two hundred people were jostling and crowding for a good look.

The bank directors manufactured "new evidence," and demanded a trial. In the summer of 1797 most of Nantucket went to Boston for the event. Fifty-two witnesses testified about a crime that everybody knew was committed by three off-islanders *who had confessed!* The one side called the other "criminal," and the other called the one "the dregs of society."

In the end, everybody was acquitted except Randall Rice. He was convicted, and it seemed he was going to go to prison and be fined $60,000—which was three times the amount of the money somebody else had admittedly stolen. This miscarriage of justice seemed irremediable, and because he was ruined Rice had no money for bail and had to stay in jail.

That conviction really did not solve much of the problem. One November day Joseph Chase met Eliakim Willis on the road. Chase belonged to the "innocent" party, Willis to the "guilty." Chase knocked Willis off his horse with his cane and then beat him when he lay on the ground. Willis sued. Chase paid fifteen dollars in damages and costs.

"The vile wretches on your island that have poisoned the fountain of your happiness," said Rice's lawyer, when he referred to the bank directors and their party. The fact that Rice was patently innocent of the crimes did not seem to help him much. He asked for a new trial, sitting there in Boston jail, but the request bogged down in administrative politics. It was now the summer of 1798, and the ridiculous, damnable case had been going on for three years.

Finally, Rice appealed to Governor Increase Sumner of Massachusetts for a pardon, and when Sumner read the facts of the case, which showed the identity of the real robbers and some of the machinations of the bankers, the governor granted the pardon. In January 1799, Randall Rice returned to Nantucket, but his troubles were far from over. He was involved in one suit after another by vindictive enemies. In the summer of 1799 he was sent to jail for debt, and his family had to live on charity of friends, which did not mean Friends.

And yet, the victors lost. The Quakers, so deeply involved in the bank robbery case through their richest and most powerful men, fell into the contempt of other islanders. Many members became half-hearted and dropped out of the Society. Those who had been neutral in the struggle gained a vague but deep distrust of the Nantucket Bank. If the bankers could be so dishonest and self-seeking, what would they not do? As if to indicate the state of affairs, in the next gubernatorial election Randall Rice got three votes for governor, and James Weatherly, one of the real robbers, got another.

In 1804 came the real hurt to the important men who had organized the bank. A new group of whaling entrepreneurs and merchants organized a new bank, the Pacific Bank. The Mitchells were then an up-and-coming whaling family on the island, and four Mitchells were among the organizers. There were Gardners and Coffins and Husseys and Swains among the others.

Oddly enough, the Quaker–Democrats who had fomented the trouble over the bank robbery in the first place came to political power in 1805 during the Jefferson years. But they had lost economic power, and the foundations of Nantucket's Quakerism were undercut at the height of its apparent influence, in part by the aftermath of the bank robbery.

Suits involving charges about the bank robbery continued for years, as for example when two Coffins got into a row over it. William Coffin tweaked Micajah Coffin's nose until the blood that ran out proved that Coffin blood ran no thicker than water where the bank robbery case was involved. Micajah sued. When Jethro Hussey died in 1808, he was a respected man, a judge, and an elder statesman. He prayed at the end for the forgiveness of his enemies who had persecuted him and the others. But there was no forgiveness. The Congregationalists and the Methodists and the Presbyterians were stealing the Quaker children of the town. The Pacific Bank was taking the non-Quaker business of the Bank. In 1818 the Bank went out of business, and even that did not end the bitterness in the town. The old enmities would continue as long as any of the principals lived, and after. For years and years, certainly up until the Great Fire of 1846 gave people something else to talk about, the robbery of the Nantucket Bank could always be used to start an argument on the island.

For example, Josiah Barker, Jr., died in 1818. For twenty-three years, since the Nantucket Bank Robbery, he had not spoken a word to Sylvanus Macy, and even on his deathbed he had nothing to say about that dearest friend of his early years.

XI

"Oh, Say, Can You See . . . ?"

NANTUCKETERS hated the War of 1812 just as much as they hated the Revolution—and for the same reason—it interfered with business. As the War Hawks screamed in Washington in May 1812 the Nantucket town meeting addressed a memorial to Congress, recalling all the unhappy past of the island: "The year 1775 . . . 150 sail . . . in the whale fishery . . . compelled to leave their peaceful occupations . . . brought to an untimely end . . . hundreds of widows . . . many fatherless children . . . harbor was frequently visited by ravaging enemies . . . once flourishing town of Nantucket was left resembling an abandoned village . . . declaration of a foreign war would be desolating to the inhabitants. . . ."

It made no difference to Washington what little Nantucket thought about affairs. The next month the American eagle seized the tail of the British lion in his talons.

Nantucketers of 1812 now knew one fact beyond all doubt: they were not like other Americans, and Nantucket's interests were hardly America's interests. Some on Nantucket had prayed vigorously for a separate peace back in the Revolutionary days, some in 1812 would have been willing to settle for re-incorporation under the Union Jack, or for independence for their island. That Nantucket cynicism about the intentions of the remainder of the country was never to leave the island. Deep suspicion of mainlanders would persist even into the twentieth century, when mainlanders were sheep to be fleeced just as thoroughly as the old ewes were shorn on the commons in the early summers. People on Nantucket in the 1970's still spoke of "going to America" when they left the island for a trip. They could hardly wait to get home to Nantucket.

82

When the war came, in June 1812, it was just as dreadful a calamity as the Nantucket fathers had expected. Nearly all Nantucket's whaling fleet was at sea, and was in danger of capture. The result might be total disaster. The proprietors of the whaling industry held a meeting of their own, in an atmosphere of gloom and near despair. Their enterprise had seen more than its share of troubles. The whaleship owners had been wiped out by the Revolution. Then they had been harried by hostile Spanish authorities in the South American ports in the nineties. They had been buffeted by the British constantly since the Revolution, and were only just getting back on their feet. Now the British would go all out against them once again. There was one sensible course for any Nantucketer to take, especially considering the silence that had followed their desperate plea to the officials in Washington who were supposed to protect the public weal. Nantucket would treat with the British independently!

How sensible a decision!

And how treasonable!

Before the meeting ended, conservative heads prevailed, and the decision was reversed. But there were many in Nantucket who said "to hell with the United States, let's be on with whaling." These men were willing to go to almost any lengths in Nantucket's interests. And, indeed, two years later Nantucketers did send a committee to the commander of the British naval force blockading the American coast: they did deal separately with the enemy! And they got away with it. Admiral Cochrane was sympathetic, and sent their plea for a separate peace off to London. This was a good deal more attention than the islanders ever got from James Madison, President of the United States, when they asked him to do something to save the whaling fleet.

On Nantucket, as the war got underway, however, the aura of despair thickened. Some people of little heart gave up altogether, and went west to escape in the wilderness. If they could not sell their property—and who wanted to buy with the British looking down your throat?—they abandoned it forever. Those faint hearts had come to the conclusion that a Nantucket belonging to the United States was untenable.

Not a month after Henry Clay of Kentucky and his backwoods, English-hating friends, had got their war going, Nantucket felt the first tremors of the disaster they knew was coming. Captain David

Cottle was out whaling in the Atlantic in the schooner *Mount Hope*. He was stopped by a British warship, the schooner was taken as a prize and burned, and the whole crew was made prisoner. They watched while 170 barrels of fine sperm oil went up in black smoke.

It was the same old story—worse even than the days of the Revolution. The British put so many ships in the Northwest Atlantic that it became really hazardous for blockade runners to try to bring food to the island, and in the fall of 1812, Nantucket actually ran out of bread. Only those provident (or hoarding) families had flour. The supply of firewood became desperately low again, and this time there was little on the moors to attract the gleaners. In November, Nantucket nearly panicked.

The very desperation caused more sailors than usual to brave the dangers of the British blockade, and some of them got through. Total panic was forestalled by the arrival in November of a blockade runner carrying flour, corn, and other staples. The buyers came aboard the ship almost before she was moored, and soon she was emptied. Some who came were without money; Nantucket's poor were reduced in this war to beggary.

As if all that war brought were not enough, natural disaster also struck Nantucket in 1812, in the form of a fire that burned the Old South Wharf and eight buildings nearby that December. It might have consumed the town, but there were no buildings to the leeward.

In 1813 the dreadful news of captures began to come to the island. The mail packet was taken off Falmouth, and the mails were broken into. *Perseverance* was captured by the British frigate *Albion*. *Hope* was taken by the frigate *Tribune*. Both were filled with precious oil. *Alligator* was captured, and Captain Jonathan Swain's *Sterling*, and they were taken to British ports for sale. Captain Seth Folger's *Edward* was captured by an armed whaler. The British had decided to destroy the American whaling fleet by tactics of stealth. Soon, four more Nantucket vessels were captured in the far seas, one sent to the Isle of France, one to Rio de Janeiro, others to British ports.

In retaliation for this scourging of the American whaling fleet, Captain David Porter in the frigate *Essex* began harrying the British whaling fleet. Soon he had captured or destroyed nearly two dozen vessels.

Early in 1814, Nantucket learned to its combined joy and woe just how badly the war was hurting the island. Captain Grafton Gardner arrived in the whaler *Charles* off the Nantucket bar. There was no possibility that he could come in over the sand, for he was carrying 1,800 barrels of whale oil—then by far the largest cargo of oil ever taken in a single voyage, and worth $80,000. They were out there, the great wonderful beasts, out there for the taking, and the dreadful war was putting an end to Nantucket's rightful business!

So serious was the Nantucket condition, that the ugly word "famine" began to surface. Disease was also a worry. Benjamin Hussey came home from Dunkirk, and suggested that all Nantucket should be inoculated against smallpox. A thousand of the people followed the suggestion, but that was only a sixth of the population of the island.

The sailors, kept home from the sea, turned to farming again. Wives, widows, orphans, and even men took to spinning and carding to make homespun for the garments they needed.

Nantucket town was badly split. That was nothing new: it had been split during the Revolution between Tories and Patriots, and it had been split wide open by the bank robbery case. The split now was between Democrats, who favored the war, and Federalists, who opposed it. When a Democrat was sent to the legislature in Boston, the Federalists ("friends of peace" they called themselves) protested the election, and were joined by powerful Federalist allies on the mainland. The words "rascal" and "scoundrel" rang through the town. There was violence, near riot, as Nantucketers quarreled over who should go to Boston to represent them.

The war continued: blockade and attack by privateers threatened the island, and caused the Nantucketers to take up the buoys that marked the bar and the shoal water, and to turn out the lights in the lighthouses. In August of 1814 Nantucketers appealed to the British blockaders on grounds of charity, to let them send vessels to the mainland for wood and provisions. Admiral David Milne on H.M.S. *Bulwark* heard the plea of three Nantucket men who came to him with a petition, and he agreed to let the vessels pass. They must carry a manifest of their cargo, and the names of the families for whom the cargo was intended.

Immediately Nantucket's sharpers were up to their old tricks. The first vessels stopped by the blockading squadron carried provision all

right, but they belonged to one proprietor, and he intended to sell
them at the kind of huge profit he could get under such conditions.
Admiral Milne was so furious he revoked the privilege.

Nantucket's Federalists and Democrats warred nearly as fiercely on
the island as the British and Americans did around it. The Democrats
were in control, there was no question of that, but the Federalists
managed to treat with the enemy, and let their feelings be known.
They told the British much the same story that their fathers had told
the British nearly forty years before. Poor people . . . infertile soil
. . . widows and orphans . . . not a tree of natural growth.

The Nantucketers were positively wicked in some representations:
"Unless we should obtain assistance from you (for we do not Expect
any from our own Government being without their protection) we
shall be destitute of fuel and provisions and our families must be
reduced to the extremes of hunger and want." Such petitions to the
English were signed by Starbucks and Husseys, and Mitchells and
Macys and Coffins and Folgers and Swains and Colemans, Nantucketers by the hundreds.

David Starbuck, Sylvanus Macy, and Isaac Coffin set out in the
summer of 1814 with a petition from their Federalist friends to find
the British Admiral Alexander Cochrane, who commanded the ships
of the blockade. Starbuck and the others sailed in the sloop *Hawk*,
and they did find the admiral, far to the south at the Patuxent River
in Maryland. This was the occasion on which the admiral agreed to
send Nantucket's petition to London, and treated the islanders with
much sympathy. When they came back from the meetings, Nantucket
town voted its separate peace with Britain. The negotiators of the
peace would be Joseph Chase, Zenas Coffin, Josiah Barker, and Aaron
Mitchell. Nantucket was going to be neutral from that time on.

Having taken so rash a step, Nantucketers worried. They sent
another committee to see Elbridge Gerry, the Vice President of the
United States, and put as good a face on their action as they could.
Gerry was a Massachusetts man, and he understood Nantucket's problem. He was very sympathetic.

Life grew incredibly complex. The Americans ordered Nantucket
to pay its taxes; the British said if Nantucket paid American taxes it
was not neutral. Nantucketers trembled, and the Federalists and
Democrats snarled at one another.

Nantucket Sound continued to be a hunting ground for the British fleet, for American privateers and blockade runners were ever there to be found if the British could track them and catch them. On October 10, 1814, the American privateer brig *Prince de Neufchatel* appeared off the south side of the island, with a prize in tow. She was the *Douglas*, a ship valued at £19,000 bearing a cargo of coffee, sugar, rum, and cotton, worth £90,000. She was, in other words, one of the great prizes of the war. Captain Ordronaux, the master of the *Prince de Neufchatel*, had taken the *Douglas* off Jamaica, and was bringing her to a New England port to be sure he reaped the precious rewards.

Ordronaux's voyage had been unusually successful. He had taken several prizes, and put crews aboard them before sending them to port. That meant the ship was unusually short-handed, and there were not really enough men aboard to sail the 310-ton brig and fight her seventeen guns at the same time.

Prince de Neufchatel and her prize were anchored off the south shore of Nantucket on the morning of October 10. A light northern breeze was blowing across the island. Captain Ordronaux had sent a boat ashore on the island to seek assistance in bringing her around into the harbor with her prize. A number of Nantucketers had volunteered to help, and they came on board the privateer. Charles J. Hillburn led them. He was the pilot who would take her into port. But before the ship could weigh anchor, a lookout discovered a sail to the southwest, and it soon turned out to be the British frigate, *Endymion*, which mounted more than twice as many guns as did the privateer.

The captain of *Endymion* knew the waters around Nantucket were full of shoals that threatened his ship; he was too wise to stand in to fight the privateer. But neither did he have an inclination to let the American vessel and her prize escape him. So the captain of the frigate loaded five boats with sailors and marines, and sent them out to board and take the privateer.

It was late afternoon when the attack began, and dark by the time the five boats came within musket range of the privateer.

The action began around nine o'clock that night. The British sent one boat against the bow, one against the stern, and the others scattered on the quarters of the privateer. More than a hundred men in all were joined in the attack, and when they were close enough they began firing.

The privateer's crew and the Nantucket men on board began firing the guns, and shooting muskets back at the British. First man to fall on the deck of *Prince de Neufchatel* was pilot Hillburn, with a musket ball through his body. The men of the privateer fired with a will, and they sank one of *Endymion's* boats. Of the forty-three men aboard, only two were saved. The crew of *Prince de Neufchatel* captured another boat, and soon the other three attacking boats were drifting, with the dead and wounded lying atop one another in the bottom.

Aboard the privateer six men were dead, and fifteen severely wounded. Most of the crew were wounded; only eight men remained aboard who were unhurt, and they could do nothing to save their enemies, even when the British cried for quarter and gave up the battle.

The fight had lasted about thirty-five minutes. When it ended, the second lieutenant of the frigate came aboard the privateer to surrender, along wtih a master's mate and three midshipmen. The rest of the prisoners were kept in a launch astern of the privateer for the night, because Captain Ordronaux was afraid they would overpower his slender force if they came aboard. He already had thirty-seven prisoners below who had been taken in other encounters. Next morning the British captives signed a parole, which interdicted them from fighting again against the Americans, at least until after they were exchanged. The prisoners were then landed on Nantucket, where two of them died and were buried on the south shore of the island.

On October 12, *Prince de Neufchatel* landed her own wounded, and the surgeons looked after them. One man had a fractured jaw. Another had a hand so badly shattered it had to be amputated. The brig then stood out to the north around the point. The prize ship, *Douglas,* was supposed to follow her. But some Nantucket man shouted that the British were coming—just as she got abreast of Squam. Panicked, the prize crew ran the ship ashore—which was just what the Nantucketers wanted.

While ashore wagons carried the wounded to Hannah Swain's house, and Captain Ordronaux headed for Boston and safety, believing his prize would be following hard after him, the *Douglas* went aground. While the British second lieutenant hired a boat to take him to join the British fleet outside, the people of Nantucket hastened to the south shore to loot the *Douglas*. They looted for five days, laughing and grinning at the sudden reversal of Nantucket's miserable fortunes of war. "They that get the most is the best fellow" wrote Kezia Fanning (daughter of the Tory diarist). The looters were furious because they could not get all the cargo. After five days the ship began to break up, and £30,000 worth of sugar was lost. It was all the fault of the agent for loading her improperly, said the angry people of Nantucket.

But even as the reverberations of the *Douglas* looting incident rang through Nantucket, to the concern of the Quaker fathers and the ministers of the other sects, the rumor spread that the war was nearly over.

On February 16, 1815, four men in a boat from Martha's Vineyard arrived at Smith Point, and made their way to Nantucket town, bringing the news that a peace had been arranged.

In the churches the sextons began to ring the bells that evening, and they rang steadily until nine o'clock at night. The houses and the town's offices were brightly lighted for the first time in months, and the people walked about congratulating one another. At last the dreadful war was over, and in the end, with the *Prince de Neufchatel* and *Douglas* affair, it had not been totally unprofitable after all.

XII

Gone A-Whaling

THE COMING OF PEACE in the early months
of 1815 brought joy and a spurt of activity to Nantucket. The harbor
was blocked with ice that year, so all the orders for the materials of
the whaling trade had to await the coming of the thaw. But with
what they had at hand, the merchants and mechanics began to pre-
pare for new whaling ventures.

The war had cut the Nantucket whaling fleet in half. Twenty-two
of the whaling ships had been captured by the enemy and sold off, but
twenty-three ships remained. It was a sufficient nucleus for a new
beginning.

By springtime, the whaling fleet was assembling. Nantucket's captains and her whaling men were coming back from other occupations,
be it work ashore, or service with the army, or with the navy or the
privateering fleet. The prisoners of war were being released, too. In
May 1815, Captain Reuben Clasby took the whaling ship *Boston* out
of Nantucket port, heading for the open sea—the first to sail.

By July most of the Nantucket whaling fleet was at sea, some heading for the waters off Brazil, but the majority trying out the new whaling grounds in the Pacific Ocean.

Nantucket suffered again that year from a lack of capital. Many of
the whaling ships went out with their cordage and their equipment
not yet paid for. The mechanics and suppliers were extending credit
to the whaling entrepreneurs because they must; otherwise the fleet
could not go out at all.

Thus, as the autumn set in with no vessels yet reporting to bring in
profitable cargoes of oil and pay off, Nantucket suffered severely. The
poor were reduced to seeking charitable donations, and the commu-

nity established a soup kitchen where those without food could come to have a hot meal.

Self-help and charity brought the island through this first difficult winter, and in the spring the whaleships that had been content with the old grounds of the Atlantic began to return, carrying their cargoes of precious oil. Old debts were paid, the mechanics and tradesmen had their wages and their bills, and the island began once again to prosper.

Unlike the years just after the Revolution, Nantucket whale oil was welcomed in England in 1816. England's southern whaling fleet had suffered in the war, and her northern fleet had bad luck for two years in a row. So Nantucket had the advantage. Nantucket's whaling fleet would soon rise to sixty-one ships. At the same time, the growth of the New England manufacturing economy created a profitable trade for coasting vessels, and Nantucket had her share, with some eighty brigs, sloops, and schooners in the mercantile trade.

In whaling the competition became stronger every year, as other ports were attracted to the trade. The Rotchs' establishment in New Bedford gave a surge to that port. New London entered the whaling trade with half a dozen vessels.

Nantucket's catch, that first year after the War of 1812, showed what could be done. The first whaler into port was the sloop *Mason's Daughter*, with 100 barrels of sperm oil from the Atlantic. She came in one July day, unloaded, and almost immediately went out again, to return in September with another 120 barrels. A week after *Mason's Daughter*'s first return, the sloop *Success* was in from the Atlantic with sixty barrels. And then came other little vessels, each bearing its small cargo. But the schooner *Parnell*, badly beaten about by storms, came home without a barrel, and had lost a boat. The *Dove*, a sloop, was lost at sea. First mate Alexander Coffin of the *Golden Farmer* was killed when he fell from aloft one day. In the spring of 1816 the results were better. The brig *Belvedere* came in with 840 tons of sea elephant oil. The *Industry* returned with 734 barrels of whale oil. And the boats continued to come in. *Essex* brought back 1,400 barrels of sperm oil.

But it was the next year, 1817, when the bounty of the postwar whaling began to show. *Dauphin* arrived in January from the Pacific with more than 1,000 barrels of sperm oil. And the others that had sailed in 1815 came in, bringing 1,000, 1,500 barrels—very satisfying

cargoes of whale oil. But a sort of millennium was reached when the
whaler *Globe* appeared on the first day of January, 1818. Captain
George Gardner was exultant, and with good reason: *Globe* brought
home 1,890 barrels of sperm oil and 125 barrels of lesser whale oil.
She was the first ship to bring back more than 2,000 barrels.

The ships that sailed in 1816 for the Pacific came home good and
heavy. Captain John Fitch's *George* brought 2,100 barrels, and *Hero*
came back with more than 2,000, too. They had gone to the whaling
grounds of the Pacific, of course. That's where the "grease" lay these
days. The trouble was, it took so long: *George* sailed on February 25,
1816, and did not reach Nantucket again until July 24, 1818, nearly 2½
years. *Vulture*, under Captain Jesse Coffin, was nearly three years at
sea after she sailed into the Pacific in August.

Even as the trade prospered, there were new concerns. Captain
George Swain went out in *Independence* in 1817 for a voyage that
lasted more than two years. He managed to take enough whales to
bring back nearly 2,000 barrels, but more than a quarter of the oil
was from right whales. He prophesied that the golden days of sperm
whaling were ended, and that no ship would again fill her hold with
sperm oil. Certainly, recent cargoes were light on sperm oil. Captain
John Brown's *Thomas* came home with a third ordinary oil this voyage. Captain George Barrett's *Tarquin* brought 1,930 barrels—not a
single barrel of sperm oil in the cargo.

There were new problems from the whaling fleet in these years.
Dove, heading into the Gulf of Mexico for whales, was boarded twice
by bandits and robbed of her provisions and her boats. She came home
empty.

In 1818 two Nantucket whalers working off the Newfoundland
banks, British waters, were captured by an English cruiser. Captain
Ziley of the sloop *Hannah* managed to recapture his ship two days
later, but Captain Pollard of the schooner *Juno* was taken into St.
John's and there released after the Americans and British worked out
a new fishing agreement.

This was the year that the far-flung Nantucket whalers first visited
the Hawaiian islands. Captain Elisha Folger in *Equator* was there in
September 1819. As the whalers traveled further and further, the
voyages grew longer and more dangerous. The men came home with
many a marvelous tale to tell. The ship *Foster* set out in 1819, headed

for the Pacific. She was successful, and brought home 1,600 barrels of sperm oil. But she was lucky to get home at all, for one day she was rammed by a swordfish, and her bottom was pierced. The sword broke off, and stuck in the hold. The cooper went below and sawed off the bill, and the water came rushing into the hold so that the pumps had to be worked at a thousand strokes an hour to keep up.

Whalers had every adventure known to the men of the sea. Their whaleboats were often stove by whales, and sometimes so were their ships, as was the *Essex* in 1820. They were attacked by pirates, as was the ship *Hero,* whose captain, James Russell, was murdered by the pirates. Mate Obed Starbuck brought her home.

In spite of dismastings, wrecks, and the bad luck that brought some ships home "clean," the whalers never lost heart. Captain Gardner proved Captain Swain quite wrong, when he went out into the Pacific and found a new offshore sperm whaling grounds hundreds of miles from the South American coast. Captain Joseph Allen did his whaling in 1821 off the coast of Japan. That was a successful voyage, but a dreadfully long one: Allen's *Maro* sailed in October 1819, and did not return until the spring of 1822. A lot could happen to a man's family in so long a time. Many a whaling man left home on a voyage to come back and find children who did not know him. Some came back to find themselves widowed, or orphaned, or the family fortunes changed, even the houses destroyed.

The year 1820 was a rough one on Nantucket whaling. *Crown Prince* was lost in the Atlantic, and *Charles* in the Pacific. The ship *Lady Adams* disappeared, and so did the schooner *Liberty.* Captain Shubael Brown took the ship *Falcon* out to the Pacific, and was killed on the voyage. His first mate, Benjamin Swain, died, and when she returned to Nantucket, *Falcon* was captained by the second mate. That is how promotion came in the whaling fleet—often through the misfortune of other men. But it was to be expected, and it was accepted by Nantucketers as a way of life.

Nantucket was growing all these years. The island housed more than 7,000 people. There was a small but vigorous colony of nearly 300 blacks—preachers and teachers, workmen and sailors. There were enough skillful whalers among them that the ship *Industry* went on one voyage manned entirely by blacks.

The whaleships were hardy and the men bold. Captain Benjamin

Worth told historian Obed Macy something of the adventurous life of the early nineteenth century when Macy was writing his history of Nantucket. Worth had gone to sea in 1783 at the age of fifteen and continued to follow the sea for forty-one years. For the last twenty-nine years he was a captain. In all his career, he estimated that he spent only seven years at home. He had sailed well over a million miles across the seven seas, he had visited forty islands and taken 20,000 barrels of whale oil.

As for the ships, they grew in size all the time, as the whalers ventured further from home. They were built of live oak and yellow pine, and in the 1820's they were fitted out for voyages of three long years, at a cost of $40,000 to $60,000. Times had changed since those early days when $10,000 would launch a successful whaling venture. The new whalers manned three or four boats, and the crews were larger, but the system was the same; the profit from the voyage was divided into "lays," and every man shared to some extent in the success or failure of the vessel.

The 1820's represented, in a sense, the high mark of Nantucket. Whaling was immensely successful, the market for the products was growing all the time, and profits were piling up. But more than that, the future looked so bright in those days that no one had any thought of failure. Nantucket, a little dot on the maps of the world, was known the world over as the home of brave and intrepid seafarers who visited all the ports of the world. As if to emphasize the success, in the spring of 1827 the ship *Sarah* sailed out under Captain Frederick Arthur, and when she came home she was carrying 3,497 barrels of sperm oil, the greatest amount ever brought into Nantucket by a single vessel on one voyage.

At home on the island, affairs also went well. The Pacific Bank was prospering. So were the insurance companies and the other island industries. The island's educational system was recovering from the dismal days of the war.

Nantucket had taken leadership in education earlier. In 1800, when the Academy—a private secondary school—was founded, there were only seventeen such academies in all Massachusetts. And on Nantucket, women were regarded as eminently educable, unlike some areas of the American mainland. In 1802 Walter Folger, Jr., advertised for an instructor for young misses and women. The teacher was to bring the girls skills in reading, writing, grammar, arithmetic, needlework, and genteel behavior. She would be called "Preceptress," and to live up to that imposing title she must have the character to match. "None need apply," said the stern Mr. Folger, "but such as are possessed of a moral character that will bear strict examination."

The applicants had to believe it. The strict examination would not cease on one look. The "preceptress" would be under the sharp gaze of the ladies of the community, day in and day out. Probably she would live with one of the island families, which would limit her social life to teas and afternoon calls by ardent swains. She would live plainly and speak plainly, according to the precepts of the Quakers. She might not be a Quaker, but she would conform.

During the early years of the nineteenth century there were many schools on the island. For the poor there was the Fragment school, so named because the good women of the community contributed "fragments" of cloth to be cut and sewn into garments for the children of the poor, so they might be decent enough to go to school. There were the "Cent schools" in which the not-so-rich paid small sums for the care and rudimentary education of their little ones. There was a Dancing School, a Mission School, a Singing School, a Writing School, a Business School and John Boadle's private school. There was a school for blacks, kept by various black preachers and educators, and called the York Street School. Blacks were not admitted to the other schools for years. They had their own African school, just as they had their own African churches.

The War of 1812 created havoc with the school system, and in 1818 a number of Nantucket townspeople complained bitterly. The Quakers were not much concerned; they had their own school system, and the doctrinal split in the town was so serious that it was hard to get them to co-operate on anything that involved unbelievers. The fact remained, however, that in 1818 three hundred children of the island were being deprived of education. The town meeting was persuaded to finance a public educational system. The fathers budgeted $104 for a schoolmistress for the year, $50 for a schoolroom, and $25 to heat it during the winter. Five schools were needed, and they were established under a committee of seven, which included two Coffins, a Bartlett, and Peleg Mitchell.

At the end of the year, half the town was in an uproar. The cost of education was becoming astronomical. The schools had spent more than a thousand dollars that year! The town fathers cut the school budget in half, and it remained low for as long as the public school venture flourished, or rather languished. So disgraceful was the general public school situation on the island by 1826 that Samuel H. Jenks, the feisty editor of the Nantucket *Inquirer,* got the town indicted by the state government for failing to provide adequate educational facilities for its children.

In time, the school situation was remedied. By the 1840's, indeed, the Nantucket public schools had become a model for the whole country, thanks to the work of the estimable Cyrus Peirce, whose story belongs to a somewhat later period. At the time, however, editor Jenks' attack on the island's schools was warranted. The Quakers and others whom he criticized struck back with the reaction of an adder. They hit Mr. Jenks where it would hurt any Nantucketer—in the pocketbook. They started an opposition paper.

Some of the teachers in Nantucket's schools, from Cent to Friends, would long remain in the memories of islanders—and not very many of them with much affection.

> *"A matron old, whom we schoolmistress name,*
> *Who boasts unruly brats with birch to tame. . . ."*

And that was the norm, it seemed.

There was Dinah Spooner, "a terror to evil doers and far from being an angel to those who did well."

There was Edward Freeman, "a savage with no redeeming trait of character," so vicious a ruler of the classroom, that one old Nantucketer, recalling Freeman when the former student was in his seventies and the teacher had long since moldered in his grave, could not help but break into tears in the memory of the indignities heaped upon him.

There was Nathan Comstock, another savage, who much preferred to use the pointer and the rule to the "repentance stool." Comstock was so unsuccessful as a teacher in the Friends school, that later he removed to New York where his qualities of character made him an eminently successful merchant. Yet the testimony rests with Comstock's son, Samuel, a Nantucket boy who grew up and went to sea.

There he led the bloodiest mutiny in the history of whaling, murdering his friend, the captain of the whaler *Globe*, two officers, and a poor black man who got on his wrong side. Nathan was a great teacher all right, and a fine example to all.

Editor Sam Jenks was possibly the most unpopular man in town in the late 1820's, with his egalitarian ideas about schools. He was called "stranger" and "coof" by the Quaker community for interfering with their ways. Things were quite good enough on the island, said the Quakers, and the implication was clear. If the dissenters did not like the social system, they could clear it all up by joining the Friends. The "Boston notions" of Sam Jenks and a handful of others were roundly lamented by the Friendly enemies.

Out of all this nastiness, of course, would come some fine educators, such as Cyrus Peirce and Maria Mitchell, and Admiral Sir Isaac Coffin, the British naval officer who founded the Coffin School and outfitted the school ship *Clio*.

Sir Isaac came to Nantucket to visit in 1826, and soon discovered that he was related to hundreds of people on Nantucket. He visited William Coffin, one of the town's most prominent citizens. Admiral Coffin arrived in the middle of the great school fight, and found that Samuel Jenks, William Coffin's son-in-law, was leading it. Sir Isaac recognized the need for good education. From his own resources he contributed £2,500, a huge sum in those days, for the Coffin School. The purpose of the school was to educate the descendants of Tristram Coffin, the old First Purchaser, and the first trustees were Coffins, a full half-dozen of them. They bought a building and established the school on as high a level as any started in Nantucket.

It was not a free school. Sir Isaac Coffin held that anything that was free people tended to despise, so the Coffin School charged a small tuition. The school opened in the spring of 1827, having no trouble at all in finding 230 Coffin descendants of school age.

It was also through the generosity and vision of Admiral Coffin that Nantucket got the school ship *Clio*, endowed by Sir Isaac to teach boys what every Nantucketer should know, the arts of seamanship and navigation. Lieutenant Pinkham was the commander of *Clio*, and he took twenty-one Nantucket boys on an educational sail to Quebec in the summer of 1829. Later the schoolboys took other trips, including one to the Rio Grande. They wore blue jackets and trousers and blue knit stockings. Their school insignia was an anchor sewed on the right sleeve of their jackets, and their hats were leather caps with anchors on them. They learned many a manly art, how to pickle and bake and slaughter, as well as how to caulk and blacksmith, and fire a naval gun. The boys aboard *Clio* also learned to swim, which was quite unusual for a day when most of the men who went to sea could not swim a lick.

The year of the founding of the Coffin School, 1827, marked a resurgence of education on the island. The public school system was well established, and ten years later came the high school. In its heyday, for the twenty years before the Civil War, Nantucket would have seventeen schools educating 1,400 children from Nantucket town to Tuckernuck. Nevertheless, it was 1847 and the height of the Abolition movement before the Nantucket town authorities could be persuaded to let blacks into the high school. Then it was done.

In spite of the remarkable oddity of the black whaler *Industry* in the 1820's, blacks and Indians on Nantucket were not equal to anyone, and they kept very much to themselves. The Indians were soon enough all gone, the last half-breed died in the middle of the nineteenth century. The blacks stayed down in New Guinea, and came forth only to labor. They were fine sailors and whalers, but that did not make them welcome in the houses of the rich.

Even so, Nantucket was probably a better place for a black man to live than almost anywhere else. The Quakers had pioneered the theory of Abolition early in the eighteenth century, and Elihu Coleman's tract against slavery was presented in 1729. At that time Sylvanus Hussey kept slaves, and so did many another Hussey, and Swains and Coffins and Starbucks all had them. With the pressure of the community on them, most of the Starbucks and Husseys divested themselves of this kind of "property," but John Swain held out until the last. In 1770, when William Rotch presented the case in Boston that won Prince Boston his freedom and ended slavery on Nantucket, there were still 5,000 slaves in the Commonwealth of Massachusetts. Everyone had to admit that Nantucket was right out there in front in social reform.

In the 1820's, Nantucket's Quakers were really pushing against slavery. Abolition was probably the most unifying factor in the social life of the island. Quakers and unbelievers, who could agree on virtually nothing else in this world except the price of whale oil, could join heartily in attempting to do something for the blacks. Nantucket captains everywhere became known as the friends of the oppressed, and when they went south, they were always suspected by the southern merchants of all kinds of rabble rousing. There was truth in it, as the case of Arthur Cooper showed in these halcyon days of the 1820's.

Arthur was a slave on a plantation of a David Ricketts, near Alexandria, Virginia, who escaped with his love, a girl named Mary. They made their way to Norfolk, where they were lucky enough to find that a Nantucket sloop lay in the harbor.

Ricketts began turning the Virginia countryside upside down in his search for the escaped slaves, and eventually he got a line on the Nantucket sloop. It took two years, but Virginia slave holders were not likely to give up their property if they could trace it. In the months between, while Ricketts searched, Arthur and Mary settled down in New Guinea on Nantucket, and got married under Massachusetts law. Soon Mary had a baby.

In 1822 Sheriff Camillus Griffiths of Virginia showed up in Boston looking for escaped slaves. He came to Nantucket. Some of the Quakers learned of his coming, and they hid the slave pair. Oliver Gardner hid them for several weeks. The sheriff poked around Boston a bit and went to New Bedford. He searched there, and heard that several escaped slaves were living in the black colony of Nantucket, so he attempted to get a writ. He could not get a writ in New Bedford, so he went back to Boston, pleading with the court there that the federal law insisted escaped slaves be returned to their owners. Did not federal law supersede Massachusetts law? he asked Judge Davis in his Boston court.

Not in this court, said Judge Davis.

Sheriff Griffiths gave up on the courts, and decided to accomplish his aim under administrative procedures, which seemed much more to his leanings. He went to the state marshal, and secured the assistance of two deputies to go with him to Nantucket and capture the escaped slaves. So Sheriff Griffiths and deputies Bass and Taylor sailed for Nantucket, arriving on the island in the middle of the night.

They went down past the Zion church on West York Street, and south and east of the three windmills on the three Mill Hills, down among the Bostons and the Painters and Pompeys—black families, some of whom had lived on Nantucket for many a year.

Sheriff Griffiths had an informant on the island who told him that the slaves could be found in a house on Angora Street, between Pleasant and North Mill. Before dawn, the sheriff and his deputies were there, knocking and demanding entrance. They pulled guns and pointed them at any who would bar their way.

The commotion aroused the black community, and soon the house was surrounded by a chattering mob. George Washington, the herder of one band of the island's cattle, slipped unseen from the edge of the crowd and hastened to the house of William Mitchell, one of the Quaker leaders of the community. Mitchell got out of bed and dressed. Meanwhile he sent Washington to arouse Gilbert Coffin, and that Quaker sent another messenger to get Oliver Gardner out of bed. They also rousted out Sylvanus Macy and Thomas Mackrel Macy to come and help.

The Quakers hurried to Angora Street, where the crowd was still milling about and the sheriff and his deputies were battering on the door and yelling. They were a bit uncertain because of the nature of the angry crowd of blacks; they intended to get their man and woman, but they wanted to avoid a direct fight with the crowd that would end in bloodshed. So they blustered and shouted and banged on the door, as the frightened pair with their baby stood inside and wondered what to do.

The Quakers came up and confronted the sheriff. He produced his Virginia warrant and waved it at them.

Was it not perhaps a forgery? asked the Quakers. They examined it by lantern light, inch by inch. It was no forgery, said the sheriff. It was a legal warrant.

Ah, legal where? asked the Quakers. Legal in Virginia, perhaps, but not legal in Massachusetts.

Under the federal law slavery was legal, said the sheriff. The Virginia planter had a right to regain his property.

Not in Massachusetts, said the Quakers.

Yes, in Massachusetts, said the sheriff.

At about this time, up came Alfred Folger, the Nantucket magistrate.

Good, said the Quakers. Could not Magistrate Folger arrest these men for disturbing the peace?

During all this argument, some of the Quakers had gone around back and lured to the front for purposes of discussion the two deputies, Bass and Taylor. Now, as Mitchell, Coffin and Gardner kept their attention in the front of the house, Thomas Mackrel Macy slipped in the back way. He put his own frock coat and his big broad-brimmed Quaker hat on Arthur Cooper, and he hustled Mary and the baby out of the house under wraps. Then Arthur walked out the back big as life, and hastened in the darkness toward upper Main Street to the house of Alfred Folger, where he and his family were hidden.

Then Sheriff Griffiths was allowed to enter the house, waving his gun.

The birds had flown, and all he could do was curse and go back to Alexandria.

XIII

The Horrors
of Whaling

YES, NANTUCKET was prospering.

The Nantucketers had learned that their particular sandspit was made a roost for whale hunters more than anything, and if they did not know it well, they had been convinced in the strange year 1816, when all the crops died. The reason was an unusually cold year, in which the island had frost in every single month, and on the Fourth of July the temperature only managed to hit 38 degrees.

But aside from such vicissitudes, the island was going very well. The Pacific Bank built its new building at the corner of Centre and Main streets in 1818. It would never need another.

The first steamer service from the American continent to Nantucket was begun in 1818, too, although it was regarded as an oddity and did not last. Those were the days before the "coofs" began to invade the island in the summers. The people who lived on Nantucket worked there, or out of there.

In the summer of 1821, Nantucket had a newspaper. An attempt had been made to establish one earlier, in 1816, but that early paper, the *Gazette,* never seemed to take root. Perhaps the town criers did that paper in: it threatened their existence in the few months that it lasted. But the *Inquirer,* begun in 1821, was a different matter. Proprietor J. T. Melcher had managed to convince some of the merchants of the community that their interests would be served by a newspaper, and so the *Inquirer* managed to survive. That summer there was something to talk about, too. A handful of wretched waifs of the sea arrived

102

in Nantucket that August, aboard the whaler *Eagle*. They were nearly all the survivors of the whaleship *Essex*, men who had suffered through the worst that nature might do to a whaling man. Their story is very much a part of the tradition of Nantucket.

Essex was a happy enough vessel when she sailed on August 12, 1819, for the Pacific whaling grounds. She was a ship of 238 tons, and had been through all Nantucket's recent whaling history. She had sailed in 1804 for the Cape of Good Hope, and came home a year and a half later with a full cargo of oil. She had sailed in 1806 for Delagoa Bay on the East African coast, and had arrived home in January of 1808 with 1,300 barrels. She had gone out again, this time to the Pacific, and had managed to stay out of the clutches of the English during the War of 1812. In 1815 *Essex* was back in the Pacific, and she came home next year with 1,400 barrels of sperm oil.

In 1817 she had done better than ever under Captain Daniel Russell, who had taken her out before. In 1819 Russell had left the ship, and the first mate, George Pollard, Jr., had succeeded to the command. *Essex* was a good old ship, as much a part of Nantucket whaling history as any vessel afloat, and she was well known to the people of the island.

Beginning her fifth voyage in 1819, *Essex* had very nearly sailed into disaster in her first weeks on the Atlantic. She had been struck by a squall one day, and bent over on her beam ends until captain and crew wondered if she would right herself again. But she had, and except for destruction of two of her four whaleboats, she was right as rain. The loss of the boats was nothing to be laughing about, though. Captain Pollard headed for the Cape Verdes, and there he ran into luck—his own good luck on top of another captain's bad. The whaler *Archimedes* out of New York had been damaged, and run aground, and she had four fine whaleboats for sale. Captain Pollard bought them.

By January, the *Essex* was around the Horn, out in the new grounds off the Chilean coast, and she had gone to whaling.

Very quickly they took eight fine whales, and then they moved on to the Peruvian coast with a thousand barrels of oil in the hold, hoping for that next thousand barrels that would make the voyage eminently successful for them all.

One November day they were a-whaling. The weather was fine and they had nothing to worry about. Or so it seemed. Then suddenly, out in his whaleboat, First Mate Owen Chase set after a whale. The harpoon was thrown, it sank into the soft flesh of the animal, and the whale gave a convulsive jerk that smashed it into the side of the whaleboat, and put a hole in the boat.

There was only one thing to do. Owen Chase seized the hatchet that lay next to the barrel of line, and cut the line that held the harpoon and the whale. Immediately, the mate began stuffing the hole in the boat with the jackets of the men. He ordered them to head for the ship, and they pulled with all their might, as one man bailed. Captain Pollard and the second mate were still out, and one of them just then struck a whale. But Chase's attention for the moment was devoted to saving his boat and his men. They reached the ship. Chase looked around. The captain and the second mate had headed off to leeward. He went forward, braced the main yard around, and put the ship in their direction. Then he ordered the whaleboat hauled, upended it, and looked at the bottom.

The mate of a whaler had to be a little of everything: shipwright, boatbuilder, handyman. Chase saw that he could repair the stove boat with a piece of canvas and put her back in the water.

He was just beginning the repairs when he saw a large sperm whale—about eighty-five feet long—approaching the ship. The whale broke water about 300 feet off the weather bow of the ship, and lay there, spouting. He remained for several minutes, then he disappeared and came up again, just off the ship. This time he headed directly for the vessel. He was moving at about three knots, and the *Essex* was moving toward him at about the same speed.

At first it seemed just another oddity of whaling. A man was likely to see any phenomenon in the behavior of whales if he remained in the trade long enough. But no, this whale seemed to have some purpose, and Chase suddenly ordered the helmsman to put the rudder hard over to avoid the creature.

He had no sooner given the order, than the whale struck, just forward of the fore chains. The impact came with such velocity that it nearly knocked the men on deck down on their faces. The ship stopped suddenly with a shock, and trembled. The whale dived under the ship, and they could hear him rasping the keel with his back as he went beneath them. He came up alongside, lay there a moment as if regaining his sense, and then headed off to leeward.

He must have been hurt. Perhaps it was the whale that Chase had harpooned. Now he was in frenzy. Chase saw him come to the top and lash the water, and smite his great jaws together again about three hundred feet off the boat.

The ship was sore hurt, and Owen Chase knew it. He ordered the pumps going, but even as they started, he saw *Essex* was settling by the head. He sent a man to run up the pennant that called the whale-boats home to the mother vessel.

Feeling his ship, Chase knew she was lost. He began getting the whaleboats ready so they might embark in them and head for safety. As he was doing this, the whale struck again, this time directly under the cathead. His head was half out of water, and the force of the blow stove in the bow of the ship. One can imagine how harsh a blow it must have been, for *Essex* was a stoutly built ship made for the northern sealing trade years before, with timbers selected to get through pack ice if need be.

Chase cut away the lashings of the spare whaleboat, which lay on two spars on the quarterdeck. He told the men to go below and take whatever they wanted for they would be leaving the ship.

They got the whaleboat into the waist of the ship. The steward went below into the cabin and got two quadrants, two practical navigators, the captain's trunk and the mate's trunk. These were put into the boat along with two compasses the mate snatched from the binnacle. The steward made one more try for the cabin, but it was full of water, and they just barely were able to put the boat over and clamber in before the ship began lying over on her beam ends. As they pushed off and cleared, *Essex* lay over to windward and settled in the water.

Not ten minutes had passed since Owen Chase first saw the whale heading toward him.

The two whaleboats of *Essex's* captain and second mate were coming toward them, the men bemused and talking to one another. The boat-steerers had taken a line on the ship earlier, and they simply followed it. But now the boat-steerer of the captain's boat looked up suddenly.

"Oh my God," he shouted. "Where is the ship?"

And then all the men turned about, and saw the wreckage of their whaling vessel, lying on its side in the water.

The boats came up to Chase's boat, and Captain Pollard sat down, pale and speechless. He sat there looking at Chase for several moments. Only then could he speak.

"My God, Mr. Chase, what is the matter?"

"We have been stove by a whale."

Chase then told the story of those dreadful minutes, and Captain Pollard recovered his strength. He then said they must cut away the masts to lighten the ship, and then get into her and find some provisions. For they would have a long voyage. They were a thousand miles from any land. The men in the boats seized the hatchets and set to work. They cut away the rigging, and then got to work on the masts. It was hard going, a hatchet does not easily do an axe's work, but in an hour they had broken them off, and the ship came up on an even keel, although she was about two-thirds full of water. The captain took a quadrant and shoved off from the ship. He made a careful observation, and deduced that they were at o degrees 40 minutes south latitude, 119 degrees 30 minutes west longitude.

Meanwhile Chase led the crew in cutting through the planks of the ship above two casks of bread, stowed high between decks, in the waist. Fortunately, when the ship went over, they were on the upper side, and they were not wet. From them, the men took 600 pounds of ship's bread for the three boats. They also took casks holding sixty-five gallons of water for each boat. They sent men into the lockers to get a musket, a canister of dry powder, a few tools and nails, and some turtles left from a supply they had captured at the Galapagos Islands weeks before.

It was late afternoon before the crew of the stricken *Essex* were finished with their preparations. They lashed the boats together and tied them all to the wreck of the ship. That way they would spend the night, before they cast loose and began the long voyage.

On November 21, they were awake at dawn. The breeze was brisk and the sea was running rugged. They visited the ship again, but found nothing more of practical use to them, until Captain Pollard decided they must take spars and cut up sails for light sails for the boats, and rig up two masts for each whaleboat. Each would carry a flying jib and two spritsails. This work took the morning. They stored their food and water in canvas under the end thwarts of the whale-boats. They took along some extra cedar boards for repairs of the boats in case they began to leak.

First Mate Chase took an observation this day, and found they and the wreck had drifted about fifty miles from their position of the previous day. They spent the rest of the day sewing sails and rigging the boats, and watching the wreck for valuables that might slip out of her. That night they slept as before, on the end of long lines attached to the hulk.

Next morning the boats hauled up to the wreck again, but found that she was about to come apart. The whale oil barrels had begun to break open, and the sea about the wreck was covered with oil, which kept the water calm. Chase saw that the ship's decks had burst during the night, and he told the captain *Essex* ought to be going down soon.

Captain Pollard wanted to wait until noon, so he could have one more observation, and so they did. He found that they had crossed the equator during the night and were just north of it, in a longitude of 120 degrees west.

The officers then assembled at the captain's boat, and he laid out the plans. There were twenty men in the three boats, six of them blacks. They were nearest to the Marquesas Islands, with the Society Islands a little further on. The captain considered the winds and the currents and their crude instruments. He decided it was much the safest to steer back east for the long coastline of South America. To use the winds, they would head due south until they struck a latitude of 25 degrees south, and there they should find the easterly winds that would blow them to the coast.

Mate Chase had the oldest boat, so he was loaded with six men, while the captain and the second mate each took seven in their newer craft. At four o'clock in the afternoon of this third day, they parted sorrowfully from the wreck, and their last contact with their Nantucket homes.

They were alone on the breast of an unfriendly sea.

The men of *Essex* anticipated that their provisions and water would last them sixty days. In less than a month they should be at the position in the south that they desired, and then in another month of traveling eastward, they should reach the South American coast. They made an allowance of about a pound of biscuit a day for each man, plus a half a pint of water.

The days began to pass, as the boats headed south.

They had hoped for moderate weather, but the wind was strong and the seas broke over their little craft. Soon much of the bread was ruined. Chase's boat sprang a leak. They repaired it, but it would be a source of worry thereafter. Then the wind changed. All their hopes were hinged on the variable winds coming anywhere but from the south. Now they sprang from the south, due south, and they continued. Bad luck multiplied: Captain Pollard's boat was struck by a shark or a killer whale in the darkness of one night, and very nearly foundered before they could drive the attacker away and make temporary repairs.

To keep to plan, they should make a degree a day. After eleven days they discovered they had made fewer than eight degrees. That was not so bad, but it was a little worrisome.

In the second week of December a storm very nearly cost them all their lives, but miraculously they managed to weather it, and even to keep together. They seemed to make some progress until December 20, when they found an island, at 24 degrees south. They were behind schedule, but at least they could stop here and rest and repair the boats. They found food and water, fish and shellfish, and birds. The captain now decided to sail for Easter Island, southeast of them, but three of the men decided to remain on this island and take their chances on rescue by a passing ship. They knew they could feed themselves and they would have water. They preferred the waiting and the loneliness to pitting themselves once more against the sea.

So two days after Christmas, the three boats set sail bravely, and were soon out of sight of the little speck of land.

As if bad luck had suddenly overtaken them again, the situation of the men in the boats deteriorated very rapidly. Less than two weeks out, Second Mate Matthew P. Joy began to grow weak, and within a matter of two or three days he died. They buried him in his clothes with a large ballast stone tied to his feet, and the captain said the solemn words of the burial service.

One day later, the boats encountered a storm, and were separated. Mate Chase looked back, but the other two boats had disappeared.

Captain's Pollard's boat and the second mate's boat managed to stay together for some time longer, but they, too, were parted, and the second mate's boat never was heard from again.

By mid-January, the survivors of *Essex* were all in a bad way. Mate Chase had pencil and paper, and he kept a little log of his terrible voyage. They ran so nearly out of food that the rations were cut. One man was caught one night stealing from the bread box, and the tensions increased. A shark followed them, then porpoises played around Chase's boat, but they could not capture any, or any fish to eat.

On January 20, the first man in Chase's boat died, a black named Richard Peterson. They buried him in the sea. But even then they were nearly starving. The night of Peterson's burial Mate Chase tried to eat a cowhide oarguard. There was no substance in it, and the chewing only tired him.

On February 8, Isaac Cole died, and the men were getting ready to put him over the side, when Mate Chase suggested they would all die without food, and that they must eat Cole for their own salvation. They cut up the flesh from the body, and put the bones over the side. Then they began to eat. They made a fire on a stone in the bottom of the boat, and roasted some flesh. They dried some in the sun. And thus they managed to survive, until they were rescued by the brig *Indian* out of London on February 18.

Owen Chase and the others from his boat were taken to Valparaiso, where a month later Captain Pollard arrived, to tell a tale of even greater horror than Chase's. The second mate's boat had run out of provisions in the middle of January, and the men had begun eating the dead. The captain's provisions had held out until the 23rd of January, and then they, too, had begun cannibalism. Worst of the captain's story was the tale of murder that followed.

Once they partook of human flesh, all the old moral principles deserted them. For when the survivors in Captain Pollard's boat had consumed the last of Samuel Reed, who died on January 28, it was but one more step for them to agree to draw lots so that another might die, by violence, to feed his fellows. The unlucky one was Owen Coffin, nephew of the captain. And then they drew lots to see who would shoot him, and Charles Ramsdell was the executioner.

Coffin was murdered on February 1, and his body provided food

until February 11. Then Barzillai Ray died, and that gave the captain
and Ramsdell enough to live on for twelve more days. They were the
last survivors in the captain's boat.

Who would murder whom? That was the question as the pair faced
one another in those last hours.

But the answer came from Nantucket. The whaler *Dauphin* was
heading for the offshore waters, having sailed from the island in
September. Captain Zimri Coffin and his men saw the derelict boat,
recognized it as a whaleboat, and bore down on it. They rescued the
poor sad figures lying on the thwarts of the battered whaleboat. They
took Captain Pollard and Ramsdell into Valparaiso, where they told
the grisly story.

In June, First Mate Chase arrived back in Nantucket aboard the
whaleship *Eagle,* and the first word of the dreadful adventure of the
Essex began to circulate around the island. The full force of it would
not be known until the captain returned, several months later. Nantucket would be a long time recovering from the horror—and Captain
Pollard never would. He took one more ship to sea; she was wrecked
and his career was ended. He spent his final days as a watchman, roam-
ing the piers of Nantucket in the night whose blackness could be no
darker than his dreams.

XIV

The Mutiny on the Globe

AFTER THE STORY of the *Essex* circulated in Nantucket, the islanders could not be shocked by much of anything. They and their trade had survived wars, piracy, and cannibalism. These were the dangers of the sea, and Nantucket men were strong enough to brave them.

Whatever else, the whaling men were mostly comrades. Aboard the whaler there was no room for petty jealousies. Most whalers were noted for their spirit of working together, partly because of the unique system of "lays" or shares, which made it obvious that the success of all depended on the work of each man.

When the word came that summer of 1821 that the whaling schooner *Mason's Daughter* had been plundered by pirates, it was accepted in Nantucket as a part of the life of the sea. Graver, more disturbing news was the word that Captain Tristram Folger had come back in *William and Nancy* "clean"—he'd made a voyage without taking a single whale. Whenever that occurred there was always the lingering fear that the whaling grounds were at last drying up. True, Folger had gone to the South Atlantic, and that ground had ceased being very productive years before. But to come back clean—it was always a shock to the ship owners and to the island.

Captain Pollard recovered from his horrible experience, and sailed again in the ship *Two Brothers* in November 1821 just a year after his *Essex* had been struck by the whale. He headed for the Pacific, a bold Nantucket sailing captain, ready to brave the odds of the sea again. That was the way of Nantucketers.

But not all of them.

In his days as a schoolmaster on Nantucket, Nathan Comstock had not aroused the admiration of many outside the Quaker faith. He was not a whaling man, he had no taste or tack for it, and after a few years as an indifferent schoolteacher he went off to New York to make his way, taking his family with him from the island.

In that family were two boys, Samuel and George. Samuel was a strange fellow, all twisted and gnarled inside. He kept his thoughts pretty much to himself, but when they came out they were likely to be surprising. On a voyage on a whaler, after he had failed at many another job, he took a liking to the South Seas. Indeed, he had the dream, shared by many a sailing man, of shipwreck in the South Seas, where he would become the king of an island, surrounded by beautiful girls and willing warriors.

There was more than a grain of fact behind the dream. The *Bounty* story, of course, was well known to all men who wrested their livings from the sea, and when a Nantucket captain found the survivors of Fletcher Christian's mutinous crew, the story was told over and over again on the island. Further, there was the true tale of David Whippey, who left Nantucket on a whaler in 1816, and went ashore in the Fiji Islands to stay. He married a native girl, and became a chief! So as Samuel Comstock was growing up in Nantucket he had this tradition to encourage him.

After a wild boyhood in which he showed a strong resistance to the strictures of several boarding schools, young Comstock signed on with Captain Shubael Chase in the whaler *Foster*, which sailed on her maiden voyage in the summer of 1819. It was an adventure all the way. They went to the Pacific, and were stove by a swordfish. They put in at the Hawaiian islands, and Comstock decided he would become an island king. He was restrained by the mate, and attempted to foment a mutiny. He was kept confined to the ship and watched, and he grew moodier as the ship stopped at Easter Island and his last chance to desert in the tropics was ended.

Home, Comstock never lost his resolve. *Foster* paid off in Nantucket in April 1822. Samuel went down to New York for a few weeks to visit his parents. He came back to Nantucket and signed on as a boat-steerer on the whaler *Globe*, with his brother George coming as a green hand before the mast. *Globe* was an historic ship and George Gardner, her captain, the most famous man of the day. In 1818 he had been first to take 2,000 barrels of oil. He had discovered the whaling grounds off the South American Pacific coast. Where Gardner went, success was said to follow.

He left the *Globe* that summer to take over the new big whaler *Maria,* and his first mate, Thomas Worth, took the *Globe* as his reward for a job well done under Gardner. It was all in the style of Nantucket. The island's whaling business was boiling with success. The rise of mates and captains was very swift, in the addition of dozens of vessels to the fleet.

The *Globe* sailed in December 1822 from Nantucket to Martha's Vineyard, where she would finish her outfitting. This was the new procedure, necessitated by the increasing size of the whaling vessels and by the bar that blocked Nantucket harbor. The largest vessels in the fleet, the *Alexander* and the *Enterprise,* were both over 400 tons. Laden with whale oil, such ships could not possibly cross the bar. For that matter, neither could *Globe,* with her 293 tons. So the ship was kept light at sailing, and picked up supplies at Edgartown. When she came home the lighter would meet her outside the bar and take off the whale oil before she crossed into the harbor.

Globe sailed around the Horn, without much whaling success on the wrong side of South America. Captain Worth decided to try the relatively unfished waters off Japan, and headed for Hawaii. The Japan fishery was a failure for him, and he returned to Hawaii for provisions. By this time, Samuel Comstock had so antagonized the members of his watch that most of them deserted the ship in the islands, and Worth had to take on seven men from the beach.

On January 26, 1823, Samuel Comstock led the new men and a few of the others in a mutiny. They intended to seize the ship and sail to a Pacific island where they would all be kings. In the mutiny Comstock and his men killed Captain Worth and the two mates of the *Globe.* A few hours later they murdered William Humphreys, one of their own gang, a black man whom Comstock did not trust. (He was, among other things, a racist.)

They headed for the Marshall Islands, where Comstock expected to become king. Ashore, they found the natives friendly, until they abused their women and their hospitality. The mutineers fell out among themselves, and they killed Comstock. But they lasted only a few days more, because they quarreled, and the natives swooped down on them and murdered most. Only two of those ashore survived, both young boys, who were adopted by the islanders.

Meanwhile, the other *Globe* boat-steerer, Gilbert Smith, and five others stole the ship from under the noses of the mutineers, and started to sail home. This venture was truly a brave one. Not one of them knew navigation, and Gilbert Smith, the closest to an officer they had, knew only that South America lay somewhere off in the direction of the rising sun. So they steered east, and a little north, until finally, miracle of miracles, they reached the Chilean coast, and others came aboard to take the ship into Valparaiso harbor.

Of course the story of the whaler men was greeted skeptically by the authorities at Valparaiso, and they were all clapped under arrest. Finally they were believed at least enough that they were freed and sent home to Nantucket, only one of them under charge of mutiny. He was brought to book, and taken to Boston for trial, but witnesses were lacking and the case was very flimsy, so it collapsed. As for the others, they went about their own business. Gilbert Smith ended up as a captain with the Dunkirk whaling fleet in France. George Comstock, the mutineer's brother, forsook the sea, never able to cleanse the dreadful night of mutiny and murder from his mind. He went to the west, and finally to California seeking gold; and there he died.

The other seamen of the *Globe* lived seamen's lives. Several were killed in the whaling trade. Others settled down. The two boys who had been left behind were rescued sometime later by an American naval vessel sent out into the South Seas.

And there lies another tale. When the survivors of the *Globe* mutiny appeared and the ship was safe, the owners began writing Washington, and particularly Secretary of the Navy Samuel Southard. He was getting many complaints from Nantucket whalemen in these times. The basic problem was the unfriendly attitude of the natives in many southern islands. Ships would put ashore, and be chased back into deep water by natives with spears and sometimes guns. There were cases of murder and injury, too. The Nantucket men wanted a show of the flag in whaling waters of the Pacific.

Of course all the troubles with the natives could be attributed to the sailing men themselves. In the beginning they had taken advantage of the peoples of the islands; they had stolen their women and sometimes enslaved their men. The sad end of the *Bounty* mutineers was a case in point; they had brought women from Tahiti for themselves, but no women for the male servants they persuaded to come with them to Pitcairn Island. Consequently the Tahitian men lusted after women, and the result was murder.

Whatever the reason, the word was passed to Commodore Isaac Hull on the Pacific Station that the flag should be shown and American whalemen protected from unfriendly natives. So a schooner, *Dolphin,* was commissioned for the job. Her captain, Lieutenant John Percival, was a daring sailor known as Mad Jack. He took the ship through the islands, stopped and showed the flag, rescued the two survivors of *Globe* left in the Marshalls, and accomplished more than anyone had ever expected of him. Then he came back to America.

The result of the *Globe* mutiny was far-reaching, in the world and in the whaling trade. Before, Nantucket whalers had lived under a loose discipline, so easy in fact that merchant sailors and navy men called whalers "undisciplined slobs." The status of the harpooners and boat-steerers was never very clear. They lived in the forecastle or in the 'tween decks with the cooper and the cook. They might eat with the officers, or they might mess with the men, depending on the ship and captain. They sometimes stood watches (mutinous Samuel Comstock had). But after the *Globe* mutiny all this changed. The boat-steerers were no longer regarded as officers of the ship. They were specialists, and their job was in whaling and very little else. The mutiny on the *Globe* brought about changes in the discipline and organization of whaling crews. And, of course, the tale was told forever after on Nantucket.

Today, the men of Martha's Vineyard have tried to take come credit for the exploits of the *Globe.* Henry Beetle Hough, editor of the Vineyard *Gazette,* would point out that many of the crewmen, including Captain Worth, hailed from the Vineyard, not Nantucket. And Hough would puff about the gravestones on the other island, that showed Vineyard men had sailed on *Globe,* and about the fact that the forces of nature made Nantucket men call at the inner island for provisioning and other resources. But the fact was that *Globe* was a Nantucket ship, and that is how it was, and no huffing and puffing from the Vineyard could change any of that.

XV

Heyday in Nantucket

AS THE 1820's WORE ON, Nantucket whaling
seemed to gain momentum. In 1824, the big ship *Alexander* came home
to the island with a cargo of 2,800 barrels of sperm oil. She had made
one of the longest voyages on record, nearly three years.

The spirit of adventure was unflagging. The ship *Oeno* sailed out
under Captain Samuel Riddell, and was wrecked in the Fiji Islands.
The captain and all but one member of the crew were murdered by
the natives. The survivor, William S. Cary, lived among the Fiji
islanders for nine years. He was adopted by a chief, and he fought in
several of the islanders' wars. He engaged for a time in the beche de
mer business—catching and drying the animal known as the sea
cucumber, which was highly prized by the Chinese throughout the
Pacific.

In these years there seemed to be a change in the climate. It had
not been so long ago that Nantucket had known frost in every one
of the twelve months of the year, but in 1825 the temperature hit
ninety-one on June 11, which set a new record for the island. More
important was the change in the intellectual and moral tone of Nantucket. The Quakers had numbered 3,000 of the 5,000 population of
Nantucket at the time of the robbery of the Nantucket Bank. Never
again would they retain the adherence of so large a proportion of the
population. Unitarians and Methodists were gaining on them fast.

In 1825, the Phoenix Bank failed. This bank had been a sort of suc-
cessor to the Nantucket Bank, organized to assure the Quaker merchants and proprietors of adequate financing. The failure of the
Phoenix was a particularly messy matter; it took ten years to settle
up the accounts, and they were never satisfying to everyone on the

island. One of the Mitchells bought the mantelpiece from the bank and installed it in his house on Vestal street—a very satisfying trophy of the wars between the island's factions.

Nantucket was booming in these years. The whaling fleet had increased to eighty-three vessels, and they were bringing home fine catches. In 1830, *Sarah* set the all-time record for sperm oil, with its cargo of nearly 3,500 barrels brought back from the Pacific after a voyage of almost three years. Captain Obed Starbuck's *Loper* came back after only fourteen months with a cargo of 2,200 barrels. The excitement about this was even greater, for the comparatively short voyage represented "mass production"—more voyages, more profits. The demand for whale oil continued to be great. Still, certain changes were being felt on the island, changes that might presage a different way of life for the future. For one thing, steamers were showing themselves to be in the sea lanes to stay. *Savannah,* a steamer owned partly by a Nantucketer, made a successful voyage across the Atlantic in 1819. In 1824 steamers were visiting Nantucket, and in 1828 a steamer was placed in service between Nantucket and New Bedford. Although this venture failed, it would be tried again and again as the years progressed.

In the 1830's, the Society of Friends began to falter on Nantucket, less through outside pressures than through its own weaknesses. At the height of Quaker power and prosperity on the island, the Hicksites made their appearance. Hicksites were Quaker followers of the dissenter Elias Hicks, who stood for more individual liberty within the church, and less sheepishness. When they came to Nantucket, the Hicksites caused a breach in the faith, and soon a separate meeting house was erected by the Hicksites on Main Street. The building would later be known as Atlantic Hall.

After the Hicksites came the Gurneyites, who arrived in 1837 to add more religiosity to the Quakers' services. Joseph John Gurney believed in reading the Bible in meetings and schools. He also believed in formal sermons. Gurney quarreled with John Wilbur, a Providence Quaker of more orthodox views, and the New England Quakers took sides. The Nantucket Meeting stood for the Wilburite faction, for the most part. But when the showdown came, the Nantucket church property was awarded in court to the Gurneyites. By arbitration the groups split the property—and thus split the Quaker faith on Nantucket. The Gurneyites, for example, began erecting small headstones on the graves of their fathers in the Quaker burying ground. Years earlier a poor young widow had been ejected from the Meeting when she tried to honor the memory of her loving husband by planting a wild rose on his grave. But Mammon was everywhere in the nineteenth century, and the Quakers were not immune to worldliness any more.

The two Quaker factions—Gurneyites and Wilburites—quarreled for years. They split the burying ground. The Gurneyites built a meeting house on Centre Street, in what is now the dining room of the Roberts House. The Wilburites kept the meeting house that was located on Fair Street until many years later when the property was sold. Naturally, all this dissension caused many of the Quakers to slip away from the Meeting altogether.

The Congregationalists on the island were having their troubles, too, as prosperity clouded the issues of the past. Not long after the beginning of the nineteenth century a group of dissenters slipped away from the First Society of Congregationalists, and formed a Second Society. Later that Second Society slipped even further, became the Unitarian church, and built the edifice they called the South Church. The Methodist Episcopals came along to build The Chapel in 1823, at the corner of Centre and Liberty streets (the pillars were added as an afterthought a few years later). The Episcopalians came to the island in about 1838, and Sam Jenks, the warlike editor of the *Inquirer,* was one of the first of them.

As Nantucket town grew it took on more of its present-day aspect. Commercial Wharf was built in the 1830's, and the library, the Atheneum, was organized and took over its present location, on the site of the old Universalist house. The Nantucket Institution for Savings was organized and began operations, and a silk factory was established on Gay Street. Originally that street had been called Coffin's Court, but in 1834 the name was changed to Gay Street, in honor of Gamaliel Gay. The silk factory was an indication of Nantucket's prosperity and its strivings for new industry. Thousands of mulberry trees were planted on the island, and silkworms were introduced to live on them. For a few years the silk factory employed twenty persons, working four looms—but for only a few years. The factory closed down in 1844. Today it is cut up into apartments—the

Great Point Light. (*Library of Congress*)

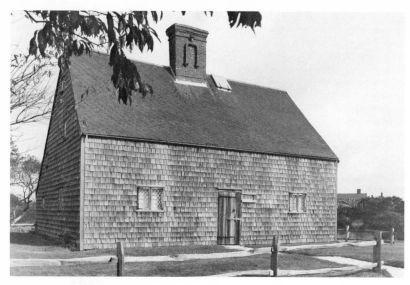

Above, The Oldest House, built in 1686 by Jethro Coffin, a grandson of the patriarchal Tristram Coffin. (*Library of Congress*) *Below,* the Swain–Mitchell House, topped by a classic "widow's walk." This was the home of Maria Mitchell. The annex to the rear of the house, at left, housed an observatory which she used for astronomical researches. (*Library of Congress*)

The Unitarian Church (1809) on Orange Street, looking west. (*Library of Congress*)

"The Three Bricks" on Main Street, built by Joseph Starbuck in 1838.

The Jared Coffin House (1845), formerly the Ocean House hotel, is today one of Nantucket's best restaurants. (*Library of Congress*)

South Mill Street, Nantucket. (*Photo by Jack E. Boucher for* The Historic American Buildings Survey—HABS)

The Quaker Burying Ground outside Nantucket. (*Photo by Jack E. Boucher for HABS*)

Above, Nantucket town, looking up Main Street towards the Pacific National Bank. *Below,* 'Sconset. Both pictures are from late in the last century. *(Collection of the Nantucket Historical Association)*

The Town of Nantucket, seen from across the harbor in a cut dated 1853. Two big windmills—for grinding grain—are in the background at left. (*Courtesy of Peabody Museum, Salem, Massachusetts*)

Main Street, Nantucket, after the tourists have fled for the winter.

A lifesaving station, part of the system of stations established on Nantucket beginning in the 1840's. The surfboat on its wheeled carriage (left) could be hustled down the beach and rowed out to assist victims of shipwreck. (*Collection of the Nantucket Historical Association*)

The Nantucket lightship today. (*Photo by Christopher Hoyt*)

The steam locomotive *Dionis* and the first Nantucket railway, 1881. The passenger cars were open-air. The first line ran from Nantucket town to Surfside and thence to 'Sconset. (*Collection of the Nantucket Historical Association*)

big house at the south corner of Gay and Westminster streets, directly across from Academy Hill School.

The thirties were the busiest years of Nantucket's history in terms of obvious improvements in the town. The fire department was organized in 1838, after a disastrous blaze on Main Street that destroyed some of the most important business houses in town. New buildings began to rise everywhere, with the successful whaling entrepreneurs each trying to outdo the other in the impressiveness of his house. Main Street and several others were paved with cobblestones.

Much more attention was paid in this period to the problems of the Nantucket town port and of the island as a whole in relation to the sea. In the 1830's the largest fleets of whalers of all time sailed out of Nantucket, and scoured the corners of the earth for "grease." So it was fitting that those at home should be concerned about the island's growing reputation as "the graveyard of the Atlantic," a reputation gained because of the shoals around the windswept island.

Brant Point and Great Point lights had been supervised by the federal government since 1789. The shoal waters around Nantucket had been charted by Captain Paul Pinkham before the turn of the nineteenth century. But still the ships kept going aground. Since Nantucket is virtually all seashore, it was quite possible for a ship to strike, and the people aboard to drag themselves ashore and then die of exposure before anyone on the island discovered they were there. So, late in the eighteenth century, several Houses of Refuge were built on the island, under the program of the Massachusetts Humane Society. And when that society began thinking about building a lifeboat to help in sea rescues, it was natural that it should turn to Nantucket, which had devised the finest cockleshell of a boat known to man, the whaleboat. The lifeboats were designed by Henry Raymond and Captain Gideon Gardner of Nantucket. They were thirty feet long and ten feet wide, with ten short oars, and two steering oars.

In the 1830's everyone in America connected with the sea was conscious of the dangers of Nantucket's waters. The growing size of ships, and their increasing number in the 1820's, had brought a whole series of disasters. At the end of autumn in 1824 the brig *Clio* went ashore near Tom Nevers Head and bilged. The sea began to break clean over her, so that the crew had to climb the rigging for safety. A boy who was sick in the cabin was drowned. The event shook Nan-

tucket when the boy's body was brought ashore for burial, and when
Admiral Isaac Coffin's floating school for seafarers was established a
few years later, it was named *Clio*.

That same year the sloop *Ranger* came ashore on the northwest
side of Great Point, and the cabin boy drowned in the attempt to reach
land. The rest of the crew made it safely, but nearly died of exhaus-
tion and exposure.

But the worst tragedy in that year was the disaster of the brig
Packet. She was sailing from St. Petersburg, Russia, to Providence,
with a cargo of hemp and iron, when she came ashore on the south
side of the island, near Miacomet Pond. The second mate got into
the ship's boat, and just as he did so, a heavy sea swept the boat away
from the vessel, and into shore. That same sea smashed *Packet*, and
even as he drifted the mate could hear the masts go down and the
men crying in their anguish.

When the boat was ashore, the mate hurried through the cold to
find help. He came to a light and knocked at a door. The house he
had chosen was a house of misery—the woman had just died and the
family were laying her out. The men were all in town. The mate came
in wild-eyed and disheveled, and the frightened women refused to
listen to him or to seek help.

When the storm subsided, the townspeople went down to look at
the wreck. There was no wreck, there was only wreckage. Blocks and
spars and bits of rigging were strewn along the shore. Part of the ship's
stern was driven up two miles away. There were not even any goods
to salvage! And all winter the bones of the captain and the nine
drowned crewmen kept washing up on the beach, grim reminder of
the dangers of Nantucket shoals.

Nantucket began building seamen's shelters then. Humane Houses,
they called them, and soon a dozen were scattered around the island,
from Smith's Point, around the south side to Great Point. A lifeboat
station was established on Tuckernuck, and later others at Coskata
and Smith's Point. Nantucket was a little safer for seamen than it
had been before.

In the 1820's, Nantucket merchants and sea captains became more
and more concerned about the bar outside the harbor. They could
see how it was already creating difficulty and expense in the management of shipping. Further, the far-sighted could see that as ships

continued to increase in size the bar would destroy Nantucket as a port. Twenty-five years earlier the federal government had recommended several projects to get around the problem of the bar, but nothing had come of any of these projects because the Nantucketers couldn't agree on the best solution to their problem. In 1828 the U.S. Engineers surveyed the island's waters again, and recommended the erection of a jetty that could create an artificial harbor. A New York promoter came up with a scheme to dig a channel, and came to try, but the money was soon exhausted, and the sand remained.

In 1831 the difficulty and danger of Nantucket's waters were emphasized again in a way that struck home with all Nantucket. The whaler *Rose* went aground one October day while outward bound, and as lightly laden as she would ever be. She stuck fast. They stripped her of spars and rigging to lighten her—and she still stayed stuck until July of 1832. A whole year had been lost by the time she was salvaged.

Other ships struck from time to time, and the islanders pursed their lips and frowned. But when a Nantucket ship was hurt, that was something else again. The whaler *Washington* was on her way home in May 1837, heavily laden with oil after a successful voyage to the Pacific. She ran as close as possible and the lighters went out of Nantucket harbor to take off the cargo so she could cross the bar. But a spring storm struck, a nor'easter with howling winds that stirred up smashing waves. The lighters stayed there as long as they could—too long—for they were driven ashore when they cast off. The *Washington* lost both anchors, and she drove onto the bar near the Cliff. She lost her rudder in the crash, and some of the stern planking was wrenched loose. The whaler began to fill with water, and in the knocking about, many of the barrels of oil were broken loose and smashed.

When the storm subsided, the ship was towed loose and brought into shore for repairs. But for the owners and crew of *Washington*, three years' profits and wages were knocked "galley west."

And as whaling entered the last great phase, in the 1840's, the danger continued.

By the forties new techniques were being introduced. Nantucket was the third largest port in Massachusetts. Its captains sailed everywhere in the world, and the whaling fleet numbered at least a hundred. The population was 10,000! The property of the island was valued at more than six million dollars, and included five wharves, thirty-six candle factories, and all the sail lofts, shipyards, and other services of a thriving port.

The whaling ships were fitted and made ready and towed to sea by steamers, which took them to Martha's Vineyard for final outfitting. Early in the 1840's the "camel" was brought into use. This device was a floating dock. A steamer towed the camels out to sea when the blue flag marked *Ship* rose on the pole in the town square. The buoyant camels were fixed to the sides of the laden ship, raising her several feet in the water. Ship and camel were then towed into harbor, over the bar, by the steamer.

In November 1842, the whaler *Joseph Starbuck* was ready for her second voyage. The occasion was something of a party; the captain's wife and other ladies had been invited to ride in *Joseph Starbuck* as far as Edgartown, where she would fit out for sea. They would come home in the steamer *Telegraph*, which was towing the whaler to the Vineyard.

The steamer took *Joseph Starbuck* in tow inside the harbor, and moved the whaler out across the bar. Suddenly what had been a strong head wind freshened into a roaring gale, so powerful that the *Telegraph* was unable to make headway. Both vessels began to drift backwards in spite of every effort to get more steam. Captain Charles Veeder of the whaler ordered the anchors dropped fore and aft. They held for a time, but the sawing of the storm soon parted both cables, and she began to drift toward the beach. Captain Veeder decided to run back into the safety of Nantucket harbor, over the bar. He set the foresail, which was certainly all he needed in this wind. The wind switched around to northwest, and *Joseph Starbuck* veered toward the eastern end of the sandbar. She struck, and soon went over on her beam ends, while the thirty-five men and women aboard clung for their lives and prayed.

In Nantucket the plight of *Joseph Starbuck* was unnoticed in the storm. Not until it had blown out did someone in the Old South Tower see her lying there. Then Nantucket moved into action.

The men of the steamer by this time had managed to come close enough to make a line fast to the lee side of the wreck—for that is what the proud whaler had become. A whaleboat was brought from the shore, and it made five trips through the heavy seas, to bring the thirty-five men and women off the hulk.

Nantucket was shaken again, but not for long. *Joseph Starbuck* was a total loss, but the Starbucks collected her insurance and went right back to business. For let no one ever forget that whaling was a business, and business was the business of Nantucket, more even than any other part of America.

Even in the forties, the apex of prosperity and adventure in the life of Nantucket, every bit of the island's effort was devoted to sensible business. There were no frills. Nantucket, the whale oil capital of the world, never lighted its own streets. That would have been a waste of their oil, a sin against frugality, and very bad business indeed.

XVI

The Faltering Forties

AS THE 1840's BEGAN, Nantucket was already
on the decline as a center of population. The whale fishery still seemed
to be profitable and flourishing, but there were signs of difficulty, none
more apparent than the use of the "camels" to bring ships over the
bar. The holder of a lofty point of view might have been able to see
the bar as the source of destruction of Nantucket's hopes.

The quarrel between the Quaker groups continued, and cost that
religious sect much of its vitality in the early 1840's. The Baptists and
the Methodists flourished, however. The Baptists built a church on
Summer Street, and the Methodists succumbed to the Greek Revival
fanaticism of the day and put up the big white pillars in front of their
church on Centre Street.

In 1837, the successful whaling entrepreneur Joseph Starbuck began
the building of three houses on Main Street for his obedient and eminently prosperous sons, George, Matthew and William. In a few years
they were all built, lasting memorials to the possibilities of enterprise
and exploitation. The Starbuck houses represented almost scandalous
spending for the time—the Three Bricks, as they would be known in
modern times, cost altogether more than $40,000. But why not? Star-
buck's ships, *Three Brothers, Omega, President* and *Young Hero,* were
bringing home thousands of tons of precious oil. Why not, indeed?

The forties were the building years. William Hadwen built the "Two
Greeks" across the street from Starbuck's Three Bricks, determined to
outdo the other ship owner. Hadwen had predicted that the Greeks
would make the people talk. They certainly did—Nantucketers and
coofs are still talking about them. They dominate Main Street now as
they did in the 1840's, reminders of the glories of the neo-Greek classi-

cism of one silly period in American spending. Hadwen built the first
house, the one on the corner of Pleasant Street, for his wife, Eunice,
who was Joseph Starbuck's daughter. He built the second for his
adopted daughter, Mary G. Swain.

These imposing buildings stirred the competitive juices of yet another successful man, Jared Coffin. This Coffin had made a fortune in
whaling in the halcyon days of the thirties, and he built a big house,
Moor's End, at Pleasant and Mill streets. But he soon tired of it when
he saw the houses that the money of Starbuck and Hadwen had
wrought, and he planned a new house, something to be larger and
finer—and taller—than any other in town. So he built the Jared Coffin
House at Broad and Centre streets, and he had the finest place in all
Nantucket, a whole story higher than any other. Having accomplished
so much, Coffin deserted the island and moved to Boston.

Hardly was Jared Coffin's house weathered in when disaster struck
Nantucket, to undo in a few hours what men had spent lifetimes building. On Sunday, July 12, Starbuck's *Young Hero* sailed for the Pacific,
and the town looked as prosperous and busy as it ever had been. True,
it was a dry year. The farmers were complaining about the drouth.
The moors were brown and dry, and the hot winds seemed to dry out
even the mud of the marshes that year.

On the night of July 13—tragedy.

At eleven o'clock that night, something set off a fire in the hat shop
of William Geary on Main Street. At first it seemed small enough. A
witness remarked that a good gout of water would have extinguished
it nicely. But the water did not come. The cry "Fire!" rang through
the streets, and men began running. It is said the two volunteer fire
companies of the town argued over which should have the honor of
putting out the fire, and so they were slow in starting their pumps and
hoses. By the time they settled the argument, the fire had leaped
through the roof of the hattery, onto the adjoining houses, and had
spread across Main Street.

It spread then, up the street as far as the Pacific Bank, whose brick
structure stopped it, down the street as far as William Rotch's countinghouse, a bank by then, where again the brick stopped it, and along
Centre Street as far as Jared Coffin's brick house. Blazing houses created winds that swirled through the town, spreading the fire, and soon
North Water Street was ablaze. The townsmen brought dynamite and

tried to blow out the fire with an explosion. They blew up two houses on Orange Street. But the explosions only spread the flames; the winds swirled more viciously, and soon men, women, and children were heading along New Dollar Lane toward Mill Hill, the safest place on the island that night.

The office of the *Inquirer* was burned down, and so was that of its competing paper, the *Mirror*. The wonderful new Atheneum was destroyed. So were the bank buildings other than the Pacific, the Episcopal church, the county building, and several hotels. Around four hundred buildings in all went up in flames that night, representing most of the wealth of the town. The estimators said that a million dollars worth of buildings went up in smoke. The drug store had burned. So had the groceries. Nantucket was in a hard way when morning came, with people huddled in the open under blankets and cradling their handful of possessions as they looked at the smoke still in the air, and smelled the acrid odor of destruction.

From all over New England help came. Goods and services and money, $100,000 worth, were soon brought to the island. The Nantucket town fathers met, and planned the rebuilding of their community. Within a few weeks construction had begun on sixty new buildings. In three months one would hardly have known that the town had been almost completely destroyed in one dreadful night. Nantucketers were somehow buoyed by disaster.

These middle years of the 1840's marked a high point in Nantucket history in several ways. First, although the island already faced decline because of the growth of size and depth of ships, it was still enjoying prosperity—as the New England maple tree turns its most glorious just before it goes dormant.

Also in these years there lived on Nantucket the three most distinguished sons and daughters of the island.

One of these was more properly coof than native, although his influence on Nantucket itself was greater than that of any other. He was Cyrus Peirce, born on the mainland in Waltham, Massachusetts, who came straight out of Harvard College in 1810 to teach private school on the island and support further studies at the Harvard Divinity School. Peirce taught on Nantucket from 1810 to 1817, with one year off to graduate from divinity school. He then cast his lot with the island, for he married a Coffin, Harriet, the daughter of William Coffin, the genealogist of the family.

At the time, Cyrus took Harriet off to northern Massachusetts where he had a church at North Reading and school at North Andover. But the mist of the islands calls loudly to its natives, and after twelve years of exile, Harriet brought her husband back to Nantucket, to teach private school once more. Soon enough, Peirce was allied with that remarkable and persistent coof, Sam Jenks, critic of Nantucket's public school system. Peirce and Jenks struggled together for public education on the island. Peirce's father-in-law was also active in the movement, and his brother-in-law was one of the first teachers in the island's public schools. But Cyrus Peirce was the leading force.

Peirce got to know Horace Mann, of the Massachusetts board of education, America's principal proponent of public schooling, and they soon became friends, laboring for the same high purposes. When the first high school was established on the island in 1838, Cyrus Peirce became principal.

But the very success of the man once more deprived the island of his services, for he was soon enough appointed to direct the first Massachusetts "normal school" or institution dedicated to the production of teachers for the public schools. This, of course, was back on the mainland. But there were to be two more years of Peirce's sterling influence on the island—1842 to 1844, when he returned to regain health strained by overwork in the cause of the people's knowledge. *Live to the Truth* was Peirce's motto, and he brought it to the island.

In his time on Nantucket, Cyrus Peirce was in contact with one of his wife's cousins who was an equally remarkable figure. He was Walter Folger, Jr., by then a very old man indeed, and well past his prime.

Folger was a direct descendant of Peter Folger, the controversial miller, poet and jailbird of the early days. He was a sickly child, and his mind thus turned to intellectual inquiries. He studied with various teachers on the island, and soon was able to teach himself. Indeed, he mastered French with the aid of a grammar and a dictionary. Soon Folger was dabbling in astronomy, and this interest would last him all his life. He married Anna Ray of the island when he was twenty years old, and then settled down in a house on Pleasant Street to study

science, fiddle with clocks and watches, and immerse himself in the
world of books. He studied medicine, chemistry, and astronomy. He
studied mathematics and history, and even theology. He built telescopes and clocks, and he earned his living by repairing watches,
while his wife occupied herself by having children. She had ten of
them before her childbearing days ended.

Soon enough, the independent Walter Folger, Jr., was disowned by
the Quaker Meeting of his forbears. He was not dismayed. This Folger
was peculiarly equipped to live on the island. Everything in the world
he wanted could be found or brought there at his convenience. He had
no desire to travel, to go whaling, to become rich. He wanted simply
to settle down in his workshop and library, and that is precisely what
he did, unfettered even by the bonds of religion. When Folger was
only twenty-five, he built an astronomical clock that was to be the
wonder of the island. It still is: in 1942 it was given to the Nantucket
Historical Association, and in 1953 it was restored by Dr. Arthur
Rawlings, a clock expert on the mainland. So even today, the eager
visitor can see the marvelous clock on the island, ticking away, telling
the year and the day of the month, showing the motion of the earth in
relation to the sun, the phases of the moon, and the tides at Siasconset.

Having accomplished this, young Folger turned to politics. He
joined the Peleg Coffin party in town affairs. In 1791 he was elected
selectman. He also served for a time as Sealer of Weights and Mea-
sures—the official whose responsibility it was to see that the island's
commercial scales did not weigh in favor of merchants or other sellers.

In 1795 young Folger became a "law expounder." In these early days
of the republic, few men went to law school, and some did not even
study under other attorneys, but secured their law directly from books
and experience. Folger was one such, an "expounder" who found his
way into court first in the aftermath of the Great Bank Robbery. For
Randall Rice sued Walter's father for libel for calling Rice a bank
robber, and Walter defended the old man. He lost the case, but Rice
hardly won; the judgment was ten dollars and costs.

Soon Folger was busy in the productive and profitable side of the
law, drawing deeds and wills and handling disputes for neighbors.
He was involved in a bitter dispute over the use of the sheep common
which arose in 1810. Old Tristram Coffin's hopes for extensive common
lands ruled by Nantucket's Men of Property were almost in ruins by

then. With the advent of prosperity, and the growth of the island, the successful merchants wanted these lands split up, so each might exploit his own property in his own way. Four years later the process of splitting up the common lands began, and Tristram Coffin's old arrangement was in collapse for certain.

Opportunity in the law was excellent for a young man of such obviously good connections as Walter Folger, Jr. His father was one of the island's more prosperous whaling merchants. Peleg Coffin, his political mentor, was in the United States Congress, and would always be high in state councils. So in 1808 it was a surprise to practically no one when Walter Folger, Jr., was appointed Chief Justice of the Court of Common Pleas for the island and county of Nantucket.

The next year he went to Boston from the island, as a representative in the Massachusetts legislature. Then he went to the state senate, where he served five years, those trying years of the War of 1812.

From 1817 to 1821, Walter Folger, Jr., served in the United States Congress, although with no national distinction. He was on the committee that supervised the rebuilding of the Capitol, which had been burned by the British, but that was about all. Much of his stay in Washington was spent in his personal pursuits, study of astronomy and science.

It was this interest that put him in close contact with William Mitchell, when he came home from Washington. William Mitchell was a Nantucket schoolteacher, and a young friend of both Folger and Cyrus Peirce. Later, Mitchell gave up teaching and took a job with the Pacific Bank at the top of Main Street. Eventually he became cashier. But, like Walter Folger, Jr., Mitchell's real interest was science, and particularly the mathematical sciences.

Folger came home in 1821. He was sixty years old, and an elder statesman. He drew William Mitchell to him as a magnet draws iron, for Folger's new ambition was to build a telescope. In the months that followed Mitchell became so familiar with Folger's work on the invention that finally he was able to write a "memoir" describing it all in detail. Together they went to meetings of the Nantucket Philosophical Institute to hear and sometimes read papers on esoteric subjects. The Institute was the pride and joy of both of them, the intellectual home of the island's thinkers. (There were lots of Folgers and a couple of Gardners in the membership, but not a single Coffin.) But

Mitchell and Folger were the leaders; one or the other of them was always prepared with a paper on some physical phenomenon, if no one else was ready.

The downfall of the Institute came in the early 1830's. So popular was science just then that the public clamored for public meetings, and the members agreed in the interests of education. Then women insisted on membership, and soon they were running the Institute, and had made a ladies' club of it. So exasperated did Walter Folger become that he finally asked that his name be taken off the membership rolls. William Mitchell's interest also was lost, and within a matter of months the Institute went out of existence. The last meeting was held in June 1832.

By that time, Folger was in his seventies, and Mitchell was the more aggressive of the two scientific students. Mitchell had married a Coleman girl, Lydia, in 1812, and was raising a family as well as working in the bank and devoting himself almost nightly to the study of the stars. In 1818 their child was born, and they named her Maria. She was to become the most famous native of Nantucket Island.

Maria Mitchell grew up in a house filled with telescopes and scientific paraphernalia. When school started for her, her father was her first teacher. Then he went into the bank, and she went to school under Cyrus Peirce. From her father and from Peirce, Maria soon gained a lively intellectual curiosity of her own. And since opportunities for its advancement were limited on the island, she naturally turned to her father's hobby, the study of the stars. At seventeen she was reading books on conic sections and navigation. At night she was helping her father with his observations.

In the 1840's, William Mitchell was well known in American astronomical circles. He owned several telescopes; the military academy at West Point had lent him some equipment. He was in contact with most of the well-known astronomers of America. He was doing some work also for the government's coast survey. Much of this work was done at the family house on Vestal Street, where Mitchell built a small observatory, and some was done at the bank, where he mixed business with pleasure: the whaling captains brought their chronometers to Mitchell at the bank when they came home from their long voyages. He made sure they were accurate before the captains set out once more.

When Maria Mitchell completed the educational requirements of

Cyrus Peirce's school, she served for a time as his assistant. Then she had a school of her own. And not long afterwards, in the 1840's, she was the librarian of the Nantucket Atheneum.

No job could have been more appropriate for a young woman of Maria Mitchell's leanings. As now, the Atheneum's hours were limited. The reading rooms and library circulation desk were open only in the afternoons and on Saturday night. (That last is one source of amusement for islanders that has been lost over the years.) Maria Mitchell checked out books to boys and girls, advised them on their reading, and talked to the old salts who came seeking information and the old ladies who walked in to find amusement.

But such effort occupied only a part of every day. The rest of the time Maria had to herself, alone in a forest of books. Even in these early years she was a tartar, a character in which she became legendary at Vassar College, where she went years later as professor of astronomy and became a chief disciplinarian. In Nantucket the signs were already out: if Maria Mitchell found that the youngsters were eagerly reading one particular book, she would snatch it up and read it herself. If she found it unsuitable, she would simply lose it. No muss, no fuss, the book was lost. It would turn up before town meeting, when the trustees examined the books and operations of the library, and then it would go missing again as soon as town meeting was over. This little exercise in censorship was unassailable, and typical of Maria Mitchell's approach. Had the genes been different, she might have revolutionized the whaling fishery.

Outwardly, the Mitchells were Quakers, but the whole family conformed merely for the sake of peace in the community. It was a sign of the times, the stern frugality and plainness of the Quakers had already passed its prime on the island as Maria Mitchell was growing up. The Mitchells kept a piano, a plain violation of the Friends' interdictions against music. No wonder the Quakers were losing their grip on Nantucket in the 1840's.

Maria, as librarian, had a tremendous influence on the cultural activity of the town. The old Atheneum, like the present building, was made for several purposes: it had a lecture hall as well as a library. In 1844, Maria Mitchell had a signal opportunity: Ralph Waldo Emerson came to Nantucket to lecture, and she was in charge of the arrangements at the Atheneum. Soon she was talking to Emerson about Walter

Folger, and taking the famous literary man to meet the town's leading intellectual.

Maria continued on at the Atheneum. She was there when the great fire of 1846 burned down the building, and she was busy with the rebuilding that came a few months later. She was in charge that spring of 1847 when Emerson came back, to give a series of six lectures in the big hall on the second floor of the present building.

The old man, Walter Folger, Jr., died two years later. By that time he was displaced in intellectual circles: Maria Mitchell was the leading figure of Nantucket, and she had put the island on the map of science as prominently as any of the whaling captains had put it on the map of the seas.

For on the night of October 1, 1847, Maria Mitchell was peering through her father's telescope when she discovered a comet. Frederick VI, the king of Denmark, had offered a gold medal a few years earlier to the first person in the world who discovered a comet by observation through a telescope. Of course elsewhere in the world, other astronomers found the same body, but Maria's claim to the award was championed by Edward Everett, the President of Harvard College, because G. P. Bond, of the observatory there, was a friend of Maria's father. So in due time the bona fides of the discovery were established and Maria had her medal. It came in the year of Walter Folger's death, and it made her internationally famous.

The next year the young lady was elected to the American Academy of Arts and Sciences, the first woman admitted. In 1849 she was asked to take charge of some computations for the American Nautical Almanac. She was soon joining astronomical expeditions around New England, too.

Maria was among the first of the feminists, railing at those who tried to keep woman in the home: "It seems to me that the needle is the chain of woman. . . ."

For Maria, from 1847 on, life was all she might have hoped; she was swept along in the rising tide of American science. She continued on in Nantucket, at the Atheneum, until 1861 when she and her widowed father moved to Lynn, Massachusetts. That is not to say that she was sedentary: she made a triumphal tour of the south, and in 1857 went to Europe, where she was welcomed by notable scientists. She went to Rome, where she was received nervously at the Vatican observatory, and eagerly by the feminist and early American woman sculptor, Harriet Hosmer. She was in constant contact with the scientific leaders of America and of Europe. She was almost as constantly involved with her work on the Nautical Almanac. She wrote scientific papers, and received more acclaim: the tiny republic of San Marino gave her a medal in 1859.

At Lynn, Maria and William Mitchell built a little observatory behind the house, and continued their work. They lived there quietly until 1865, when a rich brewer named Matthew Vassar decided to found a college for women at Poughkeepsie, New York. Maria was appointed professor of astronomy and director of an observatory that was built to rival the finest in the nation.

Maria shook them up at Vassar. Her colleagues always wanted to do what had been done before by other colleges. But not Maria: "If the earth had waited for precedent, it never would have turned on its axis!" she declared, in a letter of exasperation to the others of the faculty. She became an institution at Vassar, an irascible, brilliant, kindly, lovable spinster. She hated any kind of "side" or trumpery. Once a full-blown missionary pushed her into a religious discussion.

"And now, Miss Mitchell," said the good man, "what is your favorite position in prayer?"

"Flat on my back," came the answer.

The missionary did not wait to discover that Miss Mitchell had long since foresworn the Society of Friends, and did not join any church. What formal religious feelings she had were with the Unitarians, and she went to the Unitarian church when she was in Nantucket.

She went to see everyone who was anyone in the world of science or letters, or they came to see her. The literary Peabody sisters of Salem interested her. Dorothea Dix did, too. So did John Greenleaf Whittier, and William Lloyd Garrison. But what interested her most was the advancement of women; she was a founder of the American Association for the Advancement of Women and several times an officer.

Over the years the awards continued to come in. Maria got a Ph.D. from Rutgers Female College. She had L.L.D.s (honorary degrees) from several institutions. Her astronomical observations were disseminated throughout the world scientific community.

In 1888 she retired from Vassar, and went back to live in Lynn, and

there she lived until she died the following year, the most impressive
figure ever to come from Nantucket isle.

The period of intensive intellectualism of which Maria Mitchell was
so much a part on Nantucket, was also a period of ferment on the
island. One of the major social-intellectual interests of the time was
the struggle for abolition of slavery. The Quakers were old in this
pursuit, but in the decade of the 1840's others took up the drums as
well. Nantucket was the favorite gathering place for the anti-slavery
orators of the period, and many of them came here to make the rafters
of the Atheneum ring with their denunciations of the South.

In 1841 the anti-slavery advocates held a convention at Nantucket
for three days, and at one meeting Frederick Douglass, the escaped
slave who had taken up residence in New Bedford, made a stirring
speech. It did not stir everyone; as always Nantucket had its dissenters,
and there was enough howling and catcalling that some declared the
anti-slavery convention to be a failure. It is said that Douglass's speech
here was his first among whites, and that Nantucket put him on the
road to greatness. Perhaps it is true. At least the convention had one
historically traceable overtone: it gave a name to one of the island's
favorite restaurants.

At the convention, Stephen S. Foster arose and spoke in a fashion
reminiscent of William Lloyd Garrison and the most ardent of the
Abolitionist crowd. He accused the clergy of failing to lead the people
out of the wilderness. So annoyed did some listeners become that the
meeting broke up in a chorus of shouts, confusion and threats. Indeed,
so lasting was the effect that after the meeting ended, Nathaniel Barney and Peter Macy, a pair of unbelievers, wrote Foster a letter, asking
him to explain why he had denounced churches and clergymen for
their failure to free the slaves.

Foster replied in kind. He wrote back. Better, he seized the opportunity to elaborate on his remarks and publicize them further by printing the 68-page letter as a brochure for the anti-slavery trade. He
denounced the Baptists, the Episcopalians, the Unitarians, the Universalists, the Free Will Baptists and the Quakers. Their clergy, he said
"were thieves, adulterers, man stealers, pirates and murderers . . .
the Methodist Episcopal Church . . . more corrupt than any house of
ill fame in the city of New York . . . southern ministers perpetuating

slavery . . . for the purpose of supplying themselves with concubines . . . clergymen guilty of enormities that would disgrace an Algerine pirate. . . ." And he titled his booklet *The Brotherhood of Thieves:* or *A True Picture of the American Church and Clergy.*

Foster's diatribe was soon enough circulated throughout America, gaining every bit as much attention as he wished it to. And even today the memory of the controversy remains on Nantucket, though hardly in a way Mr. Foster would have wished. The Brotherhood of Thieves is a restaurant on Broad Street not far down toward Steamboat Wharf from the Jared Coffin house. The house advertises Good Food, Good Drink, and Good Company. And in its advertising it promotes what Mr. Foster hated, diversity of thought:

"Nantucket island," say the restaurateurs "creates the free will that permits all men and women to maintain their own personal identity, self respect, and clear perspective, which has become lost and forgotten in mainland civilizations."

That's true, but it wasn't exactly what Mr. Foster was talking about.

XVII

Dire Peril

WHALING CATCHES were encouraging in the 1840's, but still there was something not quite right about the trade. In 1842 *Constitution* was the first ship taken out by the "camels." In 1849 *Martha* was the last ship brought in by them. In between, Gardners and Coffins and Folgers and lesser men were lost, overboard, killed by whales, and even murdered by mutineers. The ships came sailing home with cargos of sperm oil, but not always very large cargos.

In 1846 the *Peru* came home with but 966 barrels; next year the 369-ton ship *Mary* had only 862 barrels in her. The *Henry* came in in '48 with but 482 barrels. Whaling was on the decline. Soon the fleet would be sold off, one by one: *Mary Mitchell* in 1847, *Walter Scott* in 1849, *Levi Starbuck* in 1850, and then many another.

The town was rebuilding after the great fire; it was not that catastrophe which had set the island on its downward course. Rather, it was the whales' becoming harder to find. The competition from Martha's Vineyard, New Bedford, Boston, New York, Sag Harbor, and the foreign ports made whaling much harder than it had been. There were also other preoccupations. The *Maria*, for example, sailed out of Nantucket on September 20, 1846, and returned with an indifferent cargo of 890 barrels of sperm oil in the summer of 1850. More telling was the rest of her story. *Maria* had stopped at California in 1849, and the whole crew had deserted her, drawn by the lure of the goldfields.

Indeed, gold called the men of Nantucket that year, and some closed down their smithies and their sail lofts and their stores, and headed Around the Horn in ships that were not whalers, "Bound for Californy."

Yes, whaling was in a decline, and the fifties showed it. In 1850 only fourteen vessels sailed from Nantucket, in 1853, only fifteen. True, in 1859, *Three Brothers* came home with 6,000 barrels and 31,000 pounds of bone, the largest cargo ever shipped into Nantucket—but of that all only 180 barrels was sperm oil; the rest was lesser stuff.

As Nantucketers were whaling, other men in other places were trying hard to find a cheap substitute for whale oil. One firm invented and marketed an oil made from lard. It thickened up in cold weather. Another group made a combination of turpentine and alcohol. It nearly burned down several establishments it was supposed to illuminate. But inventors persisted, and among them were Luther and William Atwood, who formed the United States Chemical Manufacturing Company. In a small building in Waltham, Massachusetts, they experimented with processes of refining petroleum from the earth that had been found in quantity in Pennsylvania. The Atwood brothers believed they could come up with a substance that would be as effective for lighting as whale oil, but much less expensive. They tried one formula after another, and finally they came up with an oil that would do the job: kerosene.

In 1854 kerosene production began, and then it was just a matter of time before the harbor of Nantucket would be empty of those great potbellied whaling ships that had brought her so much fame and prosperity in the past.

Before the end of the decade the Atwoods and others would perfect their petroleum refining processes, and a vast supply of petroleum would be discovered in America. With sperm oil at nearly $1.80 a gallon, the way was clear for the new oil.

To recoup the profits they had lost to kerosene, several Nantucket capitalists tried various enterprises. The silk mill had gone out of business, and the machinery was destroyed in the great fire of 1846. A shoe factory was started in the last years of the decade, but it soon burned down. A straw braid factory operated for a time in the 1840's, but a new process put it out of business. With the decline of whaling, and the knowledge that the bar would prohibit shipping, many in Nantucket lost heart, and the migration from the island became heavy in the years before the Civil War. As ships of all kinds grew larger, they had more trouble with the bar. The handwriting was certainly on the wall.

Nantucketers were each year more cognizant of the difficulties of their island. Shipping was on the increase, and shipping to Boston and points north had to negotiate the vagaries of Nantucket Sound or go far outside and waste valuable time. That meant they ran the dangers of the extensive shoals that rise south, southeast and east of the island. Walter Folger, Jr., had been instrumental in the discovery of the South shoal in 1821, a bit of shallow twelve miles off Siasconset. The inshore shoals were well known; the Fishing Rip, Bass Rip, and Rose and Crown. But well outside was another set of shoals, twenty to forty miles out from the island, and these hugged the edge of the crossroads of the western Atlantic Ocean.

New shoals were discovered from time to time, usually the hard way. In 1854 the ship *Centurion* went aground on a previously unknown shoal south of Nantucket, and her crew was taken off and moved to Boston. By the time the investigators came, the "wreckers" were ahead of them—on this occasion, the men of the area fishing fleet, who had found the stranded ship and stripped her of most of her valuables and cargo before the owners could come back.

So a new shoal was found. But finding and avoiding were two different matters. Nantucket shoals were known to Nantucket men, but not to much of the outside world. There were no government charts in the middle of the nineteenth century—those did not come until the end of the Civil War.

The increase of shipping traffic around Boston meant an increase in wrecks around Nantucket, and the Massachusetts Humane Society lifesaving program, inaugurated twenty years earlier, came to maturity in the 1840's. In that decade Nantucket had three lifesaving stations, at Tuckernuck, Coskata, and Smith's Point. In the fifties came other stations at Muskeget, Nobadeer, and Tom Nevers' Head. Surf boats and other rescuing devices came into use elsewhere on the island, including an iron mortar which fired a nine-pound shot that carried a manila line.

In 1853 the lighthouse service decided to place a lightship on Davis South shoal, twenty-five miles offshore. The keeper was Captain Samuel Bunker, a retired whaling master. Here was one way to find employment for the diminishing fleet of whaleships. One was chosen for the task, her hull painted red and her masts yellow and white, and the name *Nantucket South Shoals* printed in white against the red sides. Whale oil lamps were placed in the mastheads, and on a clear night they could be seen for fifteen miles. This lightship went into service in the summer of 1854, anchored two miles off the shoal, and there she sat, under Captain Bunker and his crew, warning of the dangers.

The summer went well enough, but as fall deepened, the storms began to come, and those who knew wondered if the lightship would survive the nor'easters of the winter. It seemed to—she bobbed and pitched and gave the men some frightful times, but she held her chains through several fierce storms that winter.

But as the old year went out, in came a more vicious storm. The winds whistled up, and the rains swept the decks of the little ship. The seas crashed across the bulwarks, and soon there was not a dry inch in the forecastle, and scarcely a haven in the cabin. For three days and three nights the storm raged about the lightship. She sawed against her anchor chains, and finally the tension was too much, the tired metal snapped, and the lightship was adrift, at the mercy of the storm.

She was no longer brig-rigged, of course; she was a hermaphrodite, half brig, half lighthouse. It was with considerable difficulty that the captain and the crew got any sail on her at all. In the teeth of the storm they ran westward, hoisting sail in what little respite they got from the force of the wind. It was not enough. Soon the lightship's sails were torn and useless, and Captain Bunker could not hold a course. The ship drove before the storm, until the night of January 5, when she came up on the sands of Montauk Point, at the southeastern claw of Long Island. There she was to stay, to be abandoned as a wreck. On Nantucket, Captain Bunker was regarded as a hero for saving the lives of himself and his crew.

The lighthouse service had established the need for a lightship at Davis South shoal, so another was to go there. This time the government built a ship for the purpose, *No. 1*, she was called. She was also a sailing ship, but she was luckier than the converted whaler. She survived many years of buffeting by the sea, long past the days of Nantucket's affluence and decline, long after the last whaling ship passed by on her way to the grounds of the Pacific.

Life on the lightship was dull, and sometimes dangerous. A storm called for the best from every man, but not only storms brought crisis. The ship was provisioned from the shore on a regular basis, but sometimes the men ran out of some provisions. Once they ran out of butter, and the captain sent a boat to Nantucket, twenty-five miles away, for a supply.

En route, the fingers of the fog slipped over them, and then the blanket came down. When they found the island, they were off Tom Nevers Head. They rowed along, keeping close to shore, and passed Siasconset, where they provided the finest amusement of the week. People came down to the shore and yelled at them, and they yelled back that the lightship was not wrecked, but that they were looking for butter.

Finally the party reached the Haulover, and pulled the boat across the beach and to the harbor. The weather was too thick to continue, they decided, after they had gone aground several times in the harbor. They stopped and caught forty winks. When morning came and the fog lifted, they went into town, got the butter, and then headed back for the lightship, where a worried captain greeted them. The perils of the fog were as great as any other hazard of the sea.

Those perils brought some unforgettable days and nights to Nantucket. In March 1846, the ship *Earl of Eglington* was on her way from Liverpool to Boston when she came in too close to Nantucket, and struck on the south shoal. That night she drifted off that shoal, and into the shoal called The Old Man. Captain John Niven saw that his vessel was not going to get off, and he beached her because she was leaking. The cargo would have to be salvaged.

The next step was to get the crew off and in to shore, in the heavy seas. The urgency was made quite plain when *Earl of Eglington* was combed by a wave—it broke clean over the decks. In the hurry to get away, two boats pulled hastily away from the ship, and one of them upset in the undertow, which whisked two of the men away and drowned them. The other two were rescued by people from the island who rushed out into the surf and grabbed the men.

By the middle of the nineteenth century, Nantucketers were used to the ways of the sea. This day, as *Earl of Eglington* had come in, the people saw and knew what they must do. Coming to the shore they had tied ropes around their waists, keeping enough men ashore to anchor those of the lifesavers who ventured into the treacherous surf. Nonetheless, Captain Watson Burgess, who went into the foam, was nearly drowned saving those two men of the boat; his legs were swept out from under him by the undertow and he was pulled away, but the rope saved him.

The four crew members in the next boat were not so lucky. The boat struck the rip when coming around the stern of the stricken ship. It overturned, and all the occupants were lost to the sea.

By this time most of the able-bodied men of Nantucket who could get there had reached the shore. By sign language they told the men still on *Earl of Eglington* to heave a line. They tried, and failed. Then they launched an oar, and the Nantucketers caught it with a fishing rig, and hauled the oar and line ashore. They sent back a message and a larger line. The men of the ship attached a cable, and soon a sling was improvised. One man at a time was hauled ashore, dunked and half drowned in the surf, until the rest of the crew were rescued. At the end, when the captain was leaving the ship, the whole rig collapsed and he nearly drowned, but the rescuers ducked into the surf again and hauled him out, spluttering but alive.

They got off just in time. The sea began to rage, and for the next three days no one could approach the stricken ship to investigate the cargo. When the weather calmed, it was too late. The wreck was total; the cargo of salt, coal, drygoods and copper was scattered and ruined. Four bodies were washed ashore, and the people of Nantucket gave them a fine funeral from the Baptist church.

For the amount of traffic that used them, Nantucket waters had relatively few wrecks, for the traffic was really intense. In 1843, for example, more than 13,000 vessels passed Cross Rip, and were logged by the lightship there. Most of these were coastal vessels, schooners and sloops, but Nantucket Sound was an important waterway, no question of that.

As far as employment was concerned, the volume of shipping that passed its shores was not much help to Nantucket. Pilots were taken aboard on the mainland or at Vineyard Haven, and while the shipping trade offered employment to many men, there was little good from it for the island. There was, of course, the question of wrecking, or salvage of wrecks, sometimes legal and sometimes not. Salvage became a major island preoccupation as the whaling trade declined, for one good wreck could set a man up. Or kill him. Two celebrated cases indicated the opportunities and the dangers.

First was the wreck of the *Louis Phillipe*, a fine New York sailing

packet on the Le Havre run. She sailed from the French port in
October 1847, and immediately encountered such stiff weather that
she was thrown off course, and fought the seas until December 16,
when one of Nantucket Sound's famous fogs settled in to finish her.
She struck a shoal northwest of Great Point, and the shock dislodged
her rudder. Captain Castoff (how apt a name) could not steer her at
all.

Nantucket waters then had their way with the crippled ship. She
was swirled along inshore, under Sankaty Head, fetching up finally
on Pochick Rip off Siasconset with a thundering crash. She struck late
in the day, and lay there in the fog until the air cleared on the morning of December 17.

As morning came, the villagers of Siasconset awoke to see a ship in
their front yard. They sent a boat, and Captain Castoff consulted his
papers and found that the insurance company had an agent in Nantucket, Peter Folger. He sent word that he needed a tow. When the
message reached Nantucket town, Folger chartered the steamer
Massachusetts, which berthed on the island and often towed whaling
ships in or out of harbor. But the fog settled in again, even as the
riders were carrying the messages. *Massachusetts* steamed out of harbor at 9:30 in the morning. By the time she had come around to
Siasconset, there was no sign of any vessel; Captain James H. Barker
could scarcely see anything at all. He turned back to the harbor.

Actually, the tide had carried *Louis Phillipe* off the shoal and out
into deeper water off Tom Nevers Head, where the captain dropped
anchor and waited for his tow. When she was located this time, the
steamer *Telegraph* set out, but it was too late in the day to make the
rescue by the time *Louis Phillipe* was found. *Telegraph* lay alongside
her all night, then returned to harbor and *Massachusetts* took her
place, for *Telegraph* had a passenger schedule to maintain.

It was Sunday—two days after the accident—before the rescue
could properly begin. Both steamships came up and put hawsers
aboard the packet, just as a southwest gale began to blow. The
steamers announced their intention of moving back to harbor, and
Louis Phillipe's crew dropped two anchors and hoped. Most of the
cabin passengers decided to go with the steamers, and they left the
ship. The *Massachusetts* and the *Telegraph* scurried for the safety of
the harbor.

The gale blew out by Monday morning, and the steamers were back again. They put the lines aboard, and together towed the packet through Muskeget channel and on to Edgartown, where they arrived safely on Monday night, December 20. The insurance company paid $26,000 for the salvage job, and every man of the crews of the two steamers got a little of it, at least.

Louis Phillipe had to count as a success story for Nantucket. But then there was the story of *British Queen,* to show the opposite side of the coin Nantucketers spun in the wreckage business.

British Queen sailed from Dublin in the fall of 1851 for America, and after she encountered storms she came up on the shoals off Muskeget Island on December 17. At night when the watchman in the Muskeget light tower closed down, he saw nothing. In the morning, going up in the northwest gale, he saw a ship on the shoals, with two masts cut away, obviously in dire distress. The watchman hurried to pass the word, but it did not do much good in this weather. All day long the storm smashed the island, and no vessels would venture out of Nantucket harbor to come around. So *British Queen* sat in the shallows, stuck fast, and aboard her sat 226 Irish immigrant passengers who were bound for the glories of the new world.

Captain Conway ran up distress signals on his mainmast—the only one standing. Many men tried to launch boats from the shore, but they could not get them through the heavy surf. So dreadful was the weather that many an old salt predicted *British Queen* would break up before the storm blew out. But night came and she held together, while the poor Irish immigrants huddled in the wet misery of the steerage and clung to one another for support. As if they needed the extra danger, it was cold, the harbor was choked with ice, and the spray froze on the deck.

In Nantucket harbor the men of the sea were debating the means of rescue that night. It seemed unlikely that the weather would soften much in the next few hours, but they got up steam in *Telegraph,* and decided to tow out the schooners *Hamilton* and *Game Cock* to try the rescue. The crews of the schooners assembled. Peter Folger, the insurance agent, came down. All was ready at dawn, except the weather. They could not take the ships out, the wind was heading down their throats from the north, and the ice and seas made it foolhardy to try before high tide. That meant they had to wait until one o'clock that afternoon. Even then it would be a close squeak, for *Hamilton* drew eight feet, and at high water the bar was only nine feet under water. The steamboat took *Game Cock* first, for she drew only seven feet. Then, precisely at high water, *Telegraph* took *Hamilton* over the bar.

Game Cock had the advantage—and advantage was what was wanted, for the schooners were competitors in the wrecking game. *Game Cock* anchored half a mile from the wreck, and *Telegraph* came up to within three-quarters of a mile of her. Shortly *Hamilton* came up.

The rescuers soon enough realized that it was a job too big for one of them alone, and they joined forces, although without much enthusiasm. Captain Thomas Gardner was one of the wreckers, the other was Captain David Patterson. They ended up in the same small boat, heading for the wreck.

When they got there, they received some really unpleasant news. *British Queen* had no cargo aboard, said the captain. All he had was 226 passengers and his crew. "They are in a horrid condition," he announced. So there was to be much danger, and little profit in this day's work. But that is how it was, and so the men of Nantucket set to work.

Horrid condition—indeed the passengers were in it. Two had died during the night, and a hundred were so weak they were near death. There was no time to be lost. *Game Cock* came alongside and began taking off people. She had some sixty passengers aboard, when Captain Gardner felt the schooner strike bottom. Now Captain Patterson suggested that the *Hamilton* be used—which meant the company's costs for salvage were going up, up, up. But there was nothing else to be done; *Game Cock* could not do the job alone.

There were complications. What was valuable was the equipment of *British Queen;* there were no payments by insurance companies for lifesaving. So Patterson wanted to be in on the salvage, and Gardner had to let him in, right then. Business matters attended to, the lifesaving continued. *Game Cock* pulled away with her sixty rescued, and *Hamilton* took off the rest of the passengers. The ships and the steamer made ready to head for harbor. The salvage of equipment would have to wait.

But others did not think so. Everybody on Nantucket knew the rules of salvage. As the ships were about to leave, up came the fishing smack *Watchman*, with a three man crew, and Captain James Maguire decided he would steal a march on the official salvagers and take off as many valuables as he could. The captain of *Hamilton* shouted at them to clear off. They paid no attention, but tied up to the bobstay and began taking off the ships' running rigging.

The official salvagers warned them that the changing of the tide might prove disastrous to the fishing boat. The fisherman smiled at the attempt to drive them off. The salvagers went back to Nantucket Straight Wharf with their worthless cargo of human lives, while the fishermen were in possession of the wreck.

In Nantucket, the townspeople rallied to the assistance of the poor refugees. Some were quartered in Sons of Temperance Hall, some in Pantheon Hall. The women, children, and the sick were taken in by Nantucket families, and soon collections were made for the poor passengers, for they had lost nearly all they owned.

As it happened the daring, or errant, interlopers from *Watchman* were not now much better off. Captain Maguire and seaman Charles Holmes were aboard the wrecked *British Queen* when the tide and weather changed. The smack was off to leeward, with seaman Jeremiah Green holding her at anchor. When the weather and water began to kick up, Captain Maguire decided to take his boat, loaded with salvage, and get back to the fishing smack. But as they pushed away, the sea pushed back, and the boat broke against the side of the wreck. Seeing, seaman Green cut his cable and ran for the bar in front of Nantucket harbor, and told the tale of what had happened.

Many a head was shaken and many a hard word was said about James Maguire's greed and folly. Nothing could be done in the renewed storm that night. The men must pay the price until the morrow.

It was three o'clock the next afternoon before anything was seen. For in the morning the light of dawn brought no sign of the wrecked *British Queen* where she had been lying. The ice extended four miles out into the sound, and no one dared go out in an unfavorable wind. But in the afternoon the men of Nantucket began to try to save the two fools who had risked everything. Someone said he saw a boat just off the beach. *Hamilton* went out past the bar, and hove to, waiting for a light from shore that would indicate where the men might be.

That night, when the light came from the beach, *Hamilton* stood in under jib alone, and came inshore. But all that anyone could see was a big piece of wreckage. There was not a man in sight.

They worked in close, and then they found the two men, in their wrecked boat, stuck in the ice about a quarter mile from the shore. Most surely they would have perished during the night had not the men of *Hamilton* found them. They were rescued and brought ashore to recover. The salvagers had to wait for the weather to abate, then they managed to get a few hundred dollars worth of lumber and hemp off the *British Queen*. They saved the quarter board when it drifted ashore onto the beach after a storm, and eventually it wound up over the front door of a house on West Chester Street.

But that was all. Except for one more gift from the sea. Most of the rescued passengers went to New York on Christmas day aboard *Telegraph*, which was chartered for the trip. But a handful of Irishmen decided they would not brave the seas again, and they settled down on Nantucket.

So that is how Nantucket got its Irishmen.

XVIII

Decline

THE STORY OF the Jared Coffin house is very much the story of Nantucket in the years after that whaling merchant built the brick building in 1846. It tells of the ups and downs, the failures and successes, and the changes that came to the island over the years.

After the fire of 1846, and the destruction of most of the town, one would think so fine a brick building as the Jared Coffin house, which was undamaged by the flames, would be of inestimable value. But it was a sign of reality that when the house sold the following year, Jared Coffin having deserted the island, it brought only $7,700. It was purchased by the Nantucket Steamboat Company, not as a private mansion, but as a hotel to accommodate the transient trade of the steamboats. It was re-christened Ocean House, and Mrs. Robert T. Parker, the organist at the Unitarian Church, was chosen to be manager. It was a handy place for traveling men, and for people who had something to offer the island when they came on a visit, like Madame Buckley, the mystic, who stayed for several weeks, on the premise that she could cure various diseases and also tell the future to her clients.

As the fifties came along, Nantucket land values began to drop. The Ocean House was sold in 1857 to Eben Allen, for whom the bar is now named, and he undertook to remodel it and make it more sufficient as a hostelry. It was then, as now, the major inn and watering place for the island's first-class tourist trade.

Nantucket's population of the fifties started in the eight thousands, and began to go down. People came and people went, the last Indians died, the boys went off to California, the girls married and left the island as their husbands sought opportunity on the mainland. By 1860 the population was down to 6,000, and the reason could be found in

147

the shipping notes in the weekly papers. Only six ships sailed from Nantucket that year. Whaling was finished.

Then came the years of Civil War, which had virtually no effect on Nantucket, save that she contributed about 350 of her sons to the war effort, including one Major General (a Macy). About seventy of them died in the service.

A handful of captains went out whaling in the war years. The sixty-five ton schooner *Samuel Chase* made five trips just offshore, taking "local" whales for the small value they now afforded. In 1862 three whalers were out, and one captain, William Cash, was so brave as to take his *Islander* to the Pacific. It was a good voyage by the old standards, with 2,400 barrels of sperm oil in the cargo and 1,800 pounds of whale bone for the corset industry, but the prices were not what they used to be, and *Islander's* success did not attract many others. In 1863 and 1864 only the little schooner *Rainbow* was a-whaling in Atlantic waters. Zenas Coleman was her captain.

The Colemans were the most stubborn of the dying breed. Zenas was whaling again in '65 and '66. In that latter year his mate, James Bunker, was killed by a whale. But that did not stop him. He sailed the 107-ton brig *Eunice H. Adams* until almost the last. Coleman sailed for the Atlantic on March 31, 1869, and came back in June 1870, with 550 barrels. The sad honor of making the last Nantucket whale voyage was left to Captain William B. Thompson of the bark *Oak*, who sailed for the Pacific on November 16, 1869, and never did come home. He shipped 60 barrels of sperm oil and 450 barrels of right whale oil, but on the way back the *Oak* was sold at Panama. She was Nantucket's very last whaler.

Toward the end there was a sadness about the voyages that permeated all Nantucket. It was as if the island itself knew it was dying, and the people looked on, and could grieve but do little else. There was no way of stopping progress, then as now. As if realizing the tragedy, when Captain William Cash sailed in 1862, and took a big whale, he felt a need unknown by captains of the old days—to bring home a trophy. He took one whale 87 feet long, which yielded 110 barrels of sperm oil. This time he took the jawbone, which measured 17 feet in length. He brought it home and kept it. Eventually the great showman P. T. Barnum came to the island, and made an offer to buy the trophy, but the family would not sell. Today, the whale's jaw is on exhibit in the Whaling Museum, one of its most highly prized of trophies of the days long gone.

By the end of the Civil War decade, Nantucket was suffering visibly. The Quakers had lost nearly all their influence. Their Meeting was rent by one controversy after another. In the middle of the decade, Christopher Hussey, their most eloquent preacher, quit the society and joined the Unitarians. The meeting house on Centre Street saw attendance grow sparser every year. The last controversy, over the publication of a journal, brought the defection of Peleg Mitchell, one of the most influential of the Quakers. He took only a small group with him—but it was large enough to bring about the downfall of the Nantucket Meeting, and the last session was held on January 10, 1867. The Meeting then transferred all activity to the New Bedford monthly meeting, and organized Quakerism nearly ceased to exist on Nantucket. Men and women held their meetings together. They would maintain a semblance of organization for another thirty years, until 1894 when the meeting house was sold to the Nantucket Historical Association.

Islanders had few illusions about what was happening to their homeland. In 1865 there was not the slightest doubt—the population dropped that year to 4,800. And what were the men and boys to do for a living? Farming was limited by the land and its misuse in the past. The island needed only a few carpenters and other specialists, because plenty of houses were vacant and it was simpler and cheaper to buy an abandoned house than build a new one. Groceries, drugs, clothing— the demand for each of these necessities was limited by the falling population.

Even in the middle of the Civil War years, the desperate plight of the island brought some to planning for a new future. The exploitation of Cape Cod as a holiday resort for Bostonians had begun already, and land prices were booming on the Cape. Mark Salom of Boston acquired a number of pieces of Nantucket real estate and began to promote the island as a vacation resort. He called a public meeting, and many of the town fathers came.

The Jared Coffin house was in the thick of it, known then as Ocean House. The proprietor put up bath houses on the Cliff Shore, near Jetties Beach, to promote the vacation idea. Other establishments began doing the same.

An attempt was made to re-establish the cod fishery on the island, and several fishing boats appeared in the harbor. But the trouble then, as later, was marketing: Nantucket could use so little of the catch that it had to be sold elsewhere, and if it was to be sold at New Bedford, then it was much brighter to base at New Bedford and not on the island. The cod fishing plan, instead of bringing new industry to Nantucket, took away its last remaining fishing men.

By the end of the 1860's the harbor was empty. A few old men sat at homemade tables near the wharves peddling the fish they caught just offshore in their little craft. Nantucket's mighty seamen were long gone.

And yet the sea remained. And the sea brought Nantucket the only gifts it was to receive. They were tragic gifts in many cases, and sometimes ghoulish, but they provided survival. They were the wrecks that came in around the island's shores.

The scarcity of money made the wreckers bold and highly competitive. After a storm, lookouts climbed the South Tower of the Unitarian church and looked around the horizon with glasses, searching for wrecks. When they found them, the race was on. During the annual town meeting in February 1861, word came that a ship had come ashore near Hummock Pond. In a moment the meeting was adjourned and the men were rushing to the scene. Soon the boats were out, and coming back loaded with sugar and molasses. The cargo was nearly all salvaged, and Nantucket had a moment of return to the good times of wealth.

At the end of the year the *May Queen* went aground between Tom Nevers Head and Nobadeer. It was a cold December day, and the crew took to the rigging as the seas broke over the hull. Captain David Patterson, who had helped rescue the steerage passengers from the wrecked *British Queen* ten years earlier, hurried to the beach with the line gun and the life cars, on pontoons, that could be used to float men off wrecks. When he got there, the men on the beach had already thrown a line to the vessel. They did it by using a bluefish drail, a one-pound lead sinker with a hook in the end, that was fished by throwing it out past the breakers and pulling in. The island's drail expert that day was William J. Ellis, who made a throw of 360 feet, and got the line to the ship. Soon the lifeboats were moving.

It was a disappointing day for the wreckers. Hardly had they gotten the crew off than the ship broke up, and nearly all was lost.

Of course it was not always that way. One time Captain Patterson salvaged all but a few bales of an entire cargo of cotton. Other times there were precious metals and iron and machinery to be saved. In the 1860's, wrecking was very much a part of island life.

On the morning of February 20, 1863, the word came that a ship in distress lay off the Cliff. Even though it was snowing heavily, Captain Patterson set out with a crew in a small boat, and so did Captain Alexander Dunham. The latter arrived first, boarded the ship, and warned Patterson away. It was Dunham's job, and no doubt about it. Six weeks later it was a different story: the German bark *Elwine Fredericke* struck on Great Point shoal during a thick fog. Captain Patterson got there first this time, and rescued the captain and fourteen men of the crew. He got a silver medal from the King of Prussia for this job, but not much else—the ship broke up shortly after the crew was taken off, and before much valuable goods could be saved.

The wrecks could bring sheer tragedy, and it was never more apparent than when women and children were involved. On November 20, 1863, the bark *Samuel A. Nichols* was blown onto Great Point Rip in a northwest gale. The ship soon showed that she was breaking up, and Captain Nichols put his wife and baby, and the baby's nursemaid into the ship's boat with the mate and two men of the crew. He then went to fetch the other men, observing the old rule of the sea that the captain was to be the last man off ship. While he was getting them, a lurch of the ship dragged the boat up against the hull and put all in the boat in danger. The line was cut and the boat drifted off, without the rest of the crew to man her, heading out before the captain's horrified eyes, not into the sound, but toward the cold open sea.

Nichols, his second mate, and three men were left on the wreck, the captain mourning his lost wife and child. They were saved through disaster. The bark broke up, they clung to the wreckage and were supported by it. A fishing sloop came along and picked up the captain and his men, and took them safe into Edgartown.

Then, two months later, the steamer *Africa* arrived in Boston from Liverpool, and there, safe and sound, were the lost ones. They had been picked up in the open sea by a ship outward bound, which had carried them to England.

In the hard wrecks, too often there was little profit for the wreckers, for Nantucket storms showed no favoritism to the islanders. But still, wrecking was a profitable business, and just about the only such on the island in lean times. Before the end of '63 the island had some major windfalls.

First was the schooner *Volant,* which came ashore at the east end of the bar on the morning of December 8. Captain Dunham and his crew discovered her at ten o'clock and went out in a boat. By using a fishing boat they managed to board, although the storm still blew. The crew was in the rigging by this time, and the vessel was iced up. But Dunham saved them, and five days later the schooner was towed in, with her cargo of lumber, salvaged.

On December 11, the steamer *Island Home* saw a vessel low in the water. She was the schooner *Odessa,* sinking in the Sound in the middle of that same storm. Four islanders boarded, and rescued the crew, who were in dreadful shape, their hands and feet frozen after two days in the rigging without shelter, food, or water. *Odessa* was brought in over the bar—another cargo saved.

In the same December of 1863, the schooner *Clara,* sailing from Baltimore to Boston, came ashore on Great Point, with no one aboard. The captain had become hopelessly lost. He and his men had seen their anchors tear away, they had bumped on shoal after shoal, and finally, off Chappaquiddick, had taken to the boats and gone in to land. Here was a classic case of an abandoned ship. The islanders were very lucky this time, for *Clara* had an assorted cargo of goods, valuable and sound. She was towed off and over to Vineyard Haven.

True, not one of these wrecks was a large vessel, but together they brought in a tidy income for the wreckers of the island.

There were a dozen wrecks on the island shoals in '64, some profitable, some tragic, and one showing the bravery and fortitude of the islanders at their very best. The most profitable was the wreck of the bark *B. Colford* in December. She was bound from the West Indies to Maine in ballast when she went ashore on Gravel Island shoal. *Island Home* steamed out in the storm, but could not come close enough for her men to board. So the bark was abandoned and sold at auction, bought by a Nantucket whaling firm for junk. After three efforts, she was gotten off the shoal in such shape that she could be towed into harbor, and, with no more than refitting, she was put into service as a whaler. She went out in 1866 to the Pacific and was sold for a fine profit before the voyage ended.

The tragedies of 1864 also involved the schooner *Haynes,* and the ship *Newton. Haynes* ran ashore in December on the south side of the island, near the head of Hummock Pond. Her crew tried to swim ashore in the storm, and drowned, every man. Had the men stayed aboard they would have been saved, for the vessel hung together, and when the storm was over, the islanders saved the whole cargo, although the weather kicked up once again and the sea took the ship before she could be salvaged.

On Christmas day, the ship *Newton* came ashore on the south side of the island, and began to break up. Next day, islanders found one member of the crew half a mile inland, lying dead, his face buried in the sand. Before the storm ended seventeen bodies washed ashore. So grave a tragedy sobered all the island. The dead were taken lovingly to the Unitarian graveyard, and buried in the order in which they had been found. On Sunday funeral services were held for them at the Methodist church. That afternoon, after the solemn funeral, nearly the whole town walked out to the Unitarian burying ground, to pay respects to these unknown dead, who had come to them in the holy season.

Ironically, the *Newton* tragedy brought the town profit. Oh, how ironically. For the islanders salvaged 2,200 barrels of oil from the wreck—coal oil!—the hated kerosene that had destroyed Nantucket! The people of so poor an island could not help but be concerned with every means of their own salvation. The wreck of the *Newton* was sold as she lay for $510, and the lumber brought ashore to add to the economy.

But the islanders were made of more than greed, in spite of their great deprivation of the sixties. No grander illustration could be found than in the tale of the schooner *Evelin Treat,* that came to strike on Miacomet Rip in the dark early hours of October 21. Captain Job Philbrick, a Philadelphia man, had been bringing her up to Gloucester with a cargo of coal. She lay there all night, and was discovered in the morning from the tower.

Evelin Treat had struck 300 feet offshore. Soon the seas were breaking over her and tore the deckhouse away. The captain ordered his men into the rigging, and there they stayed. The men of Nantucket then began to move. They brought the line gun and floats of the Humane Society, and managed to fire a line into the wind to carry across the wreck. One of the captain's sons managed to fix a hawser to it, and that was dragged ashore. Then the rescue began.

A sling was attached to the hawser. The mate got in and was drawn toward the shore. Halfway across, the rope snarled, and the pulley jammed. The men ashore threw a line, which the mate tied around his waist. He leaped into the sea, and was dragged ashore, half drowned but alive. Next came one of the captain's sons. He reported that his father, old and sick, had refused to try to come ashore. So the rescuers brought up a life car, and Daniel Folger volunteered to go to the ship and bring the captain off. But the old man refused. The life car did not work that day, anyhow, on that hawser.

There was only one way. The captain must entrust himself to the sling. He did. In his stocking feet, his head bare, the captain got into the sling and was securely trussed in by the two men in the rigging. He started across. Halfway, the rope snarled again. The captain could not extricate himself, for he was trussed like a rooster. He swung there, suspended, the sea breaking in his face, his feet dangling in the waves. Ashore, the men twisted and tugged to relieve the snarl. It would not loosen. And the minutes sped by.

It was a dark day, and by this time it was late afternoon. The captain had been hanging in midair for an hour and a half, and he could not last much longer. Frederick Ramsdell of the rescue squad saw that something must be done immediately. He tied a rope around his waist and took a knife in his teeth. He swam to the old man, and managed to make the repairs. Then he came ashore and the others hauled the captain in, saved. So too, in a little while, were the other men in the rigging.

As for *Evelin Treat*, she was a total loss. There was no profit in that rescue, save the honors paid by the Massachusetts Humane Society. Young Ramsdell was given their highest medal.

And as all the islanders agreed, sometimes just that was enough.

XIX

Tourism

THE YEAR 1870 marked what William C. Macy called the "bottom line" of Nantucket's fortunes, and Macy was not talking in twentieth century terms. The "bottom line" was very definitely bad. For years Nantucket had been having its up and downs. In the past fifteen years it had seemed more nearly all downs. And for the first time in many decades, the island was more or less unified in its approach to the world.

It may seem odd in the last part of the twentieth century, but the Nantucket of the 1830's and 1840's was a little copy of a nation. It had its "metropolis"—Nantucket town. It had its farmers, on the moors, out Madaket way, and toward Polpis. Indeed, in Nantucket jargon to be *Polpisy* was to be very hickish. Nantucket also had its fishermen and wreckers, and herdsmen, all of them living very different kinds of lives in these days when the trip from one end of the island to the other was a significant journey that would not be undertaken lightly.

The seventies brought something of a change in all this. And the reason was the realization that all the islanders were in the same boat. The decline of the whale fishing brought a loss of capital and a mutual misery that drove the islanders together as they had not been for years.

And with the misery came hope.

From the peak, Nantucket land values had dropped by more than half, as one could see by what had happened to Jared Coffin's fine house on Broad Street. Early in the seventies the house, which had been operating as the Ocean House hotel, was bought by the firm of Howe and Elmer. This time it had a *mortgage*—an appendage that would have been anathema to any self-respecting Nantucketer fifteen years earlier. Howe and Elmer had big plans. They also bought the

Samuel Swain house next door, and hoped to reap a fortune. The basis of their hopes was the presumption that the tourist trade was going to make the island rich. Yes, this was 1870, and that is what Nantucketers were doing.

These were the days of railroad promotions, and many a railroad existed that had no place in particular to go. The Massachusetts Old Colony railroad, seeing the handwriting on the wall in the consolidation and demise of small railroads at the hands of the Vanderbilts and Goulds and J. P. Morgan, came upon the happy thought that they might maintain independence and achieve considerable fortune by promoting the vacation trade on Cape Cod and the islands. They developed a particular interest in Nantucket, whose waters and airs were invested with a mystique that has never left them. The Old Colony began to promote Nantucket as a watering place. At first, the line ran from Boston to Hyannis. Then it moved to Woods Hole. Steamboats connected from Woods Hole to Nantucket and Martha's Vineyard.

In the seventies two forces were at work, both operating on the land. The well-to-do farmers were buying up agricultural lands. The old concept of the commonlands had just about gone under by this time; in the heyday of Nantucket's prosperity the rich had fought in court time and again to secure the partition of the lands, and little by little chunks had been wrested away, so that soon enough the dream of broad commons, so dear to old Tristram Coffin, would be buried deep as any Quaker in his grave.

The proprietors of Ocean House soon were doing a thriving business with tourists. The pattern that we see today on the island was emerging. In the summer of '72 the hitherto hungry fisherman found a new profitability in taking out coofs who wanted the thrill of latching onto a blue or a striper. In August of that year Captain Alexander Dunham took a fishing party on an outing clear round the island. They caught sixty blues.

Nantucket town profited from this activity, of course. But the real change was the development of Siasconset; that fishing and lifesaving community suddenly burgeoned in the land boom to become a tourist paradise.

In the seventies the most popular islanders in Siasconset were Captain William Baxter, his wife Love, and Asa P. Jones. Love Baxter was the post mistress of the new post office established in 1872 at this end of the island. That great event occurred, obviously, because there was need for it, so much so that Captain Baxter was hired at eight dollars a year to carry the mails to the patrons.

As for Asa Jones, he was largely responsible for the post office's being there in the first place. He was the "last carpenter" of Siasconset, and since 1858 he had been eking out a lonely existence at the end of the island. But in the seventies it all changed: Asa Jones became the busiest man in the community. What a change! R. B. Hussey, writing about it in the *Inquirer and Mirror* in 1912, said that Jones had been so dispirited in the fifties that when one of his assistants took all his tools off to Providence he had not even noticed it. Indeed, he had not even missed them for twenty years, and then suddenly the assistant, George Rogers, showed up again with the tools, just in time. For the building boom was about to begin.

Soon Jones was too busy to set his chickens and shear his sheep. He was building houses for the gentry. One of the early summer people was William J. Flagg, of New York, who came to Jones one day and asked the carpenter to build him a house, and a Siasconset house at that. Now there was the augury of the future: even in the 1870's there existed some driving force that led rich coofs from the mainland to recognize the peculiar values of Nantucket architecture and the Nantucket ways. Busy New Yorkers knew even then that theirs was not a viable way of life, that the crowding and ever-changing nature of the city was a huge joke on the legitimate aspirations of mankind. They knew, and in their own fumbling ways the rich men of New York and Boston tried to preserve for themselves a bit of the old that had already slipped beyond the grasp of mainlanders.

Soon houses were going up all over Siasconset. They were also going across. In the days before the telephone line, particularly after the depression of the 1850's and '60's struck the island, house moving was a constant activity. Some of the houses of Siasconset were the little shacks of the fishermen, beginning with rude walls, roof, and dirt floor, and proceeding with improvement after change. Dr. John King of Nantucket had a summer place at Siasconset even then. The idea was as prominent in the seventies as a hundred years later, when such notables as Carol, an island tour lady, and author Nathaniel Benchley would occupy one house in Siasconset in the summer, and a house in

Nantucket town in the winter. So many houses were moved in this period from Sesachacha, the other fishing village near Siasconset, that Sesachacha virtually lost its identity.

Sometimes the moving worked fine. Henry Paddack moved a cottage from Sesachacha and called it Bigenough. (These were the days of a superb puckishness in the naming of summer houses.) But when they went to move another cottage, named High Tide, from its place on Broadway, the tide went out, the cottage collapsed, and all the mover had for his pains was a load of highly seasoned lumber.

Some people made changes in modernizing the old Nantucket houses. They put on additions, which were called warts. They changed the shingling to clapboards. Well, they could afford it. In the years just before, the price of houses had been cheap enough. Captain Chandler Brown Gardner came back to the island after making his fortune in California, and bought a Siasconset house for twenty-five dollars and four quintals of fish. When Tristram Pinkham was asked how much he wanted for his Siasconset house, he allowed that it might be worth about three quintals of fish, or 300 pounds of mackerel, so to speak. Even Gardner, who owned half of it, gave Tristram Pinkham his 150 pounds of fish, and he had a house all to himself. By the end of the decade it sold for several hundred dollars.

Prices were becoming outrageous. Eagle Cottage was valued by Captain William Baxter at $200! Broadway, Siasconset, was as scandalous as its namesake down in New York.

In those days, the beach was right up in 'Sconset's back yard. Ships which ran aground at "The Head" were nearly in the community center, so close was the narrow strip of sand to the water's edge. But from the old community of some fifty fishing shacks soon evolved a summer community, made up about half of Nantucketers and half of off-islanders who discovered the place in the seventies.

The whole island became tourist oriented. In 1872 the catboat *Dauntless* was put into service, to run to and from the town bathing beach. A building boom was begun on the north shore of the island, with promise that this would be "the" place of the future. They called it Nantucket Bluffs. The boom ended with a bang, but the houses built later became extremely valuable. And it was true in Siasconset, too. Dr. Franklin Ellis and Charles H. Robinson started a land speculation there in the area south of the Gully. They were a bit premature. The land did not go like hotcakes. It did not go well at all, in fact. Next year it went a little bit, as more off-islanders came to Nantucket, and that year promoters bought up three miles of shore frontage on the south shore, and created Surfside. Not to be outdone, other promoters built the Ocean View House in Siasconset.

In 1873 and 1874 the land boom continued. A man named Tourtelot of Worcester speculated in land at Madaket, and created a 2,000-lot promotion. The islanders greeted it with a mixture of awe and revulsion—just as they greeted a similar proposal a hundred years later. The 1874 promotion fell flat; those who came to Nantucket were apparently not interested in being shunted together like oysters in an offshore bed.

But it was not just Madaket. Dr. Ellis and his partner were promoting actively that year. Building was going on on the North Shore. Surfside was developing somewhat. And at Quaise, a pair of New Haven promoters bought a tract and made 500 house lots. But that is as far as they got.

The big news that summer of 1874 was that President U. S. Grant came to Nantucket. Long Branch, New Jersey, was his special place, and sometimes he could be found at Saratoga, where the Vanderbilts and Henry Clews vacationed, but this year he visited Nantucket, and the island was delighted.

Building and speculating—that was the pattern that year. It all sounds grand, until one realizes that Nantucket's population of 1875 dropped to 3,200, or only about 900 voters. That meant most of the people on the island were women and children; the number of males was at a point about as low as it had been at any time since the middle of the eighteenth century.

There was still plenty of hope on Nantucket. Down in New York and over in Boston the steamboat men put Nantucket on their maps and began running excursion boats. These were a forerunner of the Caribbean cruise boats; they would bring the clerks and shopkeepers off on a sea vacation for a few days, and put them ashore at Nantucket to see the beautiful town and buy a few souvenirs.

There was a lively trade with New Bedford, and even intra-island, with a steamboat service inaugurated in these years from Nantucket to Wauwinet. Before anyone scoffs, let them walk it a few times—for that was the alternative for summer people without rigs and horses on the island. So busy was the summer trade at Steamboat Wharf that it even justified the building of a restaurant there, which operated profitably in 1876.

The success of steamboats on Nantucket in the summers was a reflection of a general rise in coastal shipping. And the increase in shipping brought another change; the development of the federal lifesaving service. That, in turn, brought another dividend to Nantucket's slender economic resources.

In 1874 the lifesaving service decided to build on Nantucket, because of the need of those traversing the dangers of Nantucket Sound. They chose Surfside for their first lifesaving station.

The plans were made the year before, of course, but the need was shown beyond doubt in March 1874, when ten ships were wrecked on the shoals around Nantucket. The men of the station had the duty of walking the island's south shore during storms, and firing flares if they saw reason to warn some craft. These so-called surfmen must have been effective, for it was two years before their lifesaving services were required.

Then, on March 9, 1877, the three-masted bark *W. F. Marshall* was driven onto the shore in heavy fog. She struck off Mioxes Pond. Because of that fog, surfman Horace Cash, who was on patrol, did not even see the vessel, and of course it would have done no good to fire a flare. A southeast gale was blowing, and the surf was very high on the shore. The fog parted for a moment and Cash spotted the distressed *Marshall*. He hurried back to the station for help, and as he did so, the wind blew the fog in again; it swirled around the ship and she disappeared from sight. When the surfmen reappeared, there was no ship to be seen. They fired guns to attract attention, but there was no answer. They waited, and then the fog parted once more, and before them lay the ship, broadside to the beach.

The surfmen had their boat, but they could not launch it in the heavy surf. They fired a line over the vessel, and soon had a breeches-buoy in operation. They saved the captain, the crew of thirteen, and the black steward's wife and child.

When the storm ended, the townspeople came out to see the big ship. She was soon sold as she was, hull for $185 and spars for $25 (she was in ballast, so there was no cargo). *Marshall* was a brand-new vessel, and there was hope of getting her off. But Nantucket's sands said No. Several attempts were made. On March 17, the 940-ton bark was stripped of rigging, cables, hawsers, and sails. Some of the material was brought to commercial wharf and stored in the warehouse of Captain Matthew Crosby. The insurers showed up soon, for they held about $10,000 in insurance on her. James Powers of Boston came, for he had speculated on the wreck in the hope that he might salvage her entirely and make a huge profit. He sent over a crew of wreckers, and they hired some Nantucketers, as well, to help with the work.

The Norfolk Wrecking Company sent an expert, and he reported that *Marshall* could be gotten off the shoals. He sent for a wrecking schooner and the materials necessary to do the job. They put up houses on the beach for shelter, and began work. They took the yards down from the masts, and hauled the anchor out of the hold.

In May, Powers had made the wrecking chances look so good that he was able to unload his speculation at a healthy profit, to the firm of Gibson and Bartlett of Boston. The wreckers continued the work under the new employers. They brought a lighter, and a steam engine for towing, on the schooner *Forest City*. By now it was June, and the weather should be good. But Nantucket can be unpredictably obnoxious in the weather department, and this June the water was so rough around the shore that the wrecking equipment had to be brought into harbor and put ashore at the wharf.

On June 16, Mr. Louis Forbes, the well known "submarine diver" arrived on Nantucket with his assistant, Mr. William Gillen, and the *Inquirer and Mirror* reported that he brought along his "armor." The town came out to watch as Forbes went down on the outside of the *Marshall* to make an inspection of the hull. He found three leaks between the main and the fore chains, one of them so large he could put his hand inside the hull. The swell was heavy that day and drove him up before he could make the repairs. He went down again next day to start patching.

Bad weather delayed the wrecking operation for another week. A donkey engine was gotten aboard to pump the hulk out. The leaks were stopped up, and men began taking the ballast out of the hold. In the third week of June they managed to move the wreck eight feet offshore, and the chances looked bright that they would soon have her on the way to Boston for a refit, and then a sale for thousands of dollars of profit.

But the weather remained stubbornly bad. *Forest City* nearly went aground one day in a southwest blow. Then, seeing the huge profits the Boston syndicate was about to reap, the longshoremen who were doing the hauling and movement of ballast went on strike in the last week of June. They secured a raise, to thirty cents an hour. Next day they showed how well they could work: they took a hundred tons of ballast out of the bark in one day.

But uncertain weather closed in during the first week of July and put an end to the whole operation. The heavy seas and storm brought ruin where the syndicate had seen victory. That extra eight feet offshore proved the undoing of everything, for in the heavy weather, the bark heeled over until her masts touched the water, and there was no hope that she could be righted. The donkey engines were taken back to Nantucket, *Forest City* loaded up supplies and men and headed for Boston. Gibson and Bartlett had gambled $6,000, and had lost.

J. B. Macy of the island took over the remains of the bark. He sold the cables to a firm in Nova Scotia, and shipped them out. *W. F. Marshall* was then burned late in September, and that was the end of her. She supplied an afternoon's entertainment for the people of the island that last Sunday. All had failed, and the burned wreckage of the *Marshall* ended her days on the south shore of the island, breaking up in the storms of the following year.

Two weeks later the lifesavers at Surfside were called again. This time the vessel in trouble was the Italian bark *Papa Luigi C.*, a Sicilian ship on the way to Boston with a cargo of wine. Surfman George Veeder was out in the storm, and he fired his flare, but it was too late. The ship came steadily into the shoals. By the time the lifesavers got to the wreck in force, the crew had come ashore in their own boat. Although it capsized, they were all saved. The only casualty was Henry H. Nickerson, a week later. He fell from the main topsail yard while working on the bark, and was killed.

The year 1878 was a good year for wreckers, but not much good for anyone else connected with the sea in the Nantucket Sound region. January was the worst month for storms. A gale that blew from

January 3 for four days trapped five schooners off the coast of Tucker-nuck, and two of them struck, while two more scraped their bottoms and were lucky to get off. When the *Frederick Fish* hit the shoals at the eastern entrance to Nantucket Sound, Captain, mate, crew, and the captain's wife and two children all got off safely, but drifted toward Coatue in their boat. They were all saved by two island hunters, George and John Fisher, except for the captain's brother, who died of exposure.

After the winter storms, and the spring storms, the lifesavers had a good summer. The lifesaving station closed down for those months. But in 1878 there was a wreck in May and another in July, and the bad storms came again in October, the loveliest month of the year as a rule. The October storm lasted only two days, but it sent ten ships onto the Nantucket shoals. The worst tragedy here was the drowning of the wife of the captain of one of the vessels. In another wreck, the island reaped a harvest, when after the storm an overturned vessel was discovered near Tuckernuck and the islanders salvaged 35,000 feet of good lumber.

Of course the glorious days of the seafarers were ended, but in the 1870's Nantucket began to take on a little new life. In summers it seemed more glorious than it was, for the population of islanders rose slowly, and over the decade it went up only by about 500. But there were signs of prosperity. Nantucket town had twenty grocery stores, most of them on Main and Centre streets. Then, as now, there were two drug stores, but then, not as now, there were but two restaurants. The tourists of the 1870's were the sedentary type, who rented houses or stayed at hotels, and did not venture out to eat. For rental houses, they paid an average of seventy-five dollars for the season. That was certainly another difference.

The steamboat service on the island was excellent by the end of the seventies. When the Old Colony railroad consolidated with the Cape Cod line, Old Colony bought a controlling interest in the Cape Cod Steamboat Company. Soon they put the *River Queen* on the run to Nantucket, Martha's Vineyard, and New Bedford. Now there was a vessel with a story to tell: *River Queen* had quite a history. Abraham Lincoln had met aboard her with Alexander Stephens, the former Vice President of the Confederacy. And as she ran along Nantucket

Sound in these peaceful years, the captain and crew pointed out the room in which the meeting had taken place. Soon the steamboat company was running two trips a day to and from the island, which meant the mail came in twice, provisions were plentiful, and altogether life was the easiest the islanders had known in years.

The signs of new prosperity were everywhere. The proprietors of the Ocean House (formerly Jared Coffin's house) bought the yacht *Salus*, a 6½-ton sloop with black walnut and silver mountings. They hired Captain Thomas Brown to sail her for the guests of the house in the summer months. A pair of young islanders, William Codd and William Robinson, built and ran the little steamboat Island Belle, thirty-six feet long, carrying sixty passengers to Wauwinet and on excursions.

Yes, the tourist business was the salvation of the island, and no story tells it better than that of the Henry Coffin family.

Henry Coffin was a whaling man. He and his brother ran a fleet of fourteen whaleships in the forties and fifties, until "the lights went out," when the lighting systems of the world switched to kerosene. The Coffins faced the problem in 1856 when their new ship, *Constitution II*, was ready to go a-whaling. They sent her out to the Pacific, but soon rued the day, and began selling their ships. In the three years between 1857 and 1860 they sold off all but one, *Constitution II*, and the only reason they did not sell her was that they could not retrieve her from the Pacific.

During the Civil War years, these Coffins sought opportunity, and they found it—but not in Nantucket. They invested in lands in upstate New York. They bought warehouses in Buffalo. They bought into shipping ventures, but these involved ships that sailed from the eastern cities to far places, and did not affect Nantucket.

Henry and Charles Coffin had always been careful businessmen with interests diversified. In the California Gold Rush days they had sent a ship to San Francisco with lumber and general cargo. They had built a ferry to run between the towns of Benicia and Martinez, and it was successful. Then in the 1870's, the Coffins began doing business in Nantucket land. They were the leaders of the movement to destroy the old common land holdings, and in 1872 they managed to secure thirty-five acres at the Cliff. Henry plotted a development on the Cliff to be called Sherburne Bluffs. It is said he wanted to develop the Cliffs so that a road would run along the edge, and drivers from the town could come up and look down on the beach below and out to sea. But the people who bought his lands did not like that idea at all. Charles O'Conor, a New York lawyer, refused to have anything to do with the plan. He wanted his house to command the ocean, and he did not want any lookers coming between him and the sea. So the land was sold and the dream died.

Henry Coffin then became deeply involved in the Surfside development of Nantucket, through the Nantucket Surfside Land Company, of which he was president. His development encompassed 100 acres, and so grand were the plans, including a pavilion and bandstand, that the newspapers were talking about a "city" to be developed there. Of course, the lands came from the undivided lands of the town, the Coffin shares of the old commons. The great-great-great-grandsons of Tristram were participating in the murder of the last of his old dream!

XX

The Roaring Eighties

THE 1880's BROUGHT the railroad to Nantucket, and that impetus brought more land development and more prosperity. The island was on its way to becoming a playground of the rich.

In Siasconset the developers were putting together Sunset Heights, which faces the rising sun. Dr. Ellis, who also owned one of the drug stores, was deeply involved. In Surfside, the Coffins were promoting their development. In Swain's Neck the developers were at work, as they were at work anywhere else that Nantucketers could get hold of a good piece of land.

Nantucket town was growing. Western Union established an office on the island in 1879. The next year, E. K. Godfrey began the first tourist bureau, starting it as a place where visitors could register, and there receive telegrams, packages, and letters that had formerly gone astray. He also had a reading room, a directory of services—including hotels, restaurants, and general information—and a reservations system. Altogether, Godfrey's establishment was even more elaborate than the present tourist office on Federal Street.

The eighties were marked by a new spirit on the island. In 1882 the hoteliers and others attempted to introduce liquor licensing, but the drys beat them down handily. It was a period of intensive temperance work in the pulpits of Nantucket, and, the tourist business notwithstanding, the islanders voted dry. They could see the need to improve the water system, which they did. They had to have schools and a police force. But liquor licenses? Not yet.

There were by this time six hotels in town, two in Siasconset and one in Wauwinet. But it was then, as now—Nantucket was bursting at the seams in summer, and there were not enough accommodations for all who wished to stay on the island. Jared Coffin's old house, as it does today, was sending guests over to private houses, and the guest house business was flourishing.

In 1880 Lucretia Coffin Mott, the Quaker minister, Abolitionist and advocate of women's rights, died in Philadelphia. Nantucket mourned, for she and Maria Mitchell were the island's most famous children. Mrs. Mott had less connection with the island, however. She had left Nantucket when she was eleven, and, while Maria Mitchell's fame was gained on the island, Lucretia Mott's was not.

More important to Nantucket than Lucretia Mott was the lowly scallop, which, one might say, was born in 1881, for that was the year that scalloping began on the island as a commercial enterprise. For years Nantucketers had raked clams, and oysters and steamers for the table. Some had learned that the scallop muscle, or "eye," cut away from the body of the animal, was most palatable. But it was not until the 1880's that the market for scallops developed on the mainland. Then Nantucketers discovered that in the harbor and at Madaket they had the finest scallop fishing grounds in New England. Scalloping for mainland markets became an important addition to Nantucket's livelihood in those long cold winters when the tourists were far away.

The eighties were busy years in every way. Nantucketers began to travel a bit in search of their own amusement in off months. Mrs. J. S. Doyle, wife of the proprietor of the Jared Coffin house (Ocean House), brought home a pet "crocodile" from Florida, which she kept on the premises. Erudition was coming to the island—but not to everyone. Poor ignorant, innocent young Ellen Ryan, a maid at the Jared Coffin house, found herself in a family way and did not know what to do about it. She bore a twelve-pound baby in lonely pain, and then stuffed the poor thing into the hotel's vault, where it was found when nature began to take its course. She was charged in court with homicide, but the judge took pity on her ignorance and dismissed the case. Thus the children of those Irish immigrants who came from the wreck of the *British Queen* in 1851 learned of the quality of mercy in Nantucket's courts.

The winter of '81 was a real corker. That year the harbor froze solid, and the steamer *Island Home* was caught in the ice a mile and a half behind the bar. It was so cold that winter that islanders drove five oxen pulling a load of supplies across the ice from the steamer, and she was supplied over the ice that winter, too.

That was also the year of the great Coffin Family Reunion. The scheme was dreamed up by Allen Coffin. Now, as Henry Coffin's wife Eliza pointed out with some asperity, Allen Coffin was not truly a Nantucket Coffin at all, but sprang from Coffin stock that had migrated to that lesser island inshore, Martha's Vineyard. But the island Coffins, and particularly Henry, put Eliza down when she sniffed at the idea of a grand family reunion. To be sure, Allen Coffin had his selfish interest: he was that year candidate for governor of Massachusetts on the Prohibitionist ticket, and it might well be that Coffins from all over the Commonwealth could be assembled, given the true word and sent home to elect Allen in the fall.

But Henry Coffin had his interest, too. He was still promoting Surfside, and Sherburne Bluffs up on the cliff. Charles O'Conor was building his mansion there that year, with such nice touches as fireplaces of Italian marble. Henry Coffin was planning a big resort hotel at Surfside. The good Lord alone knew how many lots might be sold at a Coffin family reunion. Why, said Henry, they might attract a thousand Coffins, all of whom regarded the island as their ancestral home.

The year was propitious. It was the bicentennial of old Tristram's death. What better time to promote a reunion of all those with Coffin blood, and sell a few lots that would bring some Coffins back to the island of their dreams for summer holidays? So the plans were made, and Coffins began writing Coffins all over the country, from Robert Barry Coffin, a well-known poet, to Maria Mitchell, who was related to the Coffins as she was to just about everybody else on the island.

As the plans matured, one of the leaders in the scheme was the Reverend Phebe Ann Hannaford, a Coffin from Siasconset who had since moved to New Jersey and become a fiery advocate of virtue and enemy of sin. She brought feminism into the picture by insisting that the reunion honor Dionis, the wife of Tristram, just as much as it did the old man. Those Coffin children, after all, were not born by immaculate conception. "Benjamin Franklin owed far more to his mother, born here on Nantucket, than to his father," she declared. "Who knows but that the Coffin traits of energy and integrity came from Dionis rather than Tristram?"

So the reunion was staged for three days beginning August 16, 1881. Five hundred Coffins assembled at Surfside, to attend a clambake, and incidentally examine Henry Coffin's land promotion scheme. They could not avoid it. Henry had seen to that. A band played, and they ate clam chowder, baked clams, sweet corn, baked fish, lobster salad and watermelon, and drank tea and coffee. Then the speeches began.

Judge Owen Tristram Coffin traced the history of the Tristram Coffins from Devonshire, England, to recent days on the island. Mary Coffin Johnson talked about the Devonshire Coffins and England, with proper obeisance to old family portraits and ivy halls. Allen and Henry Coffin just happened to have provided pictures of the old English manse for sale this day, and Coffin coats of arms, and Coffin china, all with the family imprint. On the second day there were more orations, and poems, and photographs taken by an official photographer with a big camera and a slide that flashed its powder alarmingly.

And there were speeches.

And more speeches.

"The dear little island still stands . . ."

"On Plymouth Rock stepped free our pilgrim sires . . ."

"Reverently and gratefully, then, we twine our wreaths today. . . ."

And so on, far into the afternoon.

Some Coffins went digging, to try to find the foundations of old Tristram's two houses. They found some old household utensils and put up a granite marker declaring that this was the site of the house of Tristram. Some Coffins went fishing, and like others they caught a lot of blues.

Judge Coffin took this occasion to buy the old Jethro Coffin house (today the oldest house on the island).

Some Coffins bought lots from Cousin Henry.

Some Coffins promised Cousin Allen their political support.

So it was a successful reunion, and all the Coffin coofs went away happy and full of awe and clams.

The next year, 1882, Henry Coffin persuaded the selectmen to widen Surfside Road because of the expanding development of the area. Soon enough, however, the development had its troubles. Henry had built his hotel, overlooking the sea, with its veranda nearly 300 feet from the bank. But in the middle of the eighties, erosion began to play hob with his sea frontage. In five years, the shore receded about 200 feet. The hotel was endangered, much valuable lot land was threatened.

Even the railroad track was threatened, moved, and finally washed out by a terrible storm that cut away the south shore by as much as 100 feet in November 1888.

Railroad track? Indeed.

For in the eighties Nantucket got a railroad.

Years earlier Nantucketers had been talking about railroads, but one scheme and then another collapsed. Tourism, and that almost alone, made the idea into a reality.

The promoters of the railroad were off-islanders. Philip Folger, one of them, had been a resident of Nantucket earlier, but in the 1870's he was living in Boston. There he came into contact with Joseph Veazie, Francis Amory, and Thomas Wells, and the railroad for Nantucket was born. In August 1879, Folger and several civil engineers came to the island to survey for the railroad. They spent several days on Nantucket, and aroused a good deal of interest among the islanders, who began debating the project with a considerable amount of spirit, not to say prejudice, for and against the project. The islanders, too, were interested in the development of Surfside, and some wanted the line run out to Siasconset. Something had to be done about the Siasconset road. The roadway was so bad that coaches literally came apart in transit. (On August 30, 1879, several passengers were injured when the wheels came off the Siasconset coach.) The railroad promoters promised much, including the pledge that no Nantucket money would be needed to finance the road.

In the fall, Folger and his friends were selling Nantucket railroad stock in Boston, and promoting the island for all they could get. Specifically, what they wanted was a right of way, and that involved land owners and the proprietors of the still undivided common lands of the island. At a town meeting in September the railroad issue was raised, and it was discussed further at a meeting of the proprietors. The promoters got their right of way, for a line to run from Steamboat Wharf to the corner of Easton and Beach streets, out North Beach to a point opposite the Jetties, then southwest to drop below the north head of Hummock Pond, under Trott's swamp, west of the sheep pond, and down along the south coast, skirting Miacomet and running along the edge of Surfside, past Nobadeer and Madequecham, around Tom Nevers Head, to wind up at Sunset Heights in Siasconset. The line was to be three-foot gauge, to run for seventeen miles.

By the first of May 1880, Town Crier Billy Clark was pacing the streets and announcing the coming of the wheelbarrows and shovels for the beginning of the road. Laborers came from the mainland, too, and they set to work. But the route changed, because the land owners in the north did not want to sell at the price offered by the railroad. The road ran south from Steamboat Wharf and along Washington Street, making a slow turn west of Goose Pond. The railroad was building.

When the first ties arrived from Maine, their coming was announced by Crier Billy by the sounding of his long tin horn from South Tower at 6:30 on the morning of July 19. As winter set in the roadbed was complete for 60 percent of the road. It was to be a line of a little more than ten miles, as adjusted, to eliminate the cut around Hummock Pond.

In the spring of 1881 the physical signs of the railroad began to show anew. The rails were piped in by Crier Billy late in May, and as the track was laid, a flatcar was put into service to bring rails forward. On the first day of July, in came the engine, its coal car, and two cars. The engine was a beauty from the Baldwin works in Philadelphia. It was not new, but no one minded. It had a cowcatcher, and a spark arrester to keep it from burning down the Nantucket brush and the thickets of the moors. The engine was named *Dionis*, for the promoters had tied in with Henry Coffin's family reunion, and were bent on eking out every bit of publicity value from it. No wonder—Charles F. Coffin, Henry's son, was the general manager of the Nantucket railroad. The two cars were open, with protection, front and back, against sparks from the engine, and each had fifteen benches for the passengers.

By mid-July the road was extended to Surfside, just in time for the Coffin reunion. The initial run was made on the Fourth of July, past the harbor, across the flats, along the shore of the Goose Pond, by the Clay Pits, into the fields and through the pine forest onto the broad common, and to the temporary station that had been built at Surfside for the occasion.

The invited guests on the first run included all the officials of the line and their wives, and the movers and shakers of Nantucket; bankers, newspaper publishers, the important merchants, and the town officials. Allen Coffin made a speech, very patriotic in tone, and the travelers settled down to a clambake. Coffin spoke of old Dionis, and more or less warmed up for the Coffin reunion with long quotations from his forthcoming book about old Tristram Coffin. A glee club sang, William Easton made a moribund speech that dealt with the shooting of President Garfield by an assassin two days earlier. Joseph Barney livened the passengers up by telling them that Nantucket was about to become the tourist paradise of all the western world. Mr. Barney must be forgiven, he was the agent for the Nantucket and Cape Cod Steamboat Company. That cheery message was followed by a peroration of Dr. Arthur Jenks, who gave his listeners a blow-by-blow account of the coming of the Iron Horse to America. Then everybody sang "America," and the party was over.

There was some slight delay when a coupling broke on one of the cars, but it was repaired. The passengers boarded and were back in Nantucket by 7:30.

While preparing for the celebrated Coffin Reunion, Henry and Charles Coffin were also getting ready for the general public at their Surfside development. In late July the depot and restaurant were opened formally, and soon clambakes were a regular Thursday offering. "Surfside seems destined to become the jumping off place for tourists to Nantucket," the papers opined. And it was. When the last train of the season ran on September 24, it carried the teachers and pupils of the Summer Street Baptist church to their annual outing—at Surfside this year. The party was a clambake again. Everybody had a wonderful time.

In the winter of 1881–82, the Coffins and the Folgers, and the Veazies and their friends made plans for the coming development of their lands along the railroad's right of way. Folger and Veazie owned considerable parcels, and, of course, the Coffins had the whole big Surfside tract to promote. The railroad was going to make their fortunes.

The next year the Coffins were building again. They put up bath houses, and charged ten cents a change. Surfside became the summer entertainment capital of the island, as the newspaper had predicted.

Steamboats even came from the mainland with excursionists to Surfside. Hill's Full Cornet Band of New Bedford gave concerts there. Bands came to play for dancing, fireworks shows were sent into the air, and the youngsters rollerskated on the floor of the station. People who ended a day all sunburned and full of enthusiasm were guided to the Coffin land office in the depot building, where Charles Coffin was glad to sell them lots. The promotion was successful: by the end of the season 300 lots had been sold. Even President Chester Arthur came to Surfside, although he did not buy a lot.

The Coffins continued to build. They bought a hotel on the mainland and planned to move it to Surfside. That fall of 1883 workers dug the foundations for the new hotel, and Charles Coffin went to Riverside, Rhode Island, to disassemble the hotel he had bought. It was brought over to Nantucket in pieces by sailing ship, in seven loads. Up went the Surfside Hotel, four stories with a mansard roof, furnished lavishly, for the big opening on the Fourth of July.

Allen Coffin was again the orator, and this time he spent his many minutes eulogizing the late Massachusetts Senator Charles Sumner. The land hucksters were busy again, using the delights of the new hotel's ballrooms, dining rooms, and saloons to entice the public. Surfside boomed again that year.

In 1884, the rail line was completed to Siasconset, which sent the railroad's earnings skyrocketing. That winter the line closed down, only to reopen to ship some bales of cotton from a schooner wrecked on Siasconset shore. Siasconset began to steal some of Surfside's thunder. The great storm of Christmas, 1885 caused much damage at Surfside, and many problems. The tracks of the road along south beach were under water, and the tide threatened *Dionis* and her cars in their housing in the old brass foundry house on the harbor side of Washington Street. They were moved to a safer spot that night.

That winter the railroad had its financial difficulties. It had capital problems, and the interest on its debt amounted to half the total expense. The interest was $5,000, and when it was paid, the line had operated at a deficit of $3,000 for the year. Obviously this could not continue long. What was needed was new capital to pay off the bond holders and cut down those interest charges. Then there was the problem of the erosion that threatened Surfside. The railroad's tracks had to be moved because of the forty-foot annual incursion of the tides. The Coffins were in trouble. In the summer of 1887 the 900 acres of the Surfside development were put up at auction, and a Denver man bought them at only $2.80 per acre. The Surfside bubble had just burst.

Siasconset, contrarily, was enjoying enormous prosperity. The theater crowd had begun to summer there, and the place was alive with summer theatricals, on the stage and off. As Siasconset's fortunes rose, the railroad showed signs of improving its business position. C. M. Stansbury, the presiding genius and promoter of the railroad and its affairs, was walking by one of the business houses on Main Street, Nantucket, one day when he saw a jar of beans in the window: Five dollars prize for the person who guesses the correct number of beans in the jar. Stansbury went in and guessed. When the contest was over he had won it, and the railroad seemed on the way to a new prosperity.

For as everyone in Nantucket now knew, C. M. Stansbury knew his beans.

XXI

'Sconset on a Toboggan

THE NANTUCKET RAILROAD was an off-island venture, and as such it aroused the cupidity and enmity of the island's businessmen because it was successful. By the end of the first decade of its operations, Nantucketers were determined to share in the "gravy." Macys, Husseys and Gardners lined up with the "aginers"—against the Coffins and the Folgers and their relations. Along came proposals for a horsecar line and for an electric street railway on the island, and soon the railroad was fighting such suggestions in the press and at town hall. The Electric Street Railway Company was organized to run a line from Nantucket town to Siasconset. The Nantucket Beach Street Railway was organized to run everywhere: north, south, and through the town. It fell apart in mid-passage, victim of the huge ambitions of its promoters. And so did the electric line, leaving Nantucket with very little but memories of some fearsome battles in the town hall, and a horsecar rotting near the gasworks.

By the 1890's things were not going so well for the railroads or the land promoters either. Surfside had nearly collapsed, and the Coffins had withdrawn from the venture. A New York syndicate bought most of their holdings. The new owners refurbished the Surfside Hotel, polishing it until its woodwork gleamed, and started developing land in the area of Nobadeer. The railroad enjoyed prosperity, for a while even carrying the evening mail to Siasconset. Everything went well, in spite of a derailing of the engine. *Dionis* was not hurt, and next day she was horsed back onto the tracks. No one ever discovered the cause of the accident—but over the years various attempts had been made by advocates of horsecars and electric lines to sabotage the steam railroad system. Metal and stones were placed on the tracks, and there were several derailments, although none of serious enough nature to endanger life or limb.

But nature in the winter of 1890–91 caused the railroad more trouble than mere man could. A storm tore up the tracks on the south shore, and when they were rebuilt the job must not have been done right, for next season there were three derailments, both costly in money and hurtful to the pride of the railroad.

The Surfside adventure threatened to become a total disaster. The new proprietors made a boardwalk, and put in a bowling alley, but these additions did not help attract business. The final blow came in the fall, when the railroad depot and the bath houses were flattened by a sou'wester. The manager of Surfside went quietly bankrupt, and Allen Coffin presided over the ceremonies as lawyer for the creditors.

In 1892 storms and other inequities brought the rail line into low esteem on Nantucket. Schedules were not maintained. The tracks kept washing out or falling apart. The electric franchise and the horsecar lines, which actually operated for two years, diverted public attention from the oddity value of the road. And since one never quite knew when setting out from Nantucket for Siasconset whether one would arrive or be derailed around Tom Nevers Head, only those with time to spare or excessive love of adventure went by rail if other transport was available. And it usually was. The town was full of hacks and draymen, all silently cursing the various rail lines, and some of them not bothering at all to conceal their enmity. The steamboats ran from Nantucket to various spas around the island at various times. And in the spirited competition, the railroad suffered, mostly from lack of confidence. For as the newspaper kept saying: "This running off the tracks is getting to be altogether too common. . . ."

At the moment that article was written in the *Journal, Dionis* was off the track again. And she kept on running off, until on August 21 so terrible a storm lashed the south coast of the island, that *Dionis* and her cars were stuck in Siasconset, and the management of the railroad quit. So much track had been torn up that it would not make any sense to rebuild it. The owners put the line up for sale. It went for very little—$10,800, which included the rails (under three feet of sand in some places), the right of way (washed out here and there), the franchise, and the equipment. All that could be done with the line immediately was to run the iron horse from Siasconset to Surfside, for whatever good that did anybody.

The Nantucket Railroad was dead.

But hope is the most abundant human commodity, and in 1895 a new set of optimists was ready to play for fortune in the Nantucket rail game. The Nantucket Central Railroad was incorporated in Boston that year, and a new route was laid out to avoid the pitfalls of washout that had bedeviled the old line to extinction.

In spite of natural disaster (torrential rain at Goose Pond) and human frailty (a strike of fourteen laborers in June), the road was carrying passengers before the summer was ended. There were breakdowns and disasters aplenty, and the line ran about as before, on again, off again. But it did run until the fall of 1898, when what the old-timers called the worst storm in fifty years struck the island. It was the last week in November. This was the storm in which the steamer *Portland*, from Boston, sank at sea, taking down every man, woman and child aboard, and the *Luther Eldridge* rolled over and sank in Nantucket harbor. The roadbed suffered as usual, and the pessimists around the island predicted that the trains would not run the following year. But they did, and the newspapers said the summer of 1899 was the best in history for rail service on the island. It was apparent that one never could tell what was going to happen on Nantucket.

As the century came to a close, so did the Surfside adventure. The depot was gone. The Surfside Hotel was a wreck, no longer inhabited, and in 1899 it fell down. No one even thought of rebuilding. Another Coffin dream had come to naught.

By the turn of the century, Nantucket's permanent population seemed to have stabilized at slightly over 3,000 people. They were more prosperous than they had been in the 1860's because of the tourist trade, but of course that lasted only from May through September. Everyone either saved or scratched through the rest of the year.

There had been many improvements in Nantucket town, none of them coming without spirited argument against the change. Water was brought in by pipes from a town water system, and hydrants were built on the streets for the benefit of the fire department. A sewer system was operating. Electric lighting had come in 1889, and the hotels and some of the churches were first to be illuminated in the new way. So far behind Nantucket was the brilliant past of whaling days that not many thought to emphasize the ironies. More lifesaving stations were built in these years. The traffic around the Sound brought the need for better facilities, and the lifesavers performed brilliantly year after year.

Wildlife was being introduced to the islands by those who liked hunting and wanted to promote that aspect of tourism. Pinnated grouse were brought in, and rabbits were released. The former perished, but the latter proliferated, as any islander knows today.

Some strange changes came to the island, as nature worked her way on the land with water and wind. The south shore suffered serious erosion. In the spring of 1897 a storm opened a passage through the beach at the Haulover, and the opening remained for twelve years until it was finally closed by another storm.

In 1897, the island's telephone system was organized, and the next year toll telephones were installed around the island for the public.

Nantucket Island was firmly established by the nineties as one of the most pleasant resorts in all America. The ocean breeze was its principal asset in these days before air conditioning when the cities stank in summer with the heat, and many areas brought attacks of malaria to vacationers. In the 1890's Edward Underhill began his development in Siasconset, which involved three streets of rental houses. Pochick, Lily, and Evelyn streets sprouted the Under Hill cottages, and the brochures of Mr. Underhill were sent traveling far and wide. The crafty man made a virtue of necessity: he built houses that had no room larger than ten feet square, eaved with slopes four feet from the ground, and he justified them to the renters as "replicas" of the early fishermen's houses on Siasconset. Ladders led to the attics, where children could be stuffed, and if a family was huge and needed space, why Underhill had the answer to that one, too. He had a separate "room on wheels" that could be hauled by mule to the house that had the need.

Late in the nineties, then, Siasconset had its day of glory. Writers and artists in Boston first discovered the place, and began coming for vacations. By word of mouth the news spread, and so the colony of "actors" developed on the island. Those Underhill cottages were rela-

tively cheap, which was a factor in the economy of the stage pro-
fessions. One of the first to come was George Fawcett, a well known
actor of the day. The story has it that Fawcett sent his family before
him, and then, when he arrived on the island and had to pay four
dollars for a hackman to drive him to Siasconset, he nearly moved
them off. But he stayed, and became enamored of the place, and
brought his friends the next year.

By 1900, the actors' colony was an established fact of Nantucket
life, and in the years to come it became a tourist attraction in itself,
for there is something about the people of the theater that arouses the
interest and even awe of ordinary, humdrum citizens.

Here is how the summer people came to Nantucket in those days.

They took the old Fall River steamboat line or the New Bedford
line from a pier in lower Manhattan, went down the East River to Long
Island Sound, and then around Point Judith. One way or another—
changing to a train or staying on a steamer, they reached New Bedford, and there they met the steamer for the island. In the old days the
steamer was the original *Uncatena*, a paddlewheel steamer that one
rider called "the mother duck" because it waddled its way to Nantucket.

The ship passed the crossrip lightship, where the passengers and
crew threw their old newspapers and magazines to the poor entrapped
sailors who manned the warning vessel, and even when the papers fell
into the water they were retrieved, for the printed word was almighty,
the source of man's edification and much of his amusement.

Hours later, Nantucket came in sight, the water tower, and the
Great Point Light, and then the jagged shape of steeples and buildings as the land came closer.

At Steamboat Wharf the cabbies assembled, with their cries for
the houses.

"Ocean House here."

"Sea Cliff Inn this way."

"Come to the Point Breeze Hotel."

For those going to Siasconset, the best part of the trip was about
to begin. They stowed their luggage with a carter who would bring
it along later in the day, and they plumped themselves in one of the
hacks. They might take the train, if it was running, but that seemed

problematical, and those who had experience from the past usually opted against the train, for on the railroad who knew precisely when you might arrive, if at all? The hacks were simpler, if more expensive. Along the dusty road the hackmen trotted, through the scrub and the scotch broom of the moors, until they reached Bean Hill, where Siasconset spread before them.

Then the summer fun began.

Most provisions were supplied by the island's farmers, who came in their wagons to sell produce to the tourists. A few stores sold staples, Burgess's Market on Broadway sold meat, and town shops sent out their goods with their hucksters. Nobody went into Nantucket town unless he had to for some very important reason; it was too long a trip, and destroyed as much as half a day.

The children played on the beach and built castles in the sand while adults lolled late in bed and reread the romantic novels of the day. The bicycle, then more than now, was the regular means of transportation, but even by cycle it was a long eight miles to Nantucket town.

The prosperity of Siasconset soon brought the establishment of a golf club, which in turn gave rise to a whole new way of life, including the nineteenth hole and many a party at the clubhouse.

Early in the 1900's, Siasconset became a sort of unofficial extension of the Lambs Club, the famous New York theatrical association, and for about half the season it would not have been impossible to find almost a quorum on the island. Over the years everyone who was anyone in the world of theater came there. Such now forgotten figures as DeWolf Hopper and John Drew and Joseph Jefferson brought awe to the hearts of the lesser mortals who inhabited only staid Nantucket town. Lillian Russell summered in Siasconset once. The community became famous when the Casino was built, and the actors staged benefits to pay off the mortgage.

The halcyon days continued until 1914, when the motion pictures began to destroy the legitimate theater touring companies. On top of that, the automobile had come to the island. After *that,* in the minds of the denizens of old Siasconset, everything was downhill all the way.

XXII

The Horseless Carriage and Other Woes

THE HORSELESS CARRIAGE invaded Nantucket island first in 1894 when a steam power car was built on the island by Edgard F. Whitman, a machinist. It was an oddity: it traveled twelve miles an hour if it went at all, and since it was unique it did not frighten enough horses or old ladies to create much of a fuss.

In 1900, however, the Folger family was guilty of importing a Stanley Steamer, and this was a horseless carriage of a different color. Soon there were several such vehicles on the island, and they did frighten horses. The newspapers, with a sort of grim satisfaction, reported the accidents to the cars as they occurred. It was not long before islanders were calling them a menace, and some were advocating an ordinance to prohibit their use on the island entirely.

But of course the conservatives lost, as they always have lost in these struggles. By 1903 the course was clear enough that the island's livery stables were beginning to suffer. If you can't beat them, join them, said liverymen Covil and Pease, and they began preparing to go into the automotive transportation business. The selectmen were cautious. They limited the speed of autos in the beginning. Some citizens wanted autos held down to four miles an hour, an outrageous affront to anyone who was willing to put up the money for a motorcar.

As the railroad limped along in its usual unreliable manner, proprietors on Nantucket began to think more fondly of the motor cars, and in 1906 the creation of a Nantucket Traction and Auto Transit Company was proposed to run motorized coaches to serve Siasconset.

181

That proposition was rejected by the town, but soon other men were talking about bringing autos to the island for public transportation, and others suggested that deliveries of goods could be speeded by the same method. That year Cromwell Macy began a regular motorcar service between Nantucket town and Siasconset, on the old rail tracks. The steam locomotives would be discontinued.

The inaugural run was a fizzle. Arthur Turner, the editor of the *Inquirer and Mirror,* who was aboard, reported that the car went dead two miles out of town, leaving the passengers stuck on the dusty railroad out in the middle of the pine woods. The sun went down, and the whole adventure became more eerie than anyone wanted it to be.

The passengers had to push the car back to town.

But soon enough the car, called *Siasconset,* was making two trips a day between town and village, at a rate per head of forty cents. Considering that the trip to Siasconset by horse cab had cost five dollars, it was a bargain. And that is why nobody could gainsay the progress.

Or could they?

Nantucket said they could. In the spring of 1907 the town selectmen ordered all horseless carriages excluded from the highways of Nantucket. But auto drivers were fearless men, and most of them were girded for the fray. W. V. Birney, a New Yorker, came to the island that summer with a gasoline car, and drove it to his house in Siasconset in sheer defiance of the island fathers. He was arrested and brought to trial before Justice Mooers, who threw the case out of court.

The fact that their ordinances were illegal did not stop the selectmen, who soon posted signs along the roads, announcing that auto traffic was prohibited and subject to prosecution. One would think the selectmen all owned stock in the railroad.

Various agents and entrepreneurs tried to start bus service on the island, but, given the feelings of the selectmen, they all failed to secure a franchise. Private owners continued to defy the town fathers, but as far as public transportation was concerned, the people either rode on the rails, or behind a horse. Let it never be said that Nantucket succumbed to progress without a struggle.

In the autumn of 1907 the town fathers decided to put an end once and for all to the horseless buggy craze, certain in their wisdom that the foolishness would pass, given a little injection of common sense and enough time. The council banned all horseless carriages from the

Milestone Road to Siasconset, or on any part of it. They also declared it illegal to drive an automobile on any street in the town, thus making it a clear violation of the law to have a horseless carriage in movement anywhere on the island. Since a horseless carriage not in movement was of no more value than a boarding knife or harpoon in 1907, the fathers felt secure in their wisdom and sure they had at last dealt with the mechanical age satisfactorily.

But what the islanders forgot was that the coofs who yearned for horseless carriages were not unsubstantial people, and they had re-sources—and rights—that extended beyond the boundaries of the island that liked to forget it was part of Massachusetts and of the United States.

In the spring of 1908 the outraged automobilists went to the legisla-ture in Boston, in force. But on their heels came Nantucket's finest, a delegation of some thirty citizens, ladies included, led by Representa-tive Ellenwood B. Coleman, to protest the constant invasion of the tight little island by the automobile.

They presented a petition signed by nearly 700 islanders, asking that autos be forever banned. Elsewhere there might be an excuse for autos, it could even be said that a man on the Cape, for example, might be going from Hyannis to Boston and thus had legitimate busi-ness with his horseless buggy as transportation. But Nantucket, being an island, offered no legitimacy to the auto at all. There was only one state highway in the whole island, to Siasconset, and it was the road the people liked to use on a Sunday to drive their buggies on a pleas-ant healthful outing. These days the horses were frightened by the shrieking, grinding motorcars that sped past them at speeds of twenty miles an hour. The Nantucketers invited the Committee on Roads and Bridges to come over and see for itself.

Few legislators ever turned down a free trip to a resort area, if there was the slightest indication of official business to be transacted at the taxpayers' expense. The committee members were quick to ac-cept the Nantucket invitation, and came over one spring day on the Saturday afternoon boat for a big weekend. It was a cold day, but the reception was warm and the legislators were put up at no expense to themselves at the Pitman House. They were wined and dined and shown about the island, and by the time they left they were fully in sympathy with the anti-auto claque. In a month Nantucket had its anti-automobile bill, excluding autos between June 15 and September 15, passed by both houses of the Massachusetts legislature, and signed by the lieutenant governor as acting chief of the commonwealth.

The auto haters might have won the day, if they had been a bit luckier. In Michigan, automobiles were and still are forbidden on Mackinac Island. In Virginia, the auto has never been allowed to sully the dunes of Assateague, where the wild ponies roam. But Nantucket was cursed with an incompetent rail line. The abandonment of steam locomotives and the turn to motorized cars had not worked very well, despite its early promise. By 1909 the railroad was in shambles, the stations were boarded up, the rails rusty, the ties rotting, and the rolling stock in disrepair. No one had any sympathy for the railroad, and the Macy family, who controlled it, wished it could get out from under the investment and the responsibility. Indeed, in the spring of 1909 a pair of entrepreneurs suggested turning back the clock, and bought four old Fifth Avenue omnibuses, each of which held twenty-two passengers. Each was drawn by a team of two horses, and to islanders it sounded like progress, so sour had the transportation system gone.

That spring the Nantucket railroad went into bankruptcy once more, and came out with a new set of officers and owners and a new supply of hope, the island's most ready commodity. They decided they would rebuild the whole line and make a killing, unmindful that the words had been said before on the island.

Once more Nantucket was subjected to all the old foofaraw of beginnings: including the driving of a gold spike to commemorate the rebuilding of the line. But the work train was derailed in short order, and Nantucketers settled back for more of the same old incompetence that they had been observing for years. The new steam locomotives were not going to be any better than poor old *Dionis*. In 1910 the line changed hands again.

For a few years the new owners made profits, and kept the rail line going along, with relatively good service to the island. There were various experiments, including one with a gasoline car, called "the bug," which came to an ignominious end when it crashed into the locomotive on its trial run. The locomotive started a brush fire one day on the moors, and some islanders thought the fire was going to rival the conflagration of 1846 before it ended. But it was put out in time to save the structures near by.

Meanwhile the anti-auto ban was in force, until the town fathers were overwhelmed by progress in a way that even they could not easily deny. The progress came in the form of an automotive fire engine.

For years everyone had known that the old system of horse-drawn fire engines was not the most efficient. And when it came to the matter of property, Nantucketers were just like mainland Yankees, careful as they come. So the automobile came to them this time in the guise of a fire engine, and before anyone knew it, the camel had his nose under the tent, and his hump was beginning to emerge inside. The fire engine, automotive or not, proved to be such a tremendous improvement on the ancient system that no one in his right mind suggested abandoning it just because it was an automobile. The selectmen, however, soon abandoned common sense, and here they lost the cause for which they had fought so long.

On Nantucket lived Clinton B. Folger, a hackman who sympathized completely with the idea of banning automobiles from the island during the summer months when the wild summer people wanted to bring their autos to the sacred precincts and frighten honest souls and happy horses. But Folger was a man of business. It was quite all right to keep the ban during coof season, when there was plenty of money flowing in and out of the island. Off-season was another matter. For hackman Folger had a contract to carry the U.S. Mails from Nantucket to Siasconset. In summer the volume was great enough and the other activity high enough to justify the quaint use of horses. In winter an automobile, particularly the five-passenger Overland sedan that Folger owned, was far more efficient.

Folger brought his Overland to the island, and began to use it. He was arrested by the selectmen, who had continued their own ordinances against automobiles in any month of the year. He was fined fifteen dollars and announced that he would appeal.

The next week he was caught again, fined again, although this fine was suspended, and warned that his third offense would bring a fine of sixty dollars. Such doings could wipe out all the profits from the mail contract.

Clinton Folger was an intelligent man, and skilled in the uses of publicity. He secured a dump cart, and a pair of sad eyed nags. He attached his automobile to the back of the dump cart, with signs hand lettered *U.S. MAIL*, which were hung fore and aft. Thus accoutred, the mail car was drawn from Folger's garage to the post office, and then to the Siasconset road where it became a state highway. The state law covered only the Siasconset road, that being the highway. The town ordinances held for the city streets. And so, day after day, Mailman Folger delivered the post in his odd manner, while the newspapers laughed over the story, and the selectmen seethed.

The selectmen were adamant. They passed and repassed the automotive exclusion laws. Folger was sly: he kept lending the car to doctors on emergency calls—and who could arrest a doctor for driving, even in an auto, when he was out succoring the people—and making house calls, at that?

So the struggle continued, but Nantucket was beginning to look a bit foolish. No one wanted to make the essential compromise, to permit official and public vehicles of the automotive type in the public service.

Nantucket could fight off the twentieth century only so long. In 1916 the First World War came to the island, as unbidden as the automobile, and far more sinister. Nantucket had been going through a depression caused by the state of affairs generally and the world war in particular. Indeed, Nantucket saw more of the war's brutality than any other American community. The war was brought home to the islanders in the form of a German submarine.

The Germans sent several submarines to the American coast during World War I. Most of them were on propaganda missions, or carrying dyes, for which there was a ready and high-paying market in the United States. But in October 1916, the *U-53* brought the war to the American coast. She came to Newport and appeared bold as brass inside the harbor, America being a neutral nation. Then she sailed, and next turned up on the Nantucket coast, not far from the Nantucket Shoals lightship. There she showed up on the morning of October 8. Her captain, Commander Hans Rose, was an intelligent man, and to do his duty he had chosen the crossroads of the Atlantic. More particularly, Rose had discovered where to go by intelligent questioning and deduction. His orders from Berlin were to lie off the American coast and harry British shipping. Having tried the waters off Montauk and south of Martha's Vineyard without success, he had learned from someone in Newport just the proper place. So as they went about their light-keeping business on that morning in October, the men of the lightship saw the periscope.

The first vessel that came into the U-boat's ambush was the American steamer *Kansas*. Imagine her captain's surprise when practically on America's front door a shot came across his bow and he was ordered to heave to for a German boarding party. He produced his papers, showed that he was not carrying any contraband for Britain, and was allowed to go on his way.

Then, at seven o'clock in the morning, the British steamer *Strathdene* came in sight, and the U-53 put a shot across her bow. Seeing the submarine and the deck gun, the captain of *Strathdene* ordered full steam ahead, and tried to escape. He was carrying a cargo from Glasgow to New York, and he knew very well what he faced. Already there had been rumors of German submarine warfare plans off the American coast.

The captain tried manfully, but he soon saw that he was bracketed by the German submarine's deck gun, and he hove to. He and the thirty men of the crew went into the lifeboats as ordered by the boarding officer. The Germans gave them a course that took them to the lightship, and they rowed off, as U-53 put a torpedo into their ship and sank her.

Next that day, up came the Norwegian *Christian Knudsen*, carrying a cargo of diesel oil bound for London. The German submarine held her up. The crew got off, and headed away, and the U-53 began trying to sink the Norwegian freighter. One torpedo did not do the job, for her tanks were too buoyant. So she was shelled, and another torpedo was used on her.

Then up came the British *West Point*, in ballast, heading for Newport News. Captain Rose did not want to waste torpedoes, so he sank her with demolition charges.

All this while, the Nantucket lightship was trying in a most unneutral fashion to warn the ships at sea of the danger offshore. The Germans jammed the circuits when they were surfaced, but when they went down to stalk, they could not radio. Meanwhile the *Kansas* was also calling all the world to warn.

But one captain did not heed the danger.

That morning, Captain Smith of the Red Cross line steamer *Stephano* picked up the transmissions, and knew the German submarine was lying a few miles off the lightship. But to avoid her he would have to change course and head down Nantucket Sound, which would require explanations to his owners. He was carrying a cargo of codfish oil valued at $150,000, but he decided to risk it—if there was much risk. He went on.

So as *West Point* was sinking, up came *Stephano*, and she became the *U-53*'s fourth victim. Fifth was the Dutch steamer *Blommersdyk*, headed for Liverpool. She came on the scene where Captain Rose waited so patiently, as the sky was growing dark with dusk.

Just then a flotilla of sixteen American destroyers arrived, called to sea by the Morse traffic in the air, coming to be sure that America's neutrality was not violated. The destroyers had to stand by, while Captain Rose very coolly sank the Dutch ship before them. They were neutral, there was nothing they could do.

Never had there been so much activity aboard the lightship as there was that night. The survivors of several of the vessels came up and were taken aboard. (Those of the Dutchman were picked up by the destroyers.) And as words of indignation filled the air waves, Captain Rose took the *U-53* down and steamed away toward the Gulf Stream. Eventually he would find his way safely back to Germany.

This was war, and everyone on Nantucket knew it. The war, even though America was not yet in it, did nothing to help the tourist business on the island. Tourists stayed away from Nantucket that summer, and next year, when war actually came, it was worse. In the summer of 1917, another U-boat showed up off the Georges Bank, ninety miles east of the island. The U-boat surfaced in the middle of a fleet of fishing boats and sent the fishermen into their dories. The Germans then shelled the fishing boats and sank them with the deck gun. Half a dozen of those survivors were picked up off Great Point by the patrol boat *SC 166*, and taken into Nantucket.

A few days later Nantucket learned that the British steamer *Penistone* and the Swedish freighter *Sydland* had been sunk just off the Nantucket Shoals lightship, and not long afterward another German submarine sank several barges in Nantucket Sound, a few miles off Chatham, and then disappeared beneath the frustrated eyes of a naval airplane crew who had no bombs aboard and found they could not sink a submarine by throwing monkey wrenches at it. The war was indeed with the island.

XXIII

Bootleggers, Scallops and Coofs

AFTER THE INCIDENTS of the *U-53* Nantucketers really worried about invasion by the Germans, and when the United States did enter the war, the worry increased. As the businessmen feared, tourism fell off sharply, and the island suffered. It was not like the days of the Revolution and the War of 1812, but it was bad enough, and the paucity of business proved the final blow to the faltering railroad on the island. In 1917 it lost money.

The failure of the rail line brought to the fore good old-fashioned American greed, to overturn the anti-auto ordinances. As the promoters of lands were quick to point out, if people were going to buy lots on Nantucket, they were going to have to be able to get to their sites. Without the trains, how would they get there? The war had so mechanized its society that even though horses still had their place, the day of the buggy was obviously over.

Promoters proved the undoing of the auto exclusion act, and their leader was Franklin E. Smith, who had a big land deal going at Tom Nevers Head. He went to Boston, armed with as many facts and figures in favor of the automobile as the anti-auto delegation had unleashed against it a few years before. The railroad having been junked earlier that year, the legislature saw things Smith's way. So did the voters of Nantucket, although by a fairly narrow margin. In the spring of 1918, by a vote of 336 to 296, the people decided that automobiles had come to America to stay and that Nantucket was going to have its

share of them. Had they lived sixty years later, maybe some of those
voters would not have been so quick to change.

But they did, and the change was stamped and sealed when that
spring the *Inquirer and Mirror* began printing a column devoted to
auto notes. Soon the island was roaring with the engines of autos and
taxis and omnibuses and delivery trucks. It has never been the same
since.

The twenties brought a revival of tourism lost during the war, and
a new industry, bootlegging, to the island. The bootleggers represented
various syndicates in New York and Boston, the most active of them
was a Brooklyn gang that ran a fleet of some twenty small boats
around Nantucket. European ships, loaded with Scotch whiskey and
French champagne, would make their way across the Atlantic and
heave to somewhere in the Sound. The bootleggers would go out by
night to meet them and pick up the valuable contraband cargo. The
Coast Guard was their implacable enemy, and many was the chase
off Nantucket with neighbor against neighbor, for there were the pur-
sued and pursuing living happily together during the daylight hours
on the island.

Bootlegging, scalloping, and tourism were Nantucket's industries.
The population was down again, under 3,000 in these years, and not
too well heeled at that. Some effort was made in the twenties to revive
the fishing business. The valuation of the island increased sharply—
doubled over just a few years earlier—but part of that was due to in-
flation, which hit hard on the island after World War I, as it did
everywhere else.

Of course, the transportation to the island improved in these years.
The steamship *Nobska* came to the island in the spring of 1925, and
she would serve faithfully for many years, before finally being docked
at Steamboat Wharf and then sold off to a Baltimore firm that made a
restaurant out of her in that city's harbor.

The bootleggers had a hard blow in '25 when a whole Coast Guard
fleet of eighteen patrol boats and the mother ship *Wyanda* were transferred from Greenport, Long Island to Nantucket. But the bootlegging
continued as a major Nantucket industry until 1933, when Prohibition
was repealed. The bootleggers were a resourceful lot, and as brave as
old Nantucket's blockade runners ever had been. In the middle of the

twenties, when the schooner *Waldo L. Stream* wrecked off Muskeget, the lifesaving men of the crew at Muskeget salvaged the cargo of whiskey, and stored it on the island, under Coast Guard watch. Someone cut a hole in the back of the storage shed, and next time the Coast Guard men turned around, the whiskey was gone. *Wyanda* and her fleet never made much of a dent in Nantucket's rum-running, and even if they had, they would not have stopped the liquor from flowing on the island. Out in the moors there were enough stills working to provide moonshine for any who wanted it.

In the 1920's Nantucket suddenly became sharply aware of its whaling heritage as a source of amusement and profit to the island and the town. Over the years the dedicated souls of the Historical Association had managed to preserve a number of landmarks, and as time went on these were readied for exhibit. In 1927 the Historical Association began the project to create the Whaling Museum, and the next year the restoration of the Oldest House was completed. The town bought the site of the present town offices in 1928, and also began the construction of the brick school on Academy Hill. Three years later Cyrus Peirce School on Atlantic Avenue was completed. But on the heels of all this public expenditure came the Great Depression of the 1930's, and Nantucket was not immune. Values dropped, businesses failed, and in 1933 the Nantucket Institution for Savings foreclosed on the Point Breeze and Sea Cliff hotels. Next year the Ocean House (Jared Coffin house) failed. Yet while the tourist business was hurt, it did not die. The summer residents kept coming back, they held reunions, they promoted open air art shows, they held yachting races. In the middle of the decade the island's economy began to revive. New managers hopefully took over the Point Breeze Hotel, and called it the Gordon Folger. As times changed, so did life on the island. Electrification became the rule. The sewer system was extended all through Nantucket town. A new post office was built, and air mail came to the island in the late 1930's.

It was all needed, because in the summer of 1940 the town fathers estimated that the largest number of people ever to be housed on the island were in residence in the month of August.

The next year was fine for tourism, but with the coming of war in December 1941, it all changed once again. The rationing of tires and gasoline cut down the tourist trade, and the fear of invasion did not help, either. Nantucket took the war very seriously. In the winter of 1941–42 a Public Safety Committee was organized in the new office building on Federal and Broad. An observation tower was put up on Mill Hill, and men and women volunteers manned it day and night, looking for the enemy. The streets were sandbagged, and coast watchers kept a sharp eye out for submarines. Most famous of these was Madaket Millie, who for the next thirty years refused to discuss what she had seen and what she had done during the war years, lending a certain mystery to all of Madaket.

The fact was that Nantucket's war was not nearly so exciting as the First World War had been. The Coast Guard auxiliary operated picket boats out of Nantucket, and they scoured the Sound religiously for enemy submarines. But the first incident, in 1941, involved friendly craft: the freighter *Oregon* and the battleship *New Mexico* collided forty miles offshore. Seventeen members of *Oregon's* crew were drowned, the others were rescued by a New Bedford fisherman.

In the spring of 1942 Nantucket did have a taste of the submarine menace which was threatening to deprive the allies of the means to continue to fight in Europe. In the middle of May a German submarine torpedoed the British freighter *Black Arrow* in the North Atlantic off the American shore, and the survivors took to the boats. The Coast Guardsmen saw two open boats off the south shore, and brought them in on May 24. The townspeople rallied around, supplying food and the shelter of Bennett Hall, the parish house of the Congregational Church. Next day another boat came in, and the survivors were also succored. In all, forty-two survivors of the *Black Arrow* were brought to Nantucket.

Nantucket had its war casualties, like every other community. The steamers *Naushon* and *New Bedford* were commandeered for war service, and the Navy took over the island's airport. A military police unit came to the island and set up a training station.

When the war ended, like all the rest of America, Nantucket began picking up the pieces of civilian life and making many long-delayed improvements. The old hotel on North Water Street was bought up, re-christened Harbour House, and largely rebuilt. New ferries came to the island, and the tourists began to come back.

Just before the war, Everett U. Crosby had conducted a survey of the island and its potentials for the future. While very little could be done during the war, when peace came Nantucket turned its eyes to the future. In spite of the fact that in 1946 scallops brought a record price of $10.26 per gallon, the island still depended almost 100 percent in the twentieth century on off-islander tourists for its income. Crosby shrewdly assessed the attraction of the island as its remoteness, which had prevented the development of the Coney Island atmosphere so common in other communities, and even on Cape Cod. The real treasure of the island was its 450 old buildings, representing the remnants of the old whaling community.

From Crosby's recommendations came the general policy that Nantucket would follow in the years to come. The old was to be preserved. The garish was to be avoided. Commercialism was to be disguised—shops would have quarter boards, not neon signs.

And so it came about in the 1940's and 1950's. The emphasis was on arts and crafts, and artists began to flock back to the island. At various times there had been strong art colonies on Nantucket, but they ebbed and flowed until the 1960's, when definite encouragement was given artists by residents, the town, and the financial institutions. Edouard Stackpole, the tireless promoter of Nantucket history, and student of whaling and all the memorabilia of his native island, began serious work on his history of whaling. He went to Mystic Seaport for a few years as director of the Mystic Seaport Marine museum, but then returned to Nantucket as resident historian and director of the Foulger Museum and Whaling Museum. His frequent publications and books helped put Nantucket on the map for thousands who had never heard of the place.

The 1960's saw the real boom in Nantucket properties begin. Speculators and investors began buying up lands and buildings. In 1961 the Jared Coffin house was sold again, this time to the Nantucket Historical Trust, which vowed as much as possible to restore the hotel to the likeness of Jared Coffin's house, and to keep it that way.

In the sixties, too, Walter Beinecke, Jr. interested himself in business ventures in Nantucket. For years the Beinecke family had maintained a house at Siasconset; now Beinecke saw opportunity on the island in the growth of American leisure. He bought the White Elephant, a waterfront hotel most famous at that time because Vice President Alben Barkley had slept there one night. He tore down the old hotel and built a new one. He also went to work on the wharf area, acquiring and improving properties there through his real estate operating firm, Sherburne Associates. The firm purchased and refurbished properties around the town, then rented them out for substantial sums that brought up the whole economic value of the island. Soon the wharf district was as never before, with Old South Wharf, Commercial Wharf (Swain's), and Straight Wharf all built up. Beinecke bought leases and more properties, began building studios for artists, and put in a marina to attract the wealthy yachting crowd. Soon Sherburne Associates was the largest real estate operation on the island, with 165 properties.

So the Nantucket of the 1970's became a souped-up version of the old Nantucket of a century and a half before, as much as the modern leaders could make it. The yachtsmen began to come. The artists had already arrived. The "hippies" came in the seventies, seeking unspoiled premises where they could "do their thing" and make a living. The island was soon sprouting beards and male headdress that would have put a whaler of the 1820's to shame. Blue jeans and dirty sweatshirts became the uniform of the new islanders as much as pink Nantucket trousers were to the affluent men and reed Nantucket lightship baskets (selling for three- and four hundred dollars) were to the ladies of the Cliffs and other big houses.

Real estate prices zoomed until they were beyond the reach of teachers, nurses, policemen, and the other essential citizens, and Nantucket hospitals and other institutions found that they must reckon with the problem of housing any persons they really needed. In the winter, there was plenty of housing; a big house could be had for the upkeep of it, or a rental of $150 or $200. But in summer rentals ran into the thousands for the two glorious months of July and August. These were still the key to Nantucket's economy in the 1970's. But as tourism continued and the commerce and industry of American leisure burgeoned even further, the tourist economy began to spread over more months. Dead winter, from January until April, was still dead winter. But tourists could be seen on the rainswept, wind driven streets even then, and more shops remained open more months every year in the 1970's.

As long ago as 1914, the opening of the Cape Cod Canal had decreased the deadly importance of Nantucket shoals to ocean-going traffic. Yet ships did continue to come ashore in the Nantucket shallows: tankers, freighters and fishermen. The dangers of the sea were not to be conquered in the lifetime of the island; in the winter of 1974–75 Nantucketers were reminded of this fact when a fishing boat swept ashore in a winter storm and came up on the jetties. They salvaged her later, and took her toward Hyannis, but she sank before she got there, another reminder of the uncertainties of the sea.

Times changed, the Coast Guard began using air-sea rescue techniques employing helicopters and seaplanes. The steamers were replaced on the Nantucket run by motor vessels as ferries. The old Nantucket lightship was brought to Steamboat Wharf to berth as a new tourist attraction. A new housing development began in Madaket and caused as much mumbling and speculation as ever had Henry Coffin's big plans for Surfside. The Historical Association became a major Nantucket industry. A new Nantucket Life Saving Museum was established at the old station in the Shawkemo Hills. The old Straight Wharf theater burned in the spring of 1975 and was replaced by a handful of new shops to cater to the tourist trade. That, in a sense, was symbolic of Nantucket in the 1970's, the catering to the tourists as never before, with special emphasis on the day-tourists who came each year in increasing numbers to walk or bicycle around the island between ferries.

With the exception of the tourist ghetto, however, Nantucket town remained remarkably as it had been, and the island outside the town even more so. Madaket boasted hardly any commercial establishments at all, except for the boatyard, a small garage specializing in foreign cars (shades of the Nantucket railroad!) and a small beanery on the Nantucket road. Siasconset was the same: it had a post office, whose future was in doubt in the succession of reorganizations of the postal service in the seventies; a food shop; and a handful of other little establishments. The twenty groceries of Main and Centre streets were long gone, and had given way to a pair of supermarkets. A few other shops sold foods and specialty items.

In summer Nantucket's economy was still tourist oriented to be sure —almost 100 percent. And in the winter, where Nantucket had sometimes nearly starved, things were better than they ever had been, to some extent aided by federal and state unemployment insurance, for it was a favorite device, particularly of the young off-islanders, to work all summer and spend the winter collecting their "unemployment."

As for the rest, well, there is an old Nantucket saying cited by Andrew Shunney, artist, long-time summer resident, and finally full-time real estate entrepreneur on the island. In the summer, he said, the Nantucketers sell to the tourists, and then in the winter, why they take in each other's washing.

Afterword:

"Independent People"

NANTUCKETERS have always had the name of being independent people. Anyone who doubts the fitting nature of that appellation was not reading the newspapers or watching the TV news in the winter and spring of 1977, when Nantucket, along with that "other island," moved to secede from its long and not always comfortable association with the Commonwealth of Massachusetts.

Some cynics tended to regard Nantucket's secession as a publicity stunt. Nothing could be further from the truth. Within the soul of every Nantucket man and Nantucket woman and Nantucket child lies a little kernel of rebellion. Usually it manifests itself in minor ways, such as a remark that one is "going off island," or "going to America," in a manner that means one is descending from Eden into the pit for a time, but will most certainly return, bedraggled, worn, and much the worse for the experience of mingling with *Americans* on their own shore.

Once upon a time, going "off island" might mean a two- or three-year whaling voyage, or a sailing expedition across the Atlantic for trade. Those days are gone, but Nantucket's attitude is much the same, and Nantucket people are somehow seized by the island tradition, even to the point that persons who come and set up in Nantucket and live, though born in Georgia or Oregon, quickly adapt themselves to the Nantucket ambience, and believe. Thus when they say, after only a year or so of residence, that they are "going off island," they

mean it with the same fervor as do those clamdiggers and scallop
shuckers whose parents, grandparents, and great grandparents, unto
the seventh generation, were bred and born on Nantucket soil.

Maybe it is this contagious islander's cussedness which the Commonwealth of Massachusetts underestimated when, in February 1977,
it took a momentous step. The Massachusetts General Court, or state
legislature, at that time set into motion a plan for reapportionment of
the legislature that would do away with the individual representation
of Nantucket (and Martha's Vineyard) and throw the islands into a
representational bin with part of Cape Cod. Now Cape Cod is a nice
place to visit, and some Nantucketers have friends, and even relations
there. But to be governed by a legislature in which Nantucket would
have to share a representative with Martha's Vineyard, let alone with
the mainland, was more than an island son or daughter could bear.
The thought of it wrinkled noses, and brought people down with
otherwise unexplainable cases of the grippe.

Nantucket men and women went wandering up and down the cob-
bles of Main Street, stopping in at the Sand Piper for a restorative cup
of coffee, and wandering over to complain to Mary Ellen Havemeyer
at Mitchell's book store about the indignity of it all. Of an evening
they would assemble at Cy's cozy bar for a restorative glass and discuss the evils that are sprouted only in America and other foreign
places.

"Taxation without representation," muttered Captain Jack McDonald, and then he ambled off toward the Pacific Club for a rubber of
pinochle, and commiseration with the wise old heads of that ancient
and honorable institution.

"The Cape is another world. That's America over there," said Bert
Gibbs.

Captain McDonald spat on the floor.

"Taxachusetts," grumbled another voice from a corner of the room.

"What're we gonna do?" demanded a questioner out of the gloom.

Well, what was done was the preparation of the matter for con-
sideration by the voters of Nantucket come Town Meeting time. Nantucketers voted four to one for secession from Massachusetts.

Naturally, down in Boston, the city slickers indicated that whatever
Nantucket had done was of no importance. If the bill to secede got to

the Massachusetts General Court and was passed, then Governor Michael Dukakis, a coof, would veto it. He said as much, right down there in Boston, the Hub of the Universe.

So Nantucket all spring was in a swivet, the Massachusetts legislature claiming with high rectitude that all it was doing was following the demands of the U.S. Supreme Court for true one-man-one-vote representation in congress. After all, said the legislators, giving even one representative to the two islands, with all the little Elizabeth Islands that cluster about Martha's Vineyard into the bargain, would still create a district with a population of almost sixty percent less than that required by the new norm for allotment of congressmen established by Massachusetts.

The trouble, of course, was that the city slickers of Massachusetts had lost all sense of place. The Founding Fathers carefully set up a dual system of legislative bodies federally, noting the special requirements of unique localities, like Nantucket, as well as the requirements of populations. But in the homogenization of America, place has become almost meaningless—you can travel from Portland, Maine, to Miami and hardly know that you've been anyplace at all if you go by superhighway. East, west, north and south, all have McDonald's and Dairy Queen, and John Chancellor and so forth, and every day everything gets to look, and act, and taste, and smell more like everything else everywhere on the continent. In this atmosphere, the impersonal judgment of the Massachusetts government was to be expected.

The Nantucket people did get some encouragement. New Hampshire Governor Meldrim Thompson offered Nantucket a political home in the Granite State. That was understandable: New Hampshire was behind the door when the seacoast was passed out, and it would be a pretty feather in a New Hampshireman's wool cap if he could snag Nantucket to relieve the shortage.

So as spring came and the tourists began to crowd up the ferryboats, Nantucket sprouted in Secede Now bumper stickers, and the reporters and network newsmen from the mainland pricked up their ears. "Historically, the secession movement is in the grand tradition of Nantucket," said wise old curator Edouard Stackpole of the Whaling Museum. And he pointed to a few of the facts discussed in the pages of this book: how Nantucket was fought over and raped by British and Revolutionary Yankees during the War of Independence and again in the War of 1812, and how Nantucket really never embraced either side, in either conflict.

By April there was a certain resigned disillusionment setting in among secessionists: "I don't think we've got the votes for secession," said Nantucket selectman Mike Todd, in what was probably the champion understatement of the decade. Todd went on to say he would really prefer to secede from the United States as a whole, and set up an independent government. Fire Chief John Gaspie seconded that idea. He also wanted independent Nantucket to declare war against the United States, mobilize the militia, fire two shots, and then surrender to the Coast Guard Station at Brant Point—on condition that the United States promise foreign aid for rehabilitation, and live up to it a damn sight better than it had with Vietnam.

At this writing, the Nantucket secession movement has found encouragement from Rhode Island, Vermont, and Connecticut, as well as New Hampshire. But there does not seem to be much hope. Across the water in Bean Town, Governor Dukakis has not given an inch. Nantucket hasn't given up, however. Boston and the Massachusetts legislature may find plenty of trouble ahead, in non-payment of taxes and general nuisance. For it is not Nantucket's way to resign itself to what it sees as a raw deal, from any quarter. The rest of us may take it from an impersonal Government, but we're just Americans. As readers of this book will know very well, Nantucket is an entirely different dish of tea, and it always will be.

Notes and Bibliography

I am particularly indebted to Edouard Stackpole and half a dozen of the workers at the Nantucket Historical Association museums and libraries for much assistance with this book. I also owe much to the librarians at the Nantucket Atheneum for lending me various books longer than they perhaps thought they ought to.

I talked to many people over many months in the preparation of this book, for of course at the time Nantucket was my home winter and summer, and I hope it will be again. I perused or read everything I could get my hands on that dealt with the island's history. The modern years are the most difficult, for it takes some time to develop perspective on what has happened. The changes on Nantucket are not all rung yet, but the remarkable fact is that through vigilance and care, of the kind that is represented by the now-controversial Kennedy federal land protection bill, Nantucket has remained more unspoiled than virtually any other similar place in America. Left unprotected it might become another Cape Cod or St. Augustine. God forbid.

A Brotherhood of Thieves, letter from Stephen S. Foster, July 1843, privately printed.

An Island Patchwork by Eleanor Early, Houghton Mifflin, Boston, 1941.

Bulletin No. 5, Nantucket Historic Association.

A Grandfather for Benjamin Franklin by Florence Bennett Anderson, Meador, Boston, 1941.

Early Settlers of Nantucket by Lydia S. Hinchman, W. A. Henry, Philadelphia, 1926.

"Education" by W. D. Perkins, in *Historic Nantucket,* January 1960.

"Fifty Years an Outsider" by L. F. Willard, in *Yankee,* June 1974.

Harvest Gleaning by Anna Gardner, Fowler and Wells, New York, 1881.

Historic Nantucket by W. D. Perkins, Nantucket Schools, April 1960.

Historic Nantucket, Education, W. D. Perkins, January 1960.

Historic Nantucket, October 1975. *The Wreck of the Marshall, The Coffin Saga, Will Gardner,* Whaling Museum publication, 1949.

Life Saving in Nantucket by Eduoard A. Stackpole, Nantucket, 1972.

Maria Mitchell, Life, Letters and Journals compiled by Phebe Mitchell Kendall, Books for Libraries Press, Freeport, New York, 1896.

Nantucket by Joseph E. C. Farnham, Providence, 1915.

"Nantucket Argument Settlers, 1659–1959," in *The Inquirer and Mirror,* Nantucket, 1959.

Nantucket's Changing Prosperity and Future Probabilities by E. U. Crosby, Nantucket, 1939.

Nantucket, a History by R. A. Douglas-Lithgow, G. P. Putnam Sons, New York, 1914.

Nantucket Island by Town Information Bureau, Nantucket, 1976.

Nantucket Lands and Landowners by Henry Barnard Worth, Nantucket Historical Association, 1928.

Nantucket Odyssey by Emil F. Guba, Waltham, Massachusetts, 1965.

Nantucket: the Faraway Island by William O. Stevens, Dodd Mead and Co., New York, 1966.

"Nantucket Schools" by W. D. Perkins, in *Historic Nantucket,* April 1960.

Nantucket Whole Island Catalogue by Dick Mackay, Sankaty Head Press, Siasconset, Massachusetts, 1976.

Sconset Heyday by Margaret Fawcett Barnes, The Island Press, Nantucket, 1969.

The Clock That Talks by Will Gardner, Whaling Museum Publications, Nantucket, 1954.

The Evolution of Siasconset Inquirer and Mirror Press, Nantucket, 1915.

The Far Out Island Railroad by Clay Lancaster, Pleasant Publications, Nantucket, 1972.

The Great Nantucket Bank Robbery Conspiracy and Solemn Aftermath by Emil F. Guba, Waltham, Massachusetts, 1973.

The History of Nantucket by Obed Macy, A. M. Kelley, Clifton, New Jersey, 1880.

The History of Nantucket by Alexander Starbuck, Charles E. Tuttle, Rutland, Vermont, 1969 (first published in 1924).

The History of Nantucket Island, a bibliography, Nantucket Historical Trust, 1970.

The Island of Nantucket, What It Was and What It Is by E. K. Godfrey, Lee and Shepard, New York, 1882.

The Mutiny on the Globe by Edwin P. Hoyt, Random House, New York, 1975.

The Nantucket Scrap Basket by W. F. Macy and R. B. Hussey, Inquirer and Mirror, Nantucket, 1916.

"The Robbery that Split an Island" by John W. Morgan, Jr., in *Yankee*, June 1965.

The Story of Old Nantucket by W. F. Macy, Houghton Mifflin, Boston, 1928.

The Terrible Voyage by Edwin P. Hoyt, Pinnacle Books, New York, 1976.

"The Wreck of the Marshall," in *Historic Nantucket*, October 1975.

The Wreck of the Whaleship Essex by Haverstick and Shepard, Harcourt Brace and World, New York, 1865.

Three Bricks and Three Brothers by Will Gardner, Riverside Press, Cambridge, Massachusetts, Whaling Museum Publications, 1945.

Through the Hawse Hole by Florence Bennett Anderson, Macmillan, New York, 1932.

"Wrecks Around Nantucket" by Arthur H. Gardner, in *The Inquirer and Mirror*, Nantucket, 1915.

Yankee Whalers in the South Seas by A. B. C. Whipple, Charles E. Tuttle, Rutland, Vermont, 1973.

Index

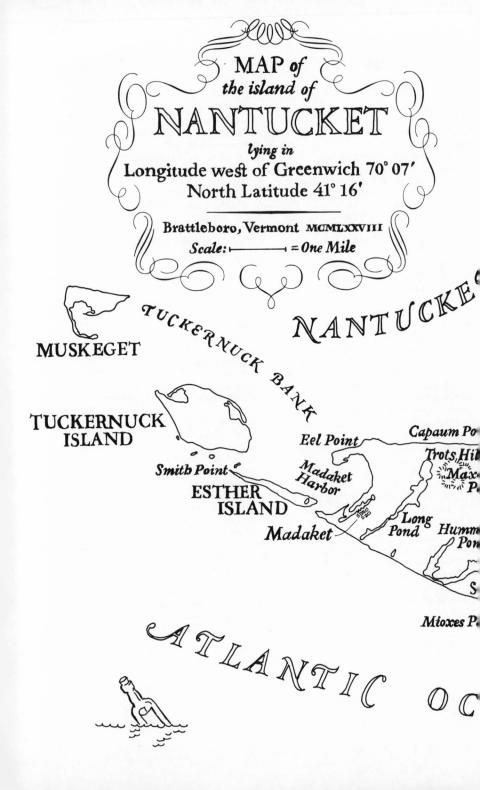

MAP of
the island of
NANTUCKET
lying in
Longitude west of Greenwich 70° 07′
North Latitude 41° 16′

Brattleboro, Vermont MCMLXXVIII

Scale: ⊢———⊣ = One Mile

MUSKEGET

TUCKERNUCK BANK

NANTUCKE

TUCKERNUCK
ISLAND

Eel Point

Capaum Po

Trots, Hil

Max

P

Smith Point

Madaket
Harbor

ESTHER
ISLAND

Long
Pond

Humm
Pon

Madaket

S

Mioxes P

ATLANTIC OC

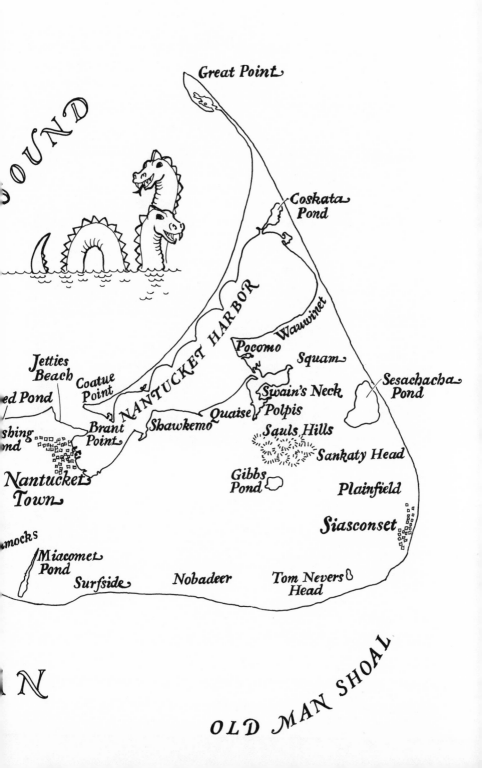

SOUND

Great Point

Coskata
Pond

NANTUCKET HARBOR

Pocomo
Wauwinet

Squam

Jetties
Beach
Coatue
Point

Sesachacha
Pond

ed Pond

Swain's Neck

Quaise
Polpis

shing
nd

Brant
Point

Shawkemo

Sauls Hills

Sankaty Head

Nantucket
Town

Gibbs
Pond

Plainfield

Siasconset

mocks

Miacomet
Pond

Surfside

Nobadeer

Tom Nevers
Head

N

OLD MAN SHOAL